GENE HELVESTON

OPERATION THUNDERSTRUCK

MARLI BAR PRESS | INDIANAPOLIS

PUBLISHED BY MARLIBAR PRESSS

Acknowledgments: Thank you to Mary Jo Zazueta, for her continued support and guidance.

MarLi Bar Press
Indianapolis, Indiana

Publisher's Cataloging-in-Publication Data

Names: Helveston, Eugene M., 1934– author.

Title: Operation Thunderstruck / an Adam Grant novel / Gene Helveston.

Description: First edition. | Indianapolis : MarLi Bar Press, [2018]

Identifiers: ISBN: 978-0-9972230-2-6 | LCCN: 2018935811

Subjects: LCSH: Terrorism—United States—Prevention—Fiction. | Terrorists—Saudi Arabia—Fiction. | Terrorists—Michigan—Fiction. | World Trade Center (New York, N.Y. : 1970-2001)—Fiction. | United States—Politics and government—Fiction. | LCGFT: Thrillers (Fiction) | BISAC: FICTION / Thrillers / Terrorism

Classification: LCC: PS3608.E39252 O64 2018 | DDC: 813/.6—dc23

Printed in the United States of America
First Printing

Cover and text design by Mary Jo Zazueta
tothepointsolutions.com

To the victims of 9/11.
May it never happen again.

The Golden Pelican—An Adam Grant Novel

*The Second Decade—Raising Kids to be
Happy, Healthy Adults through Work*

OPERATION

THUNDERSTRUCK

Prologue

The days were hot, still, and dusty. People wearing heavier clothing than what the climate called for moved about slowly. The exception to this attire were their sandals, reminiscent of biblical times. The twenty-two-year-old man, who had arrived in Yemen two years earlier, fresh from the University of Michigan, continued to be impressed by how Yemeni feet, in spite of being dusty, looked so much healthier than American feet, which were usually protected by leather shoes.

The young children he saw, and they were numerous, looked like children everywhere. Because he rarely saw teenagers walking around, he suspected there was an invisible population of them—or maybe people in this society went directly from childhood to being young adults.

The Yemenis he met in public were quiet and reserved. In private, however, they were more communicative and sometimes effusive, but never in an overbearing way. When he interacted with them in his role as an English teacher, counselor, friend, or ambassador with the Peace Corps, the young man found the people to be compliant, appreciative, and friendly. They were also justifiably concerned and almost universally disappointed because their country was neither a peaceful sanctuary nor a safe haven. Yemen was a cauldron beset with political strife and plagued with uncertainty.

Geographically, Yemen was at the end of a long peninsula that was mostly filled by Saudi Arabia. Yemen was west of Oman and across a slip of ocean from Djibouti, an African country few people have heard of. Although the population dated back more than 2,500 years, Yemen became a new country by the stroke of a pen in 1967 when the British left.

Yemenis lived in two worlds. The one that existed today had passed them by; the one that began thousands of years ago was gone. They were orphans of the millennium, with no one to take them in and nowhere to go.

Two years in the country touched Phillip Tripp's soul. He was an impressionable young man, an idealist who had embarked on a life-changing quest. His time there was broadening, redemptive, and left an indelible mark. It is where he met and lost his first true love. Powerful memories of this time lay dormant, dimming but never extinguished.

Now, nearly four decades later, Phillip Tripp, President of the United States, received a message concerning Alia.

Chapter 1

Five men huddled around a battered wooden table that had seen much use. The leader sat at the head. They were in Peshawar, in the northeast corner of Pakistan. All were attired in dirty, worn clothing. Some wore faded thobes that buttoned in the front above their waists, while others wore Western-style shirts and trousers. Everyone had a sash tied around his waist and wore leather sandals. Assoud Al Walaki, their leader and the head of Al-Fir, an offshoot of al-Qaeda, had summoned them. His purpose today was to speak while the others listened. The time was approaching for an event they hoped would pale 9/11. He needed their undivided attention and total commitment.

Assoud spoke with authority. "We have worked diligently for the past three years. In that time, due to the efforts of everyone in this room, we are nearing the time to strike. To prepare for this attack, we have used every resource available to us, even exposing the CIA operative located here in Islamabad, who has been rooting around the fringes of our organization. We have enlisted aid from our supporters, who have provided resources worth millions of dollars to help us complete our plan. We are agents of death against the infidel. We have gotten all we can from the CIA agent, who has been fed disinformation. It is now time to deal with him, before he becomes a problem. This matter will be taken care of tomorrow morning.

"For now, our wealthy businessman will be spared. We will keep him alive until we have used all of the resources he can provide in moving our team and supporting them in the United States. After that, he and his family will also be dealt with, but only after we have completed our strike against One World Trade Center. We want no one around who can talk. Are there any questions?"

"How many of us will be going to America?" asked Mihal, a dour, bearded man of about forty. He was wearing a thobe.

"I haven't decided yet."

"Thank you."

"The event will take place in November. We don't know the exact date but we will be giving the infidels another day to remember. Our plan is to kill all four thousand people inside One World Trade Center. We can only guess how many others will die trying to help.

"Because of the lesson we gave them when our comrades took down the original Twin Towers, their architects have made changes in how the new tower was constructed. Because of this, the building will be impossible to smash, even if we used planes like we did on 9/11. Instead, we will use the building as an enduring sarcophagus, a tomb for the entire population trapped inside—killed by sarin gas. We will first destroy the lower seven floors with explosives, disable the elevators, and then pump poison into the ventilation system for a clean and total kill."

"Allahu Akbar!" muttered the group.

"We must spend every minute finalizing the plan. When we succeed, we will have done more with less than any army that has ever been assembled."

"Allahu Akbar!"

———————————

Early the following morning, the Station Chief of the Central Intelligence Agency's Islamabad office sat at his desk, stunned. He had just learned that one of his agents had been killed in a car bomb explosion in the parking lot of an apartment complex. In a hoarse but audible whisper, he said, "My God, he's dead. But why?"

Chapter 2

Washington, D.C.

A month ago, after his second meeting with President Tripp, Adam Grant said good-bye to Erin O'Leary, who left for Rome to serve as the new CIA Station Chief. Adam and Erin had worked as a team on a top-secret project in North Korea and had received heartfelt thanks from the President for their successful and extraordinary work in removing Kim Il-un as a dangerous nuclear threat to the United States. Erin's reward was advancing in her career with the CIA. For Adam, it was no longer possible for him to continue active duty in the U.S. Army, which meant his reward, paradoxically, was to be unemployed for the first time since he was nine years old.

At thirty-three, Adam was now a Lieutenant Colonel in the U.S. Army Reserves. He was healthy, well-educated, and good at what he did, but his experience was narrowly focused to the military way of life and work. A West Point graduate, he had survived nearly five years in Afghanistan, been awarded the Silver Star, and underwent a brief period of training with the CIA before being deployed to North Korea for a delicate, covert operation. As a soldier, he was described by many as courageous and brave; although Adam modestly relegated his accomplishments to just doing his job. He did not seek praise.

Adam Grant's military skills were not readily transferable or applicable to many other life situations, but he did possess excellent people skills, and those around him invariably liked and trusted him. He had a knack for recognizing people's needs as well as their talents, and this skill set made him a good leader and, when appropriate, a compliant follower. Adam could willingly become part of a team. He didn't have to be the boss in every case. But, regardless of the situation, he did not suffer fools nor follow fakes.

Adam was single, loved his time in the Army, and was proud of his service. However, after meeting Erin, he realized dedication to just his job was not enough.

Nearly ten years ago, his fiancée had been killed; and since then he hadn't thought about marriage, only the challenges of the career he had chosen. Adam was sure he loved Erin. But he also knew they had bonded in an atmosphere that was serious, all-encompassing, and dangerous. He had spent more than two months by her side, almost exclusively together. During that time, survival was their implacable bonding agent. Was there more to them being together than what could be thought of as a contrived, even artificial, connection; one of convenience born out of necessity? Were they truly meant to be together? Adam had an idea, but he wasn't sure.

After their mission in North Korea, Adam and Erin had spent three wonderful weeks on a boat, cruising from Lake Michigan to the middle of Florida. But was that time even real? These thoughts filled Adam's mind as he wondered about his future.

———————

In the CIA Director's office, Robert Zinsky said, "Colonel Grant, you did an amazing job for the CIA and, more importantly, for the country. My words are insufficient to express how much we owe to you and Erin O'Leary. You've both earned our respect and deserve the opportunity to move forward in your careers. It pleases me that Erin is now in a position of responsibility where her talents and drive can serve both her and our country."

Adam knew that Erin was a good choice for the position she had accepted. "She earned the promotion and even more, Director. I am sure she is both grateful for the opportunity and eager to validate your faith in her."

"What about you, Adam? I see a very bright future for you with us, if you are interested. What I have in mind is a position that would land you in administration and training, at least to begin with. You could start as an instructor at Camp Peary and then, in a few months, be back here on campus. I don't see you being in the field just now. As important as that work is, you are more valuable and your talents can be better utilized in a leadership and consulting role. Maybe you'll be in my seat someday—who knows? You are a helluva lot further along than I was at your age!

"I don't want to make a specific offer today," the Director continued. "I just want you to know how much I value you and how much I think you can bring to the Agency. Please think carefully about what I am saying. Let's get back together in a month. I know you have a lot on your mind and you need to sort through things before making any long-term plans. Is that a deal? Can I count on you to at least give the CIA a chance?"

Adam respected the Agency and thoroughly agreed with its mission. He admired the beautiful campus and, even more, the dedicated people who worked there. He was also happy and relieved that he had been offered a job. This meant his current unemployment could end anytime he chose. If anyone asked now, he could honestly say that he was between jobs. The offer he had received was one that most people would give their eye teeth for. Not a bad place to be.

But, what about the message from the President's office? What could President Tripp possibly have to say to Adam that hadn't already been said? The last time they met, Adam had been promoted to Lieutenant Colonel, coincident with his entering the active reserves, and had received the heartfelt thanks of the Commander in Chief. A meeting was scheduled for tomorrow afternoon in the Oval Office. Adam was looking forward to hearing what the President had to say.

Chapter 3

─────────────────

For the third time in as many months, Adam Grant found himself in the Oval Office, the official working space of the most powerful man in the world. He was as nervous as a schoolboy summoned to the principal's office. What news would today bring?

Adam was scheduled to meet with the President alone. This afternoon, it was alone-alone, just he and President Tripp. Erin had been with Adam at the last meeting; having Erin at his side was essentially being alone, but in a very nice way. The connection between them was that complete. Even though Erin was in Rome, Adam felt her presence. His feelings for her were firmly entrenched.

"Thank you, Colonel Grant, for coming here today," greeted President Tripp. "How have things been going for you?"

"Very well, sir. I am gradually adjusting to the new routine. But, to be honest, it is an uncomfortable feeling for me to be unemployed." Adam strongly suspected the President was fully informed of Robert Zinsky's offer, but nothing in the President's expression revealed this. On a lighter note, Adam continued. "As I read the want ads in the newspaper and the job offerings on the internet, I don't see many listings that offer employment opportunities for a person with my skill set."

For today's meeting, the President sat in a high-backed upholstered chair at the side of the fireplace instead of behind his large, imposing desk at the farthest point in the room. Adam sat opposite, facing the President, in a matching chair. Adam knew there were many options for seating arrangements inside the Oval Office and that each implied a different level of authority and intensity. Today, the President was positioned far from the traditional seat of authority—the chair behind his heavy wooden desk. Adam suspected that the conversation he would have with the President today would include an entreaty. These ruminations were part of how Adam interpreted the seating arrangement and the President's body language. It turned out he was correct.

"Adam, the last time we met in this office, you asked if I would be willing to provide a recommendation for you when you had a job offer."

"Yes, I did, sir."

"Well, Adam, I have something I'd like you to consider before you commit to a new job," said President Tripp. "As you know, I have only been in this office for just over six months. In that time, a lot has happened—and although you assisted in one of the most important tasks we all faced during this time, there are other things going on that need immediate attention. I suspect you are aware of some of them. Anyway, the guys we beat can't seem to get the bit out of their mouths and they are thrashing around in great discomfort with me sitting here. They are not willing to accept the fact that they lost the election, and they are trying to keep the campaign going by reliving the voting process for as long as they can. Their goal is to find a way to boot me out. Am I making it clear?"

"Yes. The natives are restless, but I don't know why."

"Let me explain. The White House has a payroll of more

than thirty-five hundred people. Some are cooks and gardeners, and others provide security, administrative assistance, or technical services, and much more. There are many categories, but they are all associated with the institution and relate to this place in their own way. There is stress, excitement, responsibility, and yes, intrigue in this place because of the myriad activities and personalities. Added to this staff, there are fifteen cabinet heads who supervise tens of thousands of employees. And there is Congress, the CIA, the FBI ... And close to every President is a small group of advisors. It numbers about a dozen. These people are relied on for high-level support. Then there is another level of counselors. Most of them deal with specific issues important to the administration, like operations, the economy, strategy, communications, and speech writing. Well, you can get the idea. It's a virtually endless list."

"Yes. I think I do, sir. Although, I have to admit, I hadn't ever given much thought to the level of complexity that exists. It sounds like you sit on top of a dynamic enterprise—a house of cards," commented Adam, referring to the political drama on Netflix.

"Yes, and things can come tumbling down in a system like this, Adam. And, unfortunately, there are people who are willing to take things apart for their own benefit or for the benefit of people who have no goodwill toward us."

"Do you see this as a problem?"

"Yes."

"A severe problem?"

"Definitely. People do rash things for many reasons. They carry grudges, seek favors while doing the bidding of others, pursue personal gain—there are hundreds of other motivations. In a group as large as the one that surrounds me, there are bound to be carryovers from the previous administration who keep their job while being closet enemies. And, in some ways, possibly most serious of all, are people in the closest circles who become misguided, change their stripes, or come under the influence of others who are at odds with the administration." When he finished talking, President Tripp took a breath and sat back in his chair.

Adam knew from the news on television and reading the papers that there were a couple disaffected legislators who were calling for impeachment. It sounded like the President felt there was cause for concern. Adam decided to listen and not jump to any conclusions. The ball was still in the President's court.

Breaking the silence, President Tripp continued. "You are not asking why I am telling this to you, so I'll just tell you."

"Thank you, sir."

"I have good people around me, Adam. People who know what they are doing. Most of them are here because they are loyal, smart, and hardworking, but sometimes, even those with the very best of intentions, can get too close to what they are doing and forget that there are other people in the room or other ideas that are being floated. Now, to the reason why I called you here today."

"Yes, sir, Mr. President," Adam said as he sat up straighter.

"I want your help in dealing with a private matter, something that involves me personally. If what I suspect is behind a message that I have just received, it is unlikely the contents will remain private for long, unless we do something. Without prompt and effective action on our part there is a very real chance this thing could quickly develop into a mess. I need you to help me find some answers to questions that I am having a tough time to actually define. I don't know how long this job will take, but I know it could interfere with any immediate plans you might have now. So, first I want you to tell me if you can take on something that will put you out of commission for as long as several months. If you can, then I will tell you what I need you to do. If you can't take it on at this time, I will understand, and we will end things here."

"Sir, I have to ask the question that has been asked of me when I've meted out a task. Why me?"

"I would have been disappointed if you hadn't asked," said the President. "The reason I have chosen you is because you have looked down the barrel of a gun at a terrorist, and into the eyes of a murdering dictator, and you never flinched. You deserve the limelight but are willing to give it up for your country. You perform a deed that should earn you a medal, but accept discharge from the Army because it is for the greater good. You are mature, level-headed, and you command respect. You will not be snowed by the self-important nor overlook the self-effacing. And, if I am wrong about all of this, then you are the greatest actor I have ever met, and that in itself is something."

"Sir, I know what I will almost certainly say. I have the time. But I suspect that you would rather not hear my final answer until after I have heard the actual request and given it proper thought."

"You are right, Adam. The fact that you have the time is a good start. I will get back with you in a few days and we can discuss this further. I don't suppose I have to tell you that this is between us."

"No, sir, you don't."

Adam left the Oval Office wondering if he was heading for a life that would be relegated to piecework. His intention, when he chose a career in the Army, was so much different than what his life was now. Instead of working at a specific job with regular duties, surrounded by a large group of qualified people with a common goal, he had left a great job as Adjutant to the Chairman of the Joint Chiefs of Staff. For what? To take on an assignment that was more like a Mitch Rapp novel than real life. Would he be doing it all over again? Maybe he should call this kind of stuff quits. On the other hand, how could he say no to the President? Was it possible that he enjoyed the thrill of the chase and challenges from the unknown?

Chapter 4

Three days later, Adam was back in the Oval Office. "Mr. President," he said, "if I think I can do what you have in store for me, I am on board. At the moment, I am not in a hurry to sign on for something permanent because I don't exactly know what I want to do yet. So, for that reason, as well as my willingness to be of service, I will do what you ask; that is, if I think I can do a decent job."

"Here is what I am asking you to do, Colonel," began the President. "I would like you to determine the whereabouts of Alia Fahad. She is a woman I last saw in the port city of Aden in Yemen, the third week of June in 1982. She was eighteen at the time. Just over five feet tall, she was beautiful and bright. She was my first real love, and I think it's safe to say *we* were in love. We were desperately trying to find a way to work things out between us, when things happened to upset our plans. Actually, and it should have been no surprise to us, we ran out of time. I had to leave the country because my tour with the Peace Corps had ended and my visa would expire. Her family, or I should say her father, was not happy about our being together, and he would have been distraught if he had known what we were secretly planning. Even though I had to leave Yemen, Alia and I remained hopeful. When I left, I vowed I would find a way to return to Aden, and that somehow, we would find a way for her to come to the United States with me and we would be married. Our scheme had no foundation in reality—but tell an impressionable and idealistic twenty-two-year-old who is in love what is possible and what is not.

"When I returned home, I enrolled in graduate school and was working two jobs to save enough money to get started. Then, I received a letter from Alia with the shocking news that she had gotten married soon after I left. She said she had married an older man; he was older to us because he was almost thirty. He was a friend of her family and was working in his own family's construction business. After the wedding they would be living in Khamis Mushait, in Saudi Arabia. Her letter was simply to say good-bye. She was stolid enough under the circumstances to tell me only the facts, but I felt I knew her enough to know how she felt. She lived in a different culture, in which things like this were not uncommon, even for the daughter of an enlightened college professor. I felt like I was the one getting off easy. I was sad, and it took me a long time to get over the hurt, but eventually, reality set in. The truth is, my sadness ended up being mostly for Alia because I knew she was being forced into a marriage that might not make her happy, but there was nothing I could do, except move on, which I did." After a brief pause, the President continued. "That is the background. Now, I will tell you what has happened recently. I received a peculiar and mysterious message from someone in Saudi Arabia. It was a handwritten note sent to me on *behalf* of Alia Fahad. These kinds of notes rarely reach my desk, so someone down the line must have had a feeling that I should see it. After reading it, I do think it was the right decision.

"The sender indicated that he or she would like to speak with me personally and that, depending on the outcome, there could be serious consequences for one or both of us. When I say this, I make it sound like the message could be a threat, but that's not the feeling I got when I read it. Instead it seemed more like a warning of things to come, portending something that neither the sender nor I had much control over or wanted to have happen. I was especially taken aback by the use of Alia's family name, Fahad. I have not seen or heard from her since she wrote to tell me she had been married and had moved to Saudi Arabia. At the time, it seemed this had happened unusually fast, but I now know things like that are not uncommon in a culture ruled by the male head of the household. In hindsight, the marriage was probably already in the works with the families while Alia and I were naively making our fanciful plans. I have no reason to believe Alia hasn't remained happily married for the last thirty-seven years. I got over it and I am sure she did too."

After taking a breath, the President continued. "There are many questions, of course. Who knows Alia and I ever met, or that we were talking about getting married and her moving to America with me? These were things we shared with no one, not my family and certainly not hers. And why would they use her family name and not her married name? Of course, I don't know what her married name is. It is possible that this is a totally innocent message, or it could be from a crackpot sent for who knows what reason. To be honest, I have a weird feeling that this could be something important, even ominous. But what that could be, I have no idea. The message must be related to when Alia was Fahad and to my time in Yemen with the Peace Corps. That was almost forty years ago. Maybe I'm nuts, but I simply don't feel comfortable just brushing this off. Anyway, before something comes of this, which I doubt will happen, I want to find out who sent the note and why. The sender said that I should respond by sending a letter general delivery addressed simply to Fahad in Khamis Mushait, Saudi Arabia. After my reply acknowledging that I had read the note, the sender said we could talk about the situation in detail. Of course, that is not a path I am willing to pursue personally, but on the other hand, I don't want to leave this matter dangling. And this brings us to why you are here, Adam. What I want you to do to is take the information we have, meager as it is, and start to unravel this *thing*.

"The story begins in Yemen but I don't believe there is much to be gotten there now. It would be better if you began your efforts in Khamis Mushait. I believe that would be the place to start gathering information that could help explain both this message and identify its sender. What do you think?"

Adam tried to digest everything before he responded. "Mr. President, I am not an investigator, but you already know that. I have less experience for a situation like this than I had for my last assignment—but I am sure you know that also. As long as we both have realistic expectations about what I can accomplish, and your reasons for asking me offset the risk of my inexperience, then yes, I am willing to give it a try." On a more positive note, Adam asked, "Is there a time frame?"

"None that is specific, but I would like you to start as soon as possible."

"Can I tell anyone what I am doing or where I am going?"

"No is the essential answer, but I will rely on your judgment with the understanding that anyone you tell must be absolutely sworn to secrecy," said the President.

"Will I be on the government payroll?"

"Not per se. You will be activated from the Reserves and will receive full pay and benefits due a Lieutenant Colonel in the United States Army. Your official and on-the-record assignment will be Liaison to the President of the United States for on-the-ground intelligence affairs. If this sounds like mumbo jumbo, it's not by accident, and we'll leave it that way. For your military duty on the government's behalf, you will be on official temporary duty, which in your jargon I believe is TDY. While doing this, you will be supported for travel and living expenses.

You will travel on civilian carriers and will be functioning out of uniform. However, your current passport and all other military identification will remain your valid credentials.

"Your mission will not be secret, but you should not call special attention to yourself or what it is you are actually doing. You can ask for help from whatever U.S. government support functions or facilities you might need in order to accomplish the task at hand. I will ask you to prepare a preliminary schedule and your overall plan, and to share it with me. After we agree on the best way to proceed, you will do as you see fit. When you come up with information that you think is useful, I want you to let me know without delay. The lines of communication will remain open. For my part, if I learn anything new that might be useful to your investigation, I will share it with you immediately. I suggest that you start by trying to find anything you can about the whereabouts of Alia Fahad, which, of course, means finding out her married name. The only other information I can provide is that her husband's family was in the construction business. I suspect it was a big operation, successful and prominent in the field, but I don't know if that is still the case. Presumably the company was doing business in Khamis Mushait thirty-seven years ago, since that is where Alia said she would be moving. Not much to go on, Adam. Do you still think you can do it?"

"No promises of results, sir," said Adam, "but I'll certainly do my best. After thinking more about what you have told me, I will put together a preliminary plan and submit it for your approval in a week."

The President's face grew even more serious, before he said, "I appreciate your willingness and honesty, Adam. Now, there is one more thing I want to add ..."

When Phillip Tripp had finished, he simply said, "Okay, Colonel. You take it from here. We'll talk again next week."

Adam left the White House in deep thought about the information President Tripp had just shared. When the President first summoned Adam and they talked about a special assignment, Adam suspected something big was in the wind. Today, as he disclosed the actual contents of the strange message, President Tripp's demeanor confirmed this. When he shared the back-story, Adam's suspicions were substantiated. It was big.

Chapter 5

Erin had phoned Adam from Rome three times in the last two weeks. During each call she had a lot to tell him about what she was doing. But the conversations were more than simply catching up with a friend. Before the end of each conversation, Erin almost pleaded with Adam to hop on a plane and come to Rome to visit her for a week. Even though Adam would have liked nothing more than to spend a week with Erin, he hesitated. He knew they'd be happy just being together; sightseeing was unimportant. They both were familiar with Rome and still in the thrall of getting to know each other. The three weeks they had spent together on the boat cruising from Northern Michigan to Florida was, by mutual agreement, the best time either had ever experienced with another person. But now what? Was it fair for Adam, who felt he was no better than adrift, to move ahead with the relationship? To him it seemed Erin was grounded, and he was anything but. Adam had no established roots and no concrete plans for the future. He wanted desperately to see her but, even more, he wanted something worthwhile to offer her. Erin was too wonderful to hurt. He would never let her down.

Adam's desire to get on with his life and to do the right thing when it came to his relationship with Erin may have taken a big hit when he accepted the charge from the President. How could he deal with doing the right thing for himself, or for his career, if it harmed his relationship with Erin? The challenge he had accepted was now foremost in his mind and it rattled around, making him feel like he was trying to corner a frisky colt in a circular corral. Every time he thought he was getting close to a good idea, it just slipped away and he was back in the middle of the ring where he had started. *I guess I had better not try to out-think the situation*, Adam thought. *I just need to get down to business, and when this is done, make damn sure I will be in a position to justify offering myself to a woman like Erin O'Leary.*

———————————

Adam had promised President Tripp that he would do his best. With this pledge he would be dedicated to the task ahead. This job would now come before everything else. Then, when he was finished with the assignment, his goal would be to work toward placing the cornerstone for the rest of his life. *Fair enough, Adam*, he told himself. *Now, go for it!* He would start the process by carefully digesting what the President had told him in his final comment.

———————————

As the meeting this morning was ending, the President, with a pained look, had added, "What this note also revealed is that Alia gave birth to a baby barely nine months after I last saw her. The date of the birth of her son is emphasized, as if I should be concerned. Could the message be from her? If it is from Alia, why? Now you know why I must get to the bottom of this. And why this is personal. And private." President Tripp reached in his inside jacket pocket and brought out a small piece of paper. He handed it to Adam.

To the President of the United States:

This note is written on behalf of Alia Fahad. Her son, born Feb 1983 is in serious trouble and only you can help.

Please respond to: General delivery, Alia Fahad, Khamis Mushait, Saudi Arabia, saying you will help and we will send contact information.

Chapter 6

Adam began his research by reading everything he could find on Phillip Tripp, not the President, but the man. He found what he expected. The President was described as an intelligent, engaged, ethical, honest, and successful person. Except for the premature death of both parents, there was nothing unusual about his family. His mother died at forty-eight from colon cancer and his father at sixty-three from a heart attack. Phillip was the third child in the family. His mother died while he was still in college and his dad died after the President had completed graduate school. His oldest brother was an attorney in Indianapolis, working as general counsel for a corrugated cardboard company. His sister was married to an ophthalmologist and lived in California. He was an uncle to one niece and three nephews. He was close to his brother who lived in the same state and saw his sister and her children usually twice a year. He was the only one in the family who was politically active, but he had the wholehearted support of all in his family.

Phillip Tripp married when he was in graduate school. His wife, Arlene, also graduated from the University of Michigan and worked as a nurse for the first four years they were married.

After that, she was a stay-at-home mom until their children went off to college. She then worked for several years as a counselor in the University Health Clinic, while her husband taught. This lasted until activities in support of her husband's political career began to take more of her time. Their two children, both married, were in their early thirties, and each had two children. One son-in-law was an attorney in a large firm in Indianapolis and the other was a dentist. Both daughters were stay-at-home moms.

Although the President knew a lot of people, he had only a few close friends outside of politics and academia. Other than boating, reading, and being a moderately active sports fan, Phillip Tripp was a quiet and serious man who dug deeply into his work. Phillip Tripp's reading tastes were eclectic and included biographies, mostly of Americans. Among his favorites, though, were biographies on Winston Churchill and Napoleon. He had read all of the Vince Flynn and Lee Child novels, and all twenty-two of Patrick O'Brian's Aubrey-Maturin sea stories twice! Before becoming President of the United States, Phillip Tripp wrote an occasional op-ed. These were published in various forums, including the *Indianapolis Star* and the *Wall Street Journal*.

The courses Professor Tripp taught at DePauw University were popular and sought after. His specialty was U.S. History and the Constitution, but he also taught a survey world history course when it was his turn to teach freshman history 101. In ten years at DePauw, he had published thirty scholarly, mostly peer-reviewed, papers and numerous other invited works. He also authored two books. His best known was his last book, which was an incisive study of the signature accomplishment of each of the U.S. presidents through the twentieth century.

As Governor of Indiana and a U.S. Congressman, Tripp supported a conservative agenda that was carried out with what was described, on both sides of the aisle, as being "pursued with both conviction and goodwill." The campaign leading up to his being elected President was a matter of public record, and it was all straightforward with no evidence of any dirty dealing. For that reason, Adam relied on the information he already had, believing that in politics, if anything even remotely smelled bad, the other side would run with it.

In a word, Adam found nothing to explain the note. However, this lack of any information did not mean there was nothing behind the message. Adam would move ahead with the project.

Chapter 7

Two days after their last meeting, Adam shared his plan with the President. Because Aden had suffered nearly twenty years of fruitless civil war and was now labeled a ghost town, Adam's plan did not include going there. It was likely any official records would have been destroyed and the chance of neighborhoods, friends, and acquaintances surviving was also slim. This put Adam at a disadvantage. Under normal circumstances, he might have been able to locate Alia's parents, other family members, or neighbors, who would know her married name. But nothing in Aden could be considered even close to normal. Descriptions of the city he found online and from information Adam obtained from John Morrison, a helpful source at the CIA, told him to steer clear. Any attempts to get reliable information even from a week ago, let alone from almost forty years ago, would prove fruitless.

This meant that his search would start in Saudi Arabia, in the city of Khamis Mushait, where Alia landed shortly after her marriage. Adam's only clues were that Alia's husband's family was in the construction business—and Khamis Mushait is where the President was to send his response. After that, Adam could only guess where the trail would lead, but he felt sure it wouldn't end there.

Adam was pleased and not particularly surprised when President Tripp had nothing to add to his plan. Phillip Tripp recognized it would be necessary for Adam alone to make changes in how the investigation was carried out on a day-to-day basis depending on new and reliable information that he uncovered. This was good news to Adam because he did not want to be micromanaged by anyone, and certainly not from such a great distance. He suspected flexibility would be the key to the success of his investigation.

The information John Morrison at the CIA shared about conditions in Yemen, and his advice to start the investigation in a more stable place, was helpful. John's response also gave Adam confidence that additional information would be available and provided freely by the Agency. Adam wondered if Bob Zinsky had any idea what he was up to. The President had made it clear to Adam that this mission was for his eyes only. Had the President talked with Director Zinsky? Adam would not ask. In the brief time he had been involved in the inner workings of events in and around the White House, Adam had learned that there were multiple levels of "need to know," "how to act," and "who to tell." His suspicion was that more people knew about the mission than just he and the President, but that each person was sworn to be communicating directly with the President and no one else.

Adam was seated in the aisle seat in the exit row of a Boeing 777-200. There were only two seats in the row. This configuration allowed freer access to the window exit in the space where the third seat would have been, and there was also three extra inches of leg room that was greatly appreciated by the traveler. Because he was on TDY, it was decided that Adam should fly in coach as much as possible to avoid calling attention to an active-duty officer traveling in business or first class. This made sense given the sensitive mission he was undertaking.

Adam's usual strategy for serious travel like this was to exist in what he thought of as his personal cocoon. He avoided speaking with anyone except the flight attendants, and then only briefly and as needed; the rest of the time he quietly ate, slept, read, or worked. The few times he had succumbed to long conversations with fellow passengers bent on telling Adam their life stories had proved counterproductive and tiring. The first flight today would take him to Schiphol Airport in Amsterdam, and from there he would fly on Saudi Airlines to Jeddah.

Seventeen hours after leaving Washington D.C., the seven-hour flight from Amsterdam to Jeddah began its initial approach. Adam saw the Red Sea give way to the spread of a large city. In the center of the city's expansive harbor was a huge tower of water that appeared to lift hundreds of feet in the air. *Some pump*, thought Adam. Bordering the harbor were several ultra-modern, tall, glass-clad buildings, probably hotels. They thrust skyward above a warren of nondescript two- and three-story buildings the color of sand. As the plane flew past the city center, he saw the dozens of peaked white tents representing the Hajj terminal he had heard about. This was where hundreds of thousands of pilgrims passed through each year on the mandatory, at least once-in-a-lifetime, trek to Mecca. Beyond the white tents, across the expansive spread of runways, was the modern, brick-and-mortar of the King Abdulaziz International Airport. As the ground came up to join the plane's undercarriage in a "greased" landing, Adam and the other grateful passengers settled comfortably back to earth, a satisfying end to a long flight.

From here, Adam would take the less-than-two-hour flight on an Embraer regional jet to his final destination three hundred and seventy-eight miles south.

After a long day of travel, Adam arrived in Khamis Mushait. He had opted to find a hotel after his arrival rather than make a reservation ahead of time. This would avoid the real possibility of making a bad choice despite the best of intentions. From the in-flight magazine, he selected the Hotel Mercure. It was in the center of town and had a four out of five-star rating. That was higher than all but one hotel in the city, which was a five-star with a room rate that was three times higher than the Mercure's. Adam arrived at the hotel by 5:00 p.m. He had a quick dinner in the dining room and then went to his room to crash. He looked forward to a long and restful night's sleep. In the morning, it would be time to work.

The good night's sleep ended too early. Adam arose at 4:26 a.m. The exact time spelled out explicitly on the clock, compliments of the digital age. After a hot shower, the first order of business would be to follow the only solid lead he had. Adam looked in a combination phone book and city information directory to find a list of construction companies. The directory wasn't much help. He found listings for residential builders, underground water tanks, polyurethane water pipe installation, and other contractors that were involved in small projects, but nothing that looked big.

Adam decided to pursue a different path. Since the family business he was looking for was probably a large outfit, it was likely to be involved in commercial projects. Adam took a few minutes to consider what major construction projects had occurred in Khamis Mushait about forty years ago. He knew the answer; as did just about anyone in the U.S. military who had served in the Middle East. During the 1970s, the King Khalid

International Airport was built. It was a Saudi Air Force base built with the help of the government. The facility was used extensively by the allies in the Iraq War, and continued to be utilized to some extent in this time of chronic instability in the Middle East. Adam used Google and found that the airport's more than 12,000-foot runway was built by a Dutch company in the late 1970s. They may have directed the operation but there had to be a local company or companies involved.

In Khamis Mushait, the construction business would have been hopping while the airbase was being built. Where should he start? It didn't take long for Adam to decide that the common denominator in a project like this, with more than two miles of runway, would be concrete. Adam went back to the city directory and found the listing for the largest ready mix concrete company in the city. It was Mastophen Ready Mix. Their display ad pictured more than a dozen ready mix trucks and huge, articulated, concrete guns that could reach several hundred feet to deliver material to hard-to-reach spots. The company was large, and the ad indicated they had been in business for over fifty years, meaning they were around in the 1970s.

Adam decided to take a cab to the company's headquarters. He brought the directory with him, to show to the driver, who he anticipated would not speak English. Adam was right. The picture spoke the proverbial thousand words. After a twenty-minute cab ride, he arrived at the Mastophen Ready Mix Company. It was located in a large industrial park on the edge of the city. Adam paid the driver with a 25 Riyal coin for the 18 Riyal fare, the equivalent of a two-dollar tip.

The office building was a modest structure compared to the impressive equipment pictured in the company's advertising. *A wise allocation of their funds*, thought Adam. This outfit makes money selling concrete not providing fancy offices. Once inside, he asked the receptionist if he could speak with someone about a past project the company might have been involved in. Initially, his request seemed to cause the young woman alarm, but then she regained her composure and said she would contact a sales manager. Adam looked benignly at the attractive young woman who, like all Saudi women in public, was wearing a hijab and like most offered a look that was impassive. He knew she was not allowed to drive and was subject to what most Western women would consider oppressive rules. Adam's first impulse was to feel sorry for her, then he checked himself. What did he know?

Almost as soon as the receptionist finished with the phone, a man entered the lobby through a doorway that was situated behind her desk. He was of average height and looked no older than forty. He was attired in Western-style clothes and had a pleasant smile. Approaching Adam in front of the receptionist's desk, he asked if he could be of help. Adam realized that whatever business this man intended to conduct with him would be done on the spot and standing. This made sense, Adam thought, because he certainly didn't look like a customer. There would be no invitation from the sales manager to speak privately in his office. A suspicious mind would have made him look wary, but this man displayed only a neutral affect. A quick mental calculation also told Adam the man he was speaking with wasn't old enough to have been around when the airbase was built, but he could have knowledge of the history of the company and the region.

Adam introduced himself and explained that he was trying to locate a man whose family had been in the construction business in the city forty years ago. The man had moved here from Yemen to join the family business in 1982, about ten years after the airbase was built. Adam said he didn't know the man's name or the name of the family business. The only information he could offer that had any connection to the man or his company was his wife's name, Alia. And her family or maiden name was Fahad.

The man shook his head calmly and said, "As I am sure you

can guess, I was not around when the base was built. From what you have said, I am afraid I will not be of much help." It seemed he was ready for their conversation to end.

Adam persisted. "Is there anybody in your firm who might have been around forty years ago, and who might be able to help me?"

The man, who did not offer his name, said, "If you will excuse me a moment, I will ask Mr. Mastophen if he can help you."

The man departed through the same doorway he had entered from while Adam remained standing. In a few minutes, a considerably older man walked through the same doorway. He greeted Adam warmly and introduced himself.

"Hello. I am Ekam Mastophen. How can I be of assistance?"

"Thank you, sir," said Adam. "My name is Adam Grant and I am in search of a woman named Alia Fahad—at least, that was her family name before she married. She is said to have moved here in 1982, with her husband, whose family operated a large construction company that was either headquartered here or at least did business in this city."

"Come along with me," the man said. "We can have a cup of tea in my office. Maybe I can help."

"Thank you," said Adam. As he followed Ekam, he admired the man's sparkling white thobe. On his head, he wore a white scarf with a braided black ring holding it in place. Adam knew that this headdress for Saudi men was called a *keffiyeh*. This headpiece was usually either white or a red-and-white checked pattern. Other versions with black were either a fashion statement or had militant or political meanings. Keffiyehs were worn indoors as well as outside and occasionally even with Western-style clothes.

"Please, have a seat Mr. Grant, and tell me again what you said out in the hall."

Adam restated the purpose of his visit, adding that he was searching for a woman who was an old friend of the family, who he had lost track of, and who had lived here more than thirty years ago. He said he was sure the woman would welcome hearing from him. Even though that wasn't totally correct, Adam thought this small stretch of the truth was justified under the circumstances.

"Mr. Grant," the man said, after making sure that both he and Adam were served their tea. "I think I know the company and the family you are describing. Forty years ago, they were among the largest companies of their kind in our country, and since that time they have only grown, so now they may be the largest." Then the man reflected, "As you know, we don't have many trees in much of our country, at least not the tall, straight kind that makes good lumber, but we do have a lot of sand." He paused for effect and continued. "A lot of sand and that makes a business like ours both needed and profitable. The company I think you are speaking of was very active in the city about the time you describe. After the airfield was finished, they remained in Khamis Mushait for another fifteen years or so. Then they closed their office here, but continued doing business in Jeddah, their principal base of operation. They concentrated their efforts there to take advantage of the building boom that was just beginning.

"Khamis Mushait has grown from fifty thousand to around five hundred thousand since the time of the airfield, but the really big construction boom and population growth that hit cities like Jeddah, Riyadh, and Dammam never occurred here. The name of the company I think you are looking for is Kanaan, and that is the name of the family. I expect you will be able to find them without difficulty in Jeddah."

"Did you have any personal contact with the family?" asked Adam.

"Yes, a little," said Ekam. "I do remember a young son who came into the business around the time you are referring to, more than thirty years ago. He moved here with his new wife, and I believe they had a son. Other than seeing him once or twice while doing business with the company, I know nothing more."

"Thank you, sir," said Adam with genuine appreciation. The information he had just been provided was enormously valuable.

Adam returned to his hotel and began a search online for Kanaan Construction in Jeddah. His efforts were rewarded. From what he discovered, Adam concluded the company was a sizable operation and should be easy to find. Before going down to the restaurant, he made a reservation for a return flight to Jeddah leaving later that evening.

Chapter 8

The time, 5:36 a.m., was displayed in digital pre-cision on the clock beside Adam's bed in the Holiday Inn in downtown Jeddah. The fifteen utterances for the morning call to prayer, starting with Allahu Akbar, pierced the closed window and joined the hum of the air conditioner. Adam did not understand the words in the call but, like nearly everyone, he recognized the first two. These words called to prayer millions of peaceful Muslims who espoused lives guided by the five pillars of their faith. Sadly, a few used the same words to justify death and destruction at their bidding. Adam reflected on the amount of violence that had been committed in the name of God and religion; from the Crusades, to conflicts in Northern Ireland, and now the mayhem caused by Islamic terrorists. Virtually no place in the world had been immune.

From his online perusal, Adam learned that Kanaan Construction was a large operation. They were headquartered in Jeddah, but the company had branches in several other cities, including Riyadh, Mecca, and Dammam. They also had operations in Oman; and several locations in the Emirates, Northern Africa, and Islamabad. If there was any continued connection between Alia Fahad's husband and Kanaan Construction Ltd., that connection would probably be at or near the top. Alia's husband, who was near thirty when they were married, would be in his mid-sixties now. If he had stayed with the company, it was possible he might even be the president.

The headquarters of Kanaan Construction Ltd. could be described as understated elegance—or elegantly substantial. The building was large and Mosque-like. The dominating lines were vertical; the flat roof line was crenellated. The walls were typical of the country, stucco-colored in a light tan. A long driveway, bordered by a dozen towering palm trees, attractive shrubbery, and a well-irrigated lawn, led to the main entrance. Adam was confident he was on target. He had a definite plan and, for better or for worse, he was going to pursue it.

"My name is Adam Grant," he said to the receptionist. "I am from Washington D.C. and I have an appointment with the President of Kanaan Construction." Adam's statement was not totally truthful, but his intention was to be provocative. Even if the president of the company had no connection to the message, curiosity at this audacious announcement might get Adam a brief audience. If Adam had guessed correctly and he had identified the sender of the message, he would be ushered in immediately.

Adam took a seat in the reception area, as he was told, and waited for nearly five minutes. When the receptionist returned to her desk, she told him that Mr. Kanaan was not in his office, but he would contact Adam later that day. She said he needed to know where Adam was staying in the city, and also his cell phone number. She told Adam that if, for some reason, he hadn't heard from the president by 3:00 p.m. to call her; she gave him a business card with the number. Adam told the receptionist that he was staying at the Holiday Inn Gateway and gave her his cell phone number. Adam assured her he would be eagerly awaiting Mr. Kanaan's call.

It seemed strange to Adam that the receptionist would take five minutes away from her desk to personally determine if the president was in his office. And, if he hadn't been in his office, how could she set up the precise time that Adam would be contacted? Regardless, Adam interpreted this encounter as a positive sign that he was on the right track. If Adam's hunch was correct, the president wanted to meet with him, but he wanted the meeting to be under conditions that he set.

Back in his hotel room on the twenty-fourth floor and facing west, Adam had a view of the Red Sea, which was now calm and blue. In contrast, his mind was churning. His thoughts were directed toward what he should say and do at this meeting. If he was, indeed, dealing with the right man, Alia Fahad's husband, things might move fast. Adam thought about how he should interpret the phrase "on behalf of" that was in the note President Tripp had received. This implied that the note was not from Alia, and it begged the question why was it sent *for* her by someone else, and who would that person be? Did the note have anything to do with her husband? Was the president of Kanaan Construction her husband? The connection didn't matter at the moment. At least there was a chance the president of Kanaan Construction would be a conduit to Alia.

It was likely that useful information about the message would be forthcoming, and Adam was eager to receive it. He knew there was more that must be dealt with eventually, but this was an excellent start. The next step in the process would be to answer the questions: why did the sender mention Alia's son and why was the boy's birth date significant for the President to know? The answers would have to wait. For now, he would be satisfied if he learned Alia's married name, and he would consider it a bonus if, in the process, he would be meeting her husband.

His cell phone rang. Adam picked up the phone. "Hello."

"Is this Mr. Grant?" asked the caller.

"It is."

"Thank you, Mr. Grant. This is Ahad Kanaan. I was unable to meet with you when you visited the office earlier today, but I am available now. I would like to invite you to my home for a visit. And after that, for dinner this evening, if you are free." He spoke in an authoritative voice in clear, perfect English.

"It would be my pleasure ..." Before Adam could say more, Ahad Kanaan told Adam that a car would arrive for him at the hotel at 3:00 p.m. The driver would take Adam to his home, where they would meet.

"Thank you. I look forward to our meeting," said Adam.

"Till then, good-bye," was the response.

Adam suspected he had hit pay dirt, and early in the game at that. Still a bit jangled with the time change, along with the less-than-sound sleep he had been getting, Adam decided to take a nap. The chance that he could get some real rest was promised by the fact that his mind was more at ease. He was satisfied that the process was moving ahead.

The car arrived at precisely the appointed time, and Adam was ready. He decided to wear the best clothes he had; when he saw the car, he was glad he did. Adam wore tropical blend grey trousers; a subtly checked, long-sleeved, dress shirt with an open collar, a blue blazer, and penny loafers. The car was a Mercedes Benz S600 limousine. It was about a mile long and the backseat seemed at least a half mile from the back of the driver's head. Without turning around, the driver merely asked, "Mr. Grant?" When the response was affirmative, he drove off.

The drive was forty-five minutes and proceeded in silence. The plush leather seats smelled new and the air-conditioned temperature was perfect. The windows were lightly tinted but allowed a good view. Adam took in as much as he could. It was clear they were headed toward the sea and that they were driving south, near the coast. Once out of the city proper they passed what appeared to be scattered but sizable estates that bordered the coast. The car slowed in front of a landscaped plot and turned right onto a curved, fine-gravel drive. After completing a lazy S-shaped curve, a wall, about ten feet high, came into view. It surrounded the manicured interior grounds of a modern-looking, pink-and-white villa with stucco vertical surfaces, typical of the local architecture. It was topped by a red-tiled roof. The building looked new.

As the vehicle approached a heavy iron gate in the wall, it opened automatically, revealing a circular drive that brought the car, traveling in a counter-clockwise direction, to the front of a substantial house. It came to a halt in front of a highly varnished double front door that had massive brass fittings. As the car stopped, the left-hand side of the door opened, revealing a smiling man of medium height. He had peppered gray hair with a high forehead, or a receding hairline, it was hard to tell. He wore Western-style clothes: a tan, open-collared, short-sleeved shirt and light-brown trousers. His feet, in comfortable sandals, completed an informal, comfortable appearance. Adam got out of the car and mounted the steps leading to the ample entry.

"Ahad Kanaan," said the man framed in the doorway. As he extended his hand, he said, "I am pleased to welcome you to my home."

Chapter 9

Good start, thought Adam as they shook hands.
"Adam Grant," he replied to a smiling Ahad Kanaan.

"I hope I wasn't hurrying you with a car and a meeting this soon," said his host, showing no evidence of anything but good feeling and hospitality. "I moved ahead quickly because I have the feeling you are as eager to begin as I am." After a brief pause, with Adam remaining silent, Ahad continued "Your first visit to Jeddah, Mr. Grant?"

Adam noted that he said Jeddah and not "The Kingdom," as would be characteristic of most native Saudis. If this were an immigrant family, it went back at least three generations, based on the history of their company. "Yes, it is," replied Adam, without further comment. Adam had the feeling that this visit was expected and that Ahad Kanaan felt in complete control of the situation.

"No need for us to stand in the entry," said Ahad. "Would you like to see our little house on the Red Sea?" Without waiting for an answer, which he knew would be yes, the host began leading, and Adam followed. "We are in the construction business, Mr. Grant, and my wife likes a challenge when it comes to our home and its furnishings. Mostly because of her wishes, which I have been happy to serve, we have found ourselves changing houses more often than is customary. Of course, being in the business, as they say, makes this easier, but not totally without challenges. For example, we have been in this home for only three months and there are many small things that need to be accomplished before we are completely settled."

As they passed through a large, well-appointed living room, Adam could see next to it a dining room that would accommodate a generous group, and next to that he peeked at a large well-appointed kitchen.

"Here is where we live for the most part," said his host as he pointed to a huge veranda-like room with a fireplace and outdoor cooking facilities that included a sink and dishwasher. Windows with adjustable louvers completed three sides of the room, offering a view of a newly landscaped space with the gradually receding perspective of the Red Sea as the centerpiece. A beach, no doubt built up with imported sand, completed the scene.

Adam noticed a small pier with a stout boat hoist projecting out from the shore. It held a white-hulled fiberglass boat with generous freeboard and a cuddy cabin. The boat appeared to be in the high twenty or even thirty-foot range. Two 350-horse-power Evinrude eTech motors hung on the transom. The years he had spent in boating allowed Adam to make this rapid and accurate appraisal. *About as good as it gets*, thought Adam, whose bias for the freshwater of the Great Lakes could be seriously challenged by what he saw.

"Enough of the tour for now, Mr. Grant. Could I offer you a refreshment?"

Refreshment was the term Adam expected in a Muslim country. What followed he did not anticipate.

"We adhere to most of the customs of the society, Mr. Grant, but in my home, I can offer you a beer, a cocktail, or some wine, if you prefer."

"Coffee or tea would be fine," said Adam. "And, if it is all right with you, please call me Adam."

"And you can call me Ahad."

As Adam admired the view, Ahad explained that his family came here from Algiers, which was more than two thousand miles to the west, across the Red Sea and most of the top of Africa. His grandfather started the Kanaan Construction Company about the time the Middle East/Saudi oil boom began. The Saudis looked to the United States for help in developing the oilfields and looked to North Africa for development in medicine and other commercial ventures, such as construction. The company, under his grandfather first and then his father, flourished. Now it was said to be the largest in the Kingdom. They had thirty facilities in Saudi Arabia, Oman, Qatar, Bahrain, Pakistan, and in parts of North Africa. With a wistful look, Ahad said, "I am the third generation of Kanaan family here, and my time is winding down. But, enough of this." His face clouded ever so slightly as he continued. "Quite aside from my home and business, there is some new and unfinished business that I must deal with, and that is why I have called you here."

Ahad's comment spoke volumes to Adam. The cryptic communication the President had received, he now felt, was neither a warning nor a threat. It was a plea. Was this an opening being offered by a troubled, and even desperate, man? Should Adam now take the initiative and delve into the situation, to get to the facts? He decided the answer was yes.

"Ahad, I am here as a personal envoy of the President of the United States. When he received your message, he decided to respond by sending me. I am here on his behalf. My job is to uncover the origins of a message he received that was connected to a person who he had a relationship with thirty-seven years ago, when he was in Yemen with the Peace Corps. That person, of course, would be Alia Fahad. The sender of the message, I am guessing, was you."

"That, Mr. Grant, is astute."

"It's still Adam."

"You are correct," replied a thoughtful and noticeably relieved Ahad Kanaan. He continued. "This is a beautiful day, Adam. I noticed you observing the boat in the hoist. Am I correct in my surmise?"

"You are, Ahad. It looks like a Grady White, in the twenty-eight to thirty-foot range, with good power on the stern and ample freeboard for traveling offshore."

"You are right, Adam. And, I think, the appropriate slang from your side of the ocean is 'this isn't your first rodeo.'"

"Well, no it isn't. I enjoy pure boating. I am not much of a fisherman, but I hear fishing is excellent in this area."

"It is," said Ahad. "And to be truthful, I am not much of a fisherman either. I just like being on the water. Would you like to go for a ride?"

With his answer already on his face, Adam said, "Yes."

Since Adam was wearing leather-soled loafers, Ahad offered him a pair of soft-soled sandals, which were accepted. The two repaired to the pier. Ahad checked the water-tight drainage plugs and lowered the boat into the water. Each engine turned the instant the key was toggled to the right, and in another two seconds both Evinrudes were uttering a deep-throated purr. Adam expertly cleared the lines and fended off as Ahad eased the boat free of the now submerged rails of the hoist. In less than twenty minutes from the first suggestion of the activity, the two were away from the shore and experiencing time on the water that they both thoroughly enjoyed. After heading out from shore five hundred yards, Ahad turned north and suggested to Adam that they cruise up to Jeddah Harbor. The ride would be about ten miles each way, plus whatever time they spent in the harbor. The excursion would keep them busy until dinnertime, when his wife would be home. Adam's second invitation to dinner was implied and, in the same vein, accepted.

With the boat traveling just over ten miles an hour, at 2,800 RPM, the craft was trying to break onto a plane. Using automatic pilot, a nice touch for a boat this size, the two relaxed, with Ahad in the helm seat starboard and Adam in the companion seat across.

"Now, I should tell you how this all started," said Ahad.

Chapter 10

The engines were running at 3,500 RPM and the boat was on a smooth plane at just under twenty miles per hour. The water was like glass, not a ripple to be seen. An expanding V-shaped wake extended behind from the controlled churning of the propellers. Was it following or directing the boat? Delicate splashes of water danced from the guiding action of the strakes as the boat sliced the water like a chef with a sharp knife. The well-trimmed boat essentially drove itself. Ahad, at the wheel, looked away, slightly to his right, denying his companion a view of the concerned look that bathed his face, the result of a prolonged period of torment.

After nearly five minutes of silence, willingly afforded by Adam, Ahad spoke. "Your presence here today is because of actions taken by me, so I think it is only right that I begin." Adam remained silent but attentive. As Ahad spoke, he shifted his gaze forward, sharing more of his countenance with Adam but still avoiding eye contact. "I will start at the beginning. The story may be long because it is one I have lived for nearly forty years. I have never spoken of it, but I will now. Adam, you will be the first to hear. You come to me as a stranger and I open up to you now, as a devout person in a confessional does to an unseen voice behind a dividing screen. For this, I ask you please to understand and forgive me."

Ahad began his story. "In 1981, my father sent me to Aden, on the coast of Yemen, to start a branch of Kanaan Construction. It was one of my father's few bad business decisions when it came to the company. The country I was being sent to was born in turmoil, with no coherent history, and the people I met there had no optimism for the future. It was clear, almost from the beginning, that our company would never be successful doing business in Yemen. Soon after I arrived, the major thrust of our business plan seemed to be to get out as quickly as we could while cutting our losses. This was not a very happy time for a young man of twenty-seven embarking on his first real assignment in business.

"But my time there was not a total loss. The Fahad family took me under their wing shortly after I arrived. Mahir Fahad was a Professor at Aden University and had gone to school with my father in Egypt. He and his wife had a beautiful girl. She was a wonderful daughter, but also the cause of some concern to them. Alia was spending time with a young Peace Corps volunteer from America. They thought he was probably a nice enough fellow, but he would be there for only a limited time and they were worried he would leave their young daughter with a broken heart. Sounds dramatic, but they were deeply concerned. I didn't quite understand my role at the time, but I am sure the family was hoping I would offer some competition for this young American. I spent a fair amount of time with Alia, mostly in their home, and I was smitten.

"When the American's time with the Peace Corps ended and he left Yemen, Alia was sad, but I was there, in the wings. Almost before I even knew what was happening, I was front and center, and in just a matter of weeks, it was decided, mostly by her parents, that we should marry. And we did. Alia was young, beautiful, vulnerable, and most of all a faithful and obedient daughter. I knew she was acting mostly at her family's bidding, but Alia and I had gotten along well together, and except for the Peace Corps boy, I probably would have had no serious competition.

"After our families had communicated in the traditional way, Alia accepted my proposal and we were married within weeks. We talked frankly about the timing and Alia's relationship with the American. She accepted that he was gone and that any plans they had discussed were unrealistic. She seemed happy. Believe me, parents or not, I would not have proceeded with this arrangement without that assurance from Alia. We stayed in Aden only long enough for me to wrap up business, and then we moved to Khamis Mushait.

"Three months after our wedding, Alia told me she was pregnant. We immediately saw a doctor, and it was confirmed. Our son was born in February, a few days less than nine months from the time we were married, and only slightly over nine months since her Peace Corps friend left Yemen. I tried not to think about her relationship with the American after we spoke briefly about him before the wedding. At the time, Alia assured me she was ready to move on. I referred to him as that boy, but only in my thoughts. This, I suppose, was simply because I was jealous. It was my immature way of diminishing him. Maybe that's what jealousy really is, emotion that simmers but without reason. I began to obsess, but thankfully for only a brief time, about whether Alia became pregnant the first time we were together or the last time they were. Whatever thoughts I had, remained mine alone and were never shared.

"There was nothing in my wife's behavior that caused me to have doubts. She was a beautiful woman, a faithful wife, and a wonderful mother—who I loved very much. But she wasn't given the time she deserved to be any of these. She died of acute leukemia seven years after we were married. She was only twenty-five and our son, Fathi, was just six years old. I was sick at heart losing my beautiful wife, and when I say that I mean beautiful in every way. I regret to this day that I never apologized to Alia for holding these unfounded thoughts. All I could do after she was gone was to hope for forgiveness. After Alia died, there was nothing I could do but go on with my life, and I did. I accomplished that successfully, until now, when I once again must ask for forgiveness for defiling the memory of the woman I loved and who gave me my only son.

"Two years after Alia died, I moved back to Jeddah from Khamis Mushait, as much for family reasons as matters of business. It was not easy to raise Fathi while I was alone, even with child care and housekeepers. After three years, when Fathi was nine, I re-married. My new wife made it possible for me to provide a mother for my young son and a wife for me, a woman I am sure Alia would have approved. Now, with two daughters, I am triply blessed with my wife, Farah, and two more angels. We lived a quiet and happy life until approximately three years ago, when things changed, at least for me.

"Things became unsettled after Fathi went to Pakistan to manage a large building project for Kanaan Construction. He was involved first in a major project at the airport serving Islamabad; a project like the one we had been involved with at Khamis Mushait more than forty years ago. Fathi had demonstrated that he was a smart businessman and people liked him. He was what you might call a rising star when it came to dealing with people and in purely business matters. We decided he would be the perfect person to supervise a new venture in Pakistan. When our work at the airport was completed, we began a residential building program, mostly apartments and condominiums, but we also built a few private homes on contract. Then, something strange happened.

"Shortly after he arrived in Islamabad, my son was befriended by a man he met on the squash courts. This fellow, who seemed to be a pleasant person in the beginning, according to Fathi, in unguarded moments began spouting serious radical beliefs which he expressed more often as time went on. This began as an on-the-court friendship, initiated by an otherwise respected and intelligent businessman. One time he introduced Fathi to what he called 'professional associates,' but there was no possibility of their doing any actual business. As time went on, this fellow's behavior turned out to be worrisome, possibly even dangerous. Before Fathi knew what was happening, the man's rantings evolved into serious talk about 'retribution for the infidel,' making him sound like a fanatical jihadist. After taking Fathi into his confidence, the man described a horrific plot against the U.S. that was in the planning stage. It would be a follow-up, 'an encore' they called it, to 9/11. The plan was to attack the new tower in New York, the One World Trade Center. With this attack, their intention, he said, was to kill more people than on 9/11, and the attack would leave a radiation-contaminated building full of the dead standing as mute testimony.

"As the man talked more about this, Fathi realized that this was something that actually could happen. This man was unhinged, but not crazy. This whole thing made Fathi uncomfortable. To be safe, he avoided the man and the topic never came up again during their further contact on the courts. After about six months and hearing no more of what he now considered harmless babble, Fathi believed the whole thing had blown over and nothing would come of what he had been told. Then, my son received a call. It was from a man who identified himself as being with the U.S. Immigration Service. The man requested a meeting with Fathi, saying it was about a routine matter that was better explained in person. When they met, it turned out the meeting was anything but routine. The man identified himself as Roland Wallace, with the U.S. Central Intelligence Agency. He said that he had information indicating that Fathi had met with a man, and remained in contact with this person, who was aligned with a known terrorist organization. He then told my son that the CIA had been watching him for several months. Based on what they had observed and what they learned about his family, they knew my son was not actively involved but they believed these people were trying to recruit him.

"Fathi was shocked. As Wallace spoke further, revealing what he knew about our family and our business in such detail, Fathi was convinced that the CIA had reliable sources and were able to compile vast amounts of accurate personal information. At this first meeting, the CIA agent asked Fathi if he would be willing to work with the CIA to monitor and report on the activity of this suspected terrorist and anyone else he might put him in contact with. He said that by using information Fathi could supply, the CIA could take down Al-Fir when the time was right. He told Fathi that it was essential the CIA had enough information to be able to act with certainty before they arrested the terrorists and then prosecute them—and this information was only available from someone who was on the inside. Agent Wallace said that Fathi was in a unique position to obtain information and to share it with the authorities. Before he gave it any real thought, Fathi agreed to help. He didn't realize it at the time, but he had become what the CIA calls an asset. Roland Wallace offered to pay Fathi, but my son declined any offer of money or other favors. The only thing Fathi asked was that his involvement never be revealed. Wallace agreed to this readily.

"My son was to remain fully engaged in our company, doing business as usual and carrying on with his life in a normal way. At the same time, he would appear to be cooperating with Al-Fir and, while doing so, learn as much as he could about their plans to attack One World Trade Center. If they asked him to help in any way, he should agree to do it. CIA Agent Wallace promised Fathi that nothing he cooperated with or was aware of would result in harm to anyone. The CIA would intercede in an appropriate way but only when the time was right. By working with the terrorists, Fathi would be privy to their plans, including who would be involved, what they intended to do, and the exact timing of when they intended to carry out the attack. With this information, the CIA would be able to nab the terrorists before they had a chance to act. The plot should be allowed to develop until it brought together as many people as possible in one place. By allowing this to happen, it would be possible to capture a large group of terrorists at once. In the process of capturing the terrorists, the arrests could be made by the proper authorities in a way that would not endanger the population.

"Fathi agreed to work with the CIA, and an elaborate system for he and Roland Wallace to continue meeting in private with complete security was worked out. At first, Fathi kept this whole thing to himself. Then, things changed and Fathi began to lose trust in Wallace. That is when Fathi came to me for advice—or maybe it was just to share his concerns. The first time he did so, I offered him little more than telling him to be careful and, for now, to do what the CIA advised. After several months, Agent Wallace said he had come up with a slightly refined plan that went beyond simply nabbing the leaders. Even though Fathi was able to give the agent all the names and details of Al-Fir's plot against One World Trade Center, including an approximate date, the agent urged Fathi to continue meeting with the terrorists, so he could gather even more information. He then told my son that the net should be widened so that more terrorists, including those who would be on the front line, the bombers, could be rounded up as well. Wallace gave Fathi the impression that the CIA had big plans for a dramatic capture. Finally, the agent said it had been decided that the best plan would be to have the terrorists assemble as if they were going to travel together, for example, on a boat to America. In this way, all of them could be arrested before they even left the country. When Fathi, at the urging of Agent Wallace, offered the leaders of Al-Fir the option of the bombers traveling to the U.S. on a boat, they became so enthusiastic about this prospect there was no going back.

"By this time, which was early this year, Fathi was concerned that things had gotten out of hand, and he brought this up to me again. When he told me this, I was worried for him and urged him to immediately drop the whole thing. Fathi said he wished he could but that was no longer an option. He knew so much about Al-Fir and the plot, the only way he could extricate himself and stay alive would be for everyone in Al-Fir who knew him to be either captured or killed. Fathi didn't care if these guys lived or died, he just wanted out and to be free of these goons. With the idea of using a boat still very much on the CIA's mind, and now part of the terrorists' plans, I decided that to save my son's life, the boat had to be either a convincing ruse or the real thing. I told Fathi that he should tell the terrorists he had received an offer from an anonymous donor. This person would provide a suitable vessel but only with the guarantee that the name of the donor would never be revealed. At first, my plan was to just offer a boat for delivering the terrorists to the U.S. Once the terrorists were assembled at the dock in Pakistan, with or without a boat being there, they would then be arrested on the spot and the plot would be stopped.

"Adam, I am sure you can see that, as this complex plot moved ahead, Fathi and I were getting in so deep that there was no way we could see to get out. From the beginning, which was almost three years ago, the CIA agent had remained in regular contact with my son, who was faithfully following the agent's lead. Then, gradually, Fathi became concerned that this whole scheme was being managed at a low level within the CIA, and he even wondered about the reliability of his contact. Was Roland Wallace operating alone? Was he sharing the information with anyone else? When Fathi asked what role the CIA, as an organization, would play as the plan unfolded, Wallace put him off by saying this could be dealt with later. By this last spring, we were both getting worried. Agent Wallace, who at first indicated he would be agreeable to making the arrests in Pakistan, came up with a new plan. He wanted to have the terrorists travel to the U.S. so they could be arrested in the United States and be subject to America's legal system. An idea that we were only playing with at the time, had suddenly become a reality.

"Fathi dangled the bait and the terrorists took it. Wallace, operating under the delusion of grandeur, was depending on Fathi to make good on an offer that they both originally conceived as a hoax. Now it was Fathi's responsibility to make good on this preposterous plan, not just to save face but to save his life. All the responsibility now fell on my son's shoulders. If the scheme worked and the terrorists were apprehended on U.S. soil, the CIA agent would be considered a hero. If it failed, my son would be dead. At this point, Fathi told me he no longer trusted Agent Wallace. He even feared the agent might be consorting with Al-Fir and was acting as a double agent. We both agreed that at their next meeting, Fathi would deliver an ultimatum: that he wanted to meet with Roland Wallace and his Islamabad station chief.

"After this, I started acting perhaps too much like a father. I ramped up efforts to prepare the large but marginal vessel I had reluctantly purchased at a bargain price, and I decided to explore ways to bring this matter to the attention of higher authorities in your government—and that is why I sent the message to President Tripp. I wracked my brain and came up with nothing better than taking advantage of the connection between the man who is now the President of the United States and my first wife. Forgive me, Colonel Grant, but that is all I could think of doing. If I can find any way to justify my actions, it is to say I am using Alia's memory to enlist the aid of the only person in the world who I believe can help the son she left in my care."

When Ahad called Adam Colonel Grant, Adam knew Ahad had done his homework. Adam had given his name at the Kanaan

Construction Company office and had shown his passport at two airports since landing in the country. His using Adam's rank indicated Ahad was paying close attention and recognizing authority. "Ahad, before I say anything else," responded Adam, "there is no question in my mind about which side we are on. We are on the same side. Because that is my sincere belief, I will tell you why I am here and what I have been asked to accomplish." Adam explained that President Tripp had asked him to find Alia Fahad in order to begin unwinding whatever series of events had contributed to the note the President had received. Regarding the paternity issue, Adam had no information to offer because it hadn't been addressed in his conversations with the President, so he decided to avoid any comment. Looking at his companion, who was noticeably more relaxed, if no less serious, Adam said, "I believe we should start working together to figure out what is going on. This is the type of work I do, so I would ask that Fathi and you hold off on doing anything different for now. Just continue to listen, watch, and report to me anything that you think I need to know."

"Should I try to reach out to Al-Fir?" asked Ahad.

"Absolutely not; at least not for now. But I have a plan," said Adam.

"Can you share it with me?"

"Yes. It is this. I have contacts in the Central Intelligence Agency. That is the only organization that would have access to terrorist actions that would be organized inside Pakistan. I will contact the people I know and trust before we decide where we want to take this."

The two men had finished discussing the matter, and finally resolve and relief were felt by both. The mood lightened and Adam began to take more notice of the sights they were passing. Approaching the city from the south, he saw what looked like miles of vertical cranes suitable for unloading container ships. He guessed they were used for cargo from Europe and the West. Ahad told Adam that Jeddah's central harbor was reserved mainly for its beauty and as a natural centerpiece for the bustling downtown area. Near its center was the King Fahad Fountain, the largest such facility in the world in terms of the height of its spout, which was said to be 853 feet. Adam had seen it from the plane and from his hotel.

The marinas Adam saw in a slip beyond the main harbor were typical of many others he had seen. Each accommodated about fifty boats, ranging from thirty to fifty feet or slightly larger. Across from two of the nicer marinas were six rectangular projections, each with a dozen houses, six on each side, facing each other with an access road between them. Ahad explained that the projections were reclaimed land, built at a huge expense, and the houses, each in the two- to five-million-dollar range, had sold immediately. "I have to look at these from time to time to remind myself how lucky I am that we decided to avoid residential building like this," said Ahad. Before Adam could ask why, Ahad explained. "The builders knew a lot more about constructing houses than they did about re-claiming land, and now they are spending a fortune shoring up the falling banks of their man-made peninsulas. There is so much invested in the structures on top they have no choice but to spend whatever it takes to keep them from sliding into the water. They will get the job done eventually, but they will spend ten times what it would have cost to do the job right in the first place."

By the time they turned the boat around and headed back, dusk was approaching. Adam, who was now steering, saw the spectacular display of the King Fahad Fountain that had been promised by Ahad. They agreed that at dinner, in the presence of Mrs. Kanaan, Adam's visit would be portrayed as business-related and nothing would be said about the discussion they had just completed. Ahad assured Adam that he was not in the habit of withholding information from Farah, but this would be an exception, for now. Adam said he would make plans to briefly return to the States and that they could stay in contact via phone. Adam didn't think it was necessary to share that his trip home would include a stopover in Rome.

After the long, game-changing afternoon with Ahad, followed by a pleasant dinner that was purely social, Adam returned to his hotel with renewed confidence and a budding plan. Adam's first phone call was to Erin. It was brief. He told her he had something he needed her help with. Although they could do it over the phone, he said he could visit her in Rome on his way back to the States. She was delighted he would visit and said that she'd help in any way she could. Neither of them missed Adam's true intentions. What remained unspoken was they were both happy to have the chance to see each other again. They both knew anything else they accomplished would be a distant second on the priority scale.

After speaking with Erin, Adam contacted Saudi Airlines and booked a flight to Rome. His nonstop flight departed at 9:37 a.m. and would arrive in Rome at 1:28 p.m. local time. He would not even miss a day at work, and he would get to see Erin!

He called Erin back, told her the time of his arrival, and she gave him the address of her apartment. With the seriousness and secretiveness of his mission in Saudi Arabia, and soon in Pakistan, it would be better if he avoided being seen at the CIA office in Rome. Anything official that would be accomplished during his visit could be carried out between the two of them and would pale in importance to their own personal business. Neither mentioned the need for Adam to book a hotel room.

Chapter 11

August 12, Friday

Adam had always been able to do some of his best thinking while in an environment many would consider distracting; for example, like being on a crowded airplane. Anticipating a full flight, and with no traveling companion, he was thoughtful about his seat selection. Adam's intention was to station himself in a place that would be most conducive to getting some productive work accomplished. For this, he chose the very last row and an aisle seat. He would not be able to recline his seat back, but that was of no concern. He would not be sleeping. Also, there was a better than even chance that the middle seat next to him would remain empty and, possibly, no one would be seated at the window meaning he would have the row to himself. The last row was considered by many to be the worst on an airplane; sometimes it didn't even have a window. That was just fine for Adam today. His goal, for the next five hours, was to pull together all the meaningful facts he had assembled. It would start with his conversations with the President and proceed through all that Ahad had told him yesterday.

After his meeting with Ahad, Adam felt the challenge he had been given by the President had gained the other half of the symbolic arch he envisioned. Before yesterday, with only questions, just half of the arch was in place. It was big, but incomplete and unstable, an unsupported segment towering but unfinished. What it had lacked in stability, in this case credibility, now made sense. It was as though the other half of the arch was in place based on what he had learned from Ahad Kanaan, but some of his nagging questions still needed answers. Every arch needs a keystone and that was the information Adam was looking for.

Vital information garnered by the investigator, as Adam now pictured himself, was that Alia Kanaan née Fahad had died thirty years ago. Anything she could have offered was buried with her. The key to the issue at hand, as Adam saw it, lay with her son, Fathi. Who was his biological father and what could be done about the situation he had become embroiled in? Fathi Kanaan was operating in dangerous waters. He was between a group of ruthless individuals bent on bringing death and destruction to the United States and a CIA agent he scarcely trusted, and all of this was compounded by his being essentially alone in a country that was rife with terrorist activity.

A lot of work lay ahead. On the plus side, it was a great relief that Ahad Kanaan seemed to be a man who was reasonable, competent, and capable of action, and who had well-founded concerns about the safety of his son and his son's family and the horrific acts intended by ruthless terrorists. Adam could appreciate how Fathi's situation had gotten out of hand. And he believed Ahad had acted in a way that only a father could, albeit at the eleventh hour, with his desperate attempt to help his son by the audacious act of reaching out to the President of the United States. Fathi should consider himself fortunate to have a person like this on his side.

What would a father do? That word, *father*, with all of its implications, was operative, especially when considering Ahad's motives and actions. Adam truly believed Ahad was Fathi's father, and he believed Ahad thought the same. Comparing the two men as he recreated his discussions with the President, there was nothing Adam could glean from what the President said or did to convince him that Fathi was Phillip Tripp's biological son. But the only way to know with absolute certainty would be to ask the President if Alia and he had had relations and then use DNA testing to confirm or deny a connection—but these were not issues Adam could easily pursue with the President of the United States. Although it was essential that the paternity issue be resolved, it was not the critical issue now.

The pressing issue at hand was real, imminent, and dangerous. Adam felt he had to meet with Fathi Kanaan as soon as it could be arranged without endangering him. It was important for Adam to speak with Fathi face to face, but it was too dangerous to do so in Islamabad. While considering this, Adam's thoughts turned to Pakistan, a country that was often in the news, and not in the best light. It is one of nine nuclear powers in the world and the United States seemed to have a love/hate relationship with its government.

The United States maintains a large, six-story embassy in Islamabad. It was completed in 2015, at a cost of eighty-five million dollars. A much larger complex had been planned, with a projected cost of one billion dollars. It was to have facilities for a contingent of Marines supported by mobile combat-related equipment. The Pakistani government, after originally agreeing to this, blocked the plans, ostensibly to avoid being considered a U.S. military outpost. They apparently believed their own interests would be better served if they continued to straddle the divide in world power.

Despite generous financial support to Pakistan from the United States, over three billion dollars in 2011, relations with this Muslim country that borders Afghanistan on the north, Iran to the east, and India to the south, have been uneven and problematic. In contrast, India, the other part of the former British-Indian Empire, has been a consistently loyal ally of the U.S. With a largely Hindu population, India has a difficult relationship with Muslim Pakistan. That led to a limited war between these two nuclear powers and continues with relentless ongoing tension.

The fact that India and Pakistan, countries that are politically and culturally divided, and have a serious territorial dispute in Kashmir, can refrain from *total* war has been touted as evidence of the peaceful use of nuclear arms—that is, having them be just a *threat*. But anyone who is encouraged that nuclear weapons are a safe deterrent adds the disclaimer: restraint also requires at least a modicum of common sense. Using nuclear force pre-emptively in the face of possible mutual destruction takes a madman, a dysfunctional government, or an unrestrained ter-rorist. The burden for a responsible government is to use all means possible to avoid the risk of nuclear war.

Adam concluded that the best place to start looking for any dealings Fathi Kanaan might have with the CIA would be at the Agency's headquarters at Langley. If Fathi was providing infor-mation about the terrorists' plot while functioning as an asset working with a CIA agent, this could eventually be confirmed. However, to get answers it would be necessary for Adam to gain the confidence of whoever at Langley was in the know. And, if Fathi was actively working as a useful, functioning asset, his handler would protect him; even including the use of deflection. This could go so far as to brand Fathi, at least for outside con-sumption, as a terrorist they were watching. Any outing of an asset would have to be approved by the asset himself. In that case, it would be necessary for the CIA to take appropriate measures to keep the asset safe from any reprisal at the hands of the terrorists they were exposing. A change of status or sharing of information would be done only at the discretion of the handler. While an asset was active and useful, the handler would not divulge information that would expose his charge. Adam knew he was dealing with a delicate situation. The tasks at hand would be difficult but not impossible.

From what he had learned about the CIA Directorate of Operations, the formal name for the group that handles spies, nothing in the organization was guarded more jealously than the identity of people like Fathi. These individuals were recruited and developed over months and even years and were the crown jewels of the spy game. The continued usefulness and safety of an asset depended entirely on confidentiality and stealth.

Sharing what he had learned with Erin would be a good place to start when it came to entering the inner workings of the CIA, but it would only be a start. The best Adam could hope for would be for Erin to provide him a useful contact at Langley. Adam would have to carry on from there.

After a short visit with Erin, Adam would fly to the States, where his first stop would be CIA Headquarters. After that, he would go to the National Institutes of Health where he would learn what he could about DNA and paternity testing. But the best thing Adam had in store was seeing Erin after three months of them being apart.

Chapter 12

August 12, Friday

Ahad had promised Adam that he would not discuss the situation with anyone, but in Ahad's mind, that did not include his son. After Adam left Jeddah, Ahad phoned Fathi and told him what had transpired at his meeting with Adam. Ahad did not provide any names, only the gist of what had been discussed. He described meeting with a man who was a personal envoy of a highly placed person in the United States. That person's recommendation, for now, was for both Fathi and Ahad to continue working as they had been with Al-Fir. Fathi should make no changes in how he behaved because too much was at stake. The son understood and agreed.

Fathi was eager to see his father and to meet this mysterious envoy but he knew it was critical that he remain calm, focused, and accountable. He sensed things were coming to a head with Al-Fir, and it was becoming uncomfortable for him to interact with them. The way things were unfolding, he would deal with crazy terrorists one day; Roland Wallace, the CIA agent he did not trust, on the next; and then go to Kanaan Construction and try to conduct business—not an easy life. Fathi was glad he had confided in his father, and also that his father had reached out for help. But he knew there was only so much that either he or his father could do, and time was running out.

Any hope Fathi had about ending his ties with Al-Fir and capturing the whole lot of the organization's leaders and the bombers on Pakistani soil evaporated when Wallace said the CIA had no authority for such action in Pakistan and that they couldn't rely on local support. The take-down had to occur in the United States. It would make a bigger splash, Wallace said, and would ensure capture of a larger number. With this decided, there seemed to be no viable alternative—the boat option was confirmed. It was a good thing his father had gone as far as he had acquiring and prepping the boat, including lining up a captain and crew. Ahad's condition for agreeing to acquire a boat that would actually transport the terrorists from Pakistan to the U.S. was that Fathi obtain a guarantee from Roland Wallace that all of this was being done with the full knowledge and sanction of the U.S. government and the CIA, as Roland had assured Fathi from the beginning.

Fathi remembered his first meeting with Assoud Al Walaki, the head of Al-Fir. At that meeting, Fathi learned that Al-Fir was recruiting people who were willing to inflict damage on the United States. At the time, Fathi was not yet considered a part of the team, only a consultant. It was now almost three years since that first meeting, and Fathi continued to meet regularly with both the terrorists and Wallace. Fathi had provided Wallace with enough ancillary information for the CIA agent to justify to his boss, the station chief, the time he spent with his asset while hiding the real purpose of the relationship. The station chief was pleased that through Wallace's efforts, several dangerous terrorists had been dealt with. But Fathi's involvement with the bigger plot, that Wallace had never disclosed to his superiors, was Wallace's top priority, and it would soon be reaching its conclusion.

Fathi Kanaan was unaware that Roland Wallace was only a mid-level CIA agent with a stalled career. He wanted to make a big and truly consequential arrest, which is why he told Fathi the arrests had to occur on U.S. soil. He assured Fathi that the arrests of Al-Fir suicide bombers *before* they could act would be a signal accomplishment in the war on terror. It would require persistence and dedication to pull off, and working with the CIA, Fathi could play a vital part. What Roland did not say was that this operation was known to only one man in the CIA, and that man was Roland Wallace. Success with this operation would put Roland in the books as one of the most effective operatives in the history of the CIA. *Maybe not a statue at Langley*, he mused, *but recognition and fame, and that would be great.*

———————

Fathi was called to an urgent meeting with the team that would be traveling with and supervising the bombers who would carry out the attack on One World Trade Center. The meeting would be held in the usual place, a time-worn, two-story concrete structure with peeling painted walls and a large, though mostly unused, second-story balcony perched above graffiti-splashed muddy exterior walls. Five men sat on mismatched chairs around a battered wooden table. Four wore dark, slightly ballooned trousers; loose-fitting, light-colored, long-sleeved shirts; and sandals. They had omitted the headpiece and sash over one shoulder, as had been worn by the late al-Qaeda leader, Osama bin Laden. Their heads were thrust toward the center of the table, in a conspiratorial pose. They spoke softly, even though there was nobody nearby to hear them, not even if they had shouted. This house was safe, they were sure. Their attention was directed at a fifth man who, except for his heritage, had little in common with them. He wore Western-style clothing, was well-groomed, and spoke in an educated and clipped pattern.

The four men Fathi was addressing had recruited and trained the men and women who would complete the attack on One World Trade Center. They would accompany the bombers to the U.S., providing them support and direction. They respected and obeyed the supreme leaders in the movement, especially Assoud Al Walaki. The fifth man was a consultant and facilitator. Fathi had the knowledge and experience to formulate the necessary plans to achieve their grand scheme. Because he was not one of them, they listened to him grudgingly.

Today's meeting began with the discussion of an issue that had become all too common at their meetings. Two more leaders had been killed by drone strikes, delivered in what had been thought to be a secure enclave near the Afghan border. And, almost as bad, three bomb-making facilities in northern Pakistan had been knocked out in the last two months. The men agreed it was fortunate that there had been civilian casualties in all of the raids because when women and children were killed it helped demonstrate the ruthless behavior of the U.S.-led infidel forces. Mihal, Abdul, Fazeez, and Mohammad wracked their brains to think of who could be leaking information about the whereabouts of their leaders. They admitted it was possible, but not likely, that the CIA had located the enclave on its own. Their gut told them it was the work of an informant, and if this was true, the traitor had to be found and destroyed. The fifth man maintained a calm demeanor as he observed their zealous fanaticism. Silently, he was pleased that the information he had provided to the CIA had been used effectively to stall their actions.

After several minutes and now calmer, the men joined hands and pledged undying support for the quest to find the traitor. "Enough bitching!" said Mihal. "Now, let's get down to business." Mihal was the leader of the four. "We are not here to talk about losses. Our job is to make plans for how we can carry out the ultimate *destruction* project." As he said this, Mihal smiled at his use of *destruction* because of what he would say next. "We have an expert at *construction* with us. He tells us he can build things. Now, let's see how much he knows about knocking things down." Mihal assumed a triumphant grin as he directed his gaze at a man he didn't like or trust. Mihal couldn't decide if it was jealousy or something else about this man who lived in Saudi Arabia but whose family was from Algeria. "Tell us what we should know."

Fathi nodded in assent and began to speak in a professional and analytical way. "Although the task we have ahead of us is not made any easier by the monumental success in 2001, the infidels are still vulnerable. This time when we strike, there won't be the massive physical destruction, but there will be an even greater loss of human lives. And the infidels will suffer in the process." Fathi paused and looked at the satisfied faces around him. Even though Fathi knew they considered him an outsider, they listened to him because Assoud Al Walaki said they should.

Fathi continued, "The plan that we have decided on is this ..." He took a deep breath and paused long enough to reassure himself that none of the terrible things he was about to say would ever happen. And to remind himself that his life depended on his delivering a convincing performance. "We will primarily attack the base of the building, at its core. The main central hall on the ground floor has a sixty-foot ceiling which will become an inferno littered with debris after the simultaneous detonation of twenty explosive vests, each of which will be laced with radioactive material, making them dirty bombs. In the atrium area, one thousand gallons of flammable material will be released from irrigation carts intended for the building's live plants. Our team will prepare these carts on site after neutralizing the regular maintenance crews. In each of the lower seven floor lobbies and in the elevators, personal explosive devices will be detonated, killing as many people as possible and disabling the elevators and the stairways."

"What about the building?" asked Fazeez, who was getting more comfortable with the direction of the meeting.

"We will not be able to fully destroy the building because of how it has been constructed. Although the building will remain standing, this attack will kill at least four thousand people, which is even more than were killed on 9/11. We will accomplish this by killing as many as possible in the lower seven floors and trapping everyone above them and pumping one hundred pounds of sarin gas into the ventilation system. Anyone who survives the blasts will be poisoned."

"This is an ambitious plan," said Mihal.

"Ours is a sacred mission," replied Fathi, who uttered this more convincingly than he thought he was capable of.

"Will we have enough people in New York to take a meaningful part in this project?" asked Abdul.

"Yes. We have a dozen people in Manhattan who are prepared to work alongside your team. They will be there to assist the people you will be bringing as they make the ultimate contribution to our cause—the glory will go to the group of men and women that you will be leading to martyrdom, Mihal."

This recognition of his special role pleased Mihal, but he still didn't like Fathi. Mihal didn't trust the manhood of someone he hadn't seen kill one of the enemy while looking them in the eye. "That will be a big job," Mihal agreed.

Fathi continued. "These men, as they leave this earth, will meet the seventy-two virgins promised in the Quran, and the women will have their reward too. They will be reunited with their husbands, choose their favorite if they had several, or choose any man they want if they have never married. All of these heroes will leave this earth and meet their reward in heaven. Our group will be larger than in 2001, but Manhattan is a crowded city of more than eight million people. On the journey to the U.S., all of you will be changing your looks so you blend in and become invisible. Men will shave their beards, wear Western clothing, and have haircuts like the Americans. It is okay to copy the infidel when it is for the right cause."

Concluding, Fathi said, "The bombs will be stored in a safe and secure place on the ship; there will be no accidents or a repeat of our factories being destroyed accidentally. Our team, which you have been training for more than a year, will enter the U.S. on a boat traveling in the waters between Canada and the United States. The infidels do not monitor these waterways closely and will not be suspicious of the boat. Then our people will land far enough away from the target to allow them the opportunity to assemble and attack in a safe and deliberate way. You are all doing a fine job." After answering a few not very important questions, the group seemed satisfied with what they had just heard. The meeting disbanded and Fathi left.

The leaders of Al Fir had turned to Fathi because they had no other ready alternative. He was intelligent, knowledgeable, and a successful businessman, who was committed to the Jihadist cause. They knew that this combination of abilities was essential and realized that they must make a concession to a person who had been born in Saudi Arabia to Algerian and Egyptian parents from a family that for two preceding generations had assumed a Western lifestyle. They were counting on what was in his heart and head and not on the clothes he wore. Fathi was smart and had the talents they needed to complete their task. They were pleased when he agreed to help in the planning of the event and accepted his choice to not travel to the United States.

All of this was moot. They would take care of him when his services were no longer needed.

Chapter 13

Adam gave the cab driver the address of Erin's apartment. He was satisfied with what he had accomplished on the flight. He would tell Erin only as much as she wanted to hear about the mission, but his guess was that she would want to know it all. After everything the two of them had experienced in North Korea, there was no separation between them in terms of their professional lives, and, Adam thought, a lot more.

The cab stopped in the middle of the block in what was Rome's central historic district. The building entrance was unremarkable. The double doors with smudged glass windows were flanked by retail shops, one that sold luggage and the other shoes. There were no clues of what might be behind the doors, but they had to lead to apartments of some sort if this is where Erin lived.

Out of the cab and on the sidewalk with his one bag, Adam opened the door he had spied. It revealed a well-used foyer. He saw the name E. O'Leary on a directory that included ten other names. There was a button next to each, but no numbers. It was nearly four o'clock and he wondered if Erin would be home. He suspected she might be, since she knew his arrival time and had told him to come here straight from the airport. He buzzed and waited. There was no apparent intercom connection.

Before he had time to digest that thought, the elevator door opened. Erin popped out, ran up to him with a big smile, and planted a big kiss on his lips. She grabbed his bag, but he chivalrously grabbed it back, and they both entered the elevator. On the second floor, Erin walked to an apartment door directly across from the elevator and opened it. The ceiling, in what Adam guessed was the living room, was high, a pre-air-conditioning design. The place looked well-used, but that was to be expected in a city as old as Rome. The space was functional and probably affordable. He also guessed the best feature of the apartment was its location.

The two of them started to talk at once. When they stopped, there was nothing said, and then the situation repeated itself, twice.

Adam took charge. "Erin, you have the floor. Tell me what the heck you are doing."

Erin gave Adam a thorough rundown of who she was working with at the office; the type of not exactly cloak-and-dagger activities they were engaged in; and, best of all, she told him that she had the next three days off. She told Adam that her work schedule, since she had arrived in Rome, had been ten plus hours a day, six days a week, and she had earned some time off. While she was talking, Erin went into a small but functional kitchen and got each of them a can of Diet Coke. Changing gears, Erin said, "Now, Adam, what do you want to see in Rome?"

"I'm looking at her."

"Come on! Really, what do you want me to show you?"

"All of you. *Really.*"

"Okay, I promise that will happen later, but what kind of plans do you want to make?"

"What do you suggest?"

Erin took a deep breath. "Okay, cowboy. Oops! I think I

called you that once and I had to fight off getting pregnant. Okay, Adam, we have two options."

"I'm game," Adam replied.

"There is so much to see in Rome, we could take a month, but we don't have that much time. Tell me what you would like to see, and we can make up our own tour schedule."

"Before I answer that, what is option two?"

"We spend three days at the Britannia Hotel at Lake Como."

"No contest, Erin. When do we leave for Lake Como?"

"Adam, I am so happy you said that! We can leave in the morning. Now, another choice: train or car?"

"How many miles and time for each?"

Erin said, "It is about 350 miles north. It will take maybe six plus hours by car and nine hours by train."

"No question. I prefer we drive. We can be together and alone, stop for a nice lunch along the way, and we will have a car there if we want to see anything. I hear the area is beautiful."

With nothing to do until dinner, Erin led Adam into the other room and he collected on the promise she had made. Totally relaxed and satisfied, Erin said, "I could stay here all night with you, but we must eat something, and I have a place I want to show you."

"Erin, I am ready for anything you suggest."

At seven o'clock, the two got into a cab and Erin directed the driver to Alfredo alla Scrofo. "The restaurant is just beyond the Tiber River, about ten blocks from the Vatican," Erin explained to Adam. "This is where they invented fettuccini Alfredo. And that's what you must order. I know you will enjoy it."

"As you wish," said Adam.

The restaurant had an impressive entry. A garland of flowers wrapped around the door and extended on either side above broad windows. Erin insisted the atmosphere was better inside, so they were seated at a corner table for two directly under black-and-white pictures of 1950's movie stars Spencer Tracy and Tyrone Power. The restaurant had three large rooms and a few of the tables could hold eight people or more. It was obvious that the restaurant benefited from the tourist trade, but Adam wasn't going to comment and spoil Erin's pleasure in introducing him to this experience. Like many legendary New York restaurants, the walls were covered with hundreds of photos of famous people from around the world, mostly actors, athletes, and politicians.

When the server came to their table, each ordered the dish the restaurant was famous for. Soon a different server, young and full of enthusiasm, arrived with an ample white platter with a generous mound of flat, broad noodles covered with a yellow sauce. At the table, the server used two large forks to mix the cheese, which was on top of the noodles, employing an expertise no doubt gained from a considerable amount of practice. He placed half of the food on a large clean plate that he gave to Adam. And then, with a flourish, he gave the original plate heaped with the fettuccini noodles and cheese sauce to Erin. "The lady gets the honor of having the extra treat of the delicious cheese sticking to the plate's rim," said the triumphant server.

This was like no other pasta Adam had tasted. The cheese was stronger and had a mild grainy but pleasant texture. There was less cream than he was used to, but it turned out to be a plus and just the right amount. Erin enjoyed a glass of Chianti and Adam had sparkling water. The meal was everything Erin had promised; another bonus for Adam, although being with Erin was the real prize. A hamburger at McDonald's would be dining paradise for him as long as Erin was across the table. On the way home, they had the cab driver take a detour along the Via Veneto, so they could check out the dressed windows of the extravagant shops. This short trip turned out to be the extent of their sightseeing in the city.

Before they turned out the lights, it occurred to Adam that

he hadn't asked Erin what they were going to do for a car. Erin must have read his mind, as she said, "Adam, as you probably already guessed, I don't have a car. But I rented one and it will be delivered here at eight o'clock in the morning. I hope it's okay."

"I'm sure it will be," said Adam.

They were asleep in minutes.

The car was a dark-blue Fiat 500X four-door. It was small but sufficient for their needs. The driver's seat was comfortable, with plenty of leg room, and Adam noticed it had a 2.4 Liter engine which, for a car that small, promised some pep. After checking Google Maps, they decided to take state road E35 instead of the autostrada. It would take a bit longer, but they would be able to enjoy the towns in between and avoid the traffic that Adam knew traveled at breakneck speed with no limits on the highway. The trip, as Adam planned, would take the slower but more interesting route, that would take them to Florence, Bologna, and Milan, as well as a bevy of potentially interesting smaller towns in between. Both travelers were looking forward to a leisurely and pleasant day together.

After fighting traffic for a half hour while getting out of Rome, and now officially on their way, Adam decided the drive would be a convenient time to get their business done. "Erin, you haven't asked me why I am here, and I appreciate that—but it's now time for me to explain."

"I'm all ears."

Adam recited to Erin, verbatim, the note sent to the President of the United States and explained Phillip Tripp's concern over its meaning. Adam told Erin about the President's time in the Peace Corps in Yemen, where he met his first true love, Alia Fahad. He also gave Erin a rundown on who he had met and what he had learned since leaving the United States and while visiting Jeddah. With the background established, Adam said, "My job for the President is to confirm that Ahad Kanaan is Fathi's biological father and, more critically, meet with Fathi and get the details about what is happening with Al-Fir and their plot to attack One World Trade Center."

"That's putting it succinctly," said Erin. "If I were you, I would ask the President if there is any possibility he is Fathi's father. We both know there is only one way he can say no. And, regardless of President Tripp's answer, there is only one sure way to confirm who is the biological dad, and that, of course, is DNA testing. You will have to find a way to get Fathi's DNA sample, or maybe Ahad can be of assistance. Ethically, since everyone is an adult, you should get permission from all of them—but maybe you don't consider that as being an option.

"From what you have told me so far, the very best scenario is that a couple of amateurs are getting in way over their heads. The plot may be fact or fantasy, or even a little bit of both. The CIA agent's involvement sounds a little weird, but there could be some disconnect in the telling. If the story is true, it should be possible to confirm that when you get back to D.C. And I can help with that if you want. Finally, if these guys are simply whackos, all bets are off."

She gets it, Adam thought. He was happy to give this smart lady credit. "You nailed it, Erin. When I get to D.C., I will visit Langley and after that maybe the National Institutes of Health to speak with someone about DNA testing. When it comes time for me to check out what might be going on with the CIA in Islamabad, do you know who I should contact at Langley? I have already consulted with John Morrison about Yemen and he was helpful."

Erin, as usual, was a step ahead. "My recommendation for that is Fred Billson. He is up on everything on our watch in Pakistan, so speaking with him would be the place to start. I will contact Fred and give him a heads up, if that is okay with you."

"Please do, Erin," said Adam. "Now, let's find a place for lunch and consider this the end of our business."

Erin agreed.

The Hotel Britannia, on the shores of Lake Como, was perfect. Carefully maintained and updated, the hotel combined Old-World charm with modern conveniences. It was large, more than two hundred rooms, but once inside their room, the parquet floors, king size bed with a companion single bed abutted, and tasteful furnishings was just right. The bathroom was small and European, with a free-standing tub and a jury-rigged shower curtain.

The three days passed in what seemed like an hour. Erin and Adam were as comfortable with each other as was humanly possible. The idyllic setting took a distant second place to the pure joy each experienced being together. On the drive back to Rome, Erin's demeanor changed from pleased and satisfied to wistful and distant. She finally broke the comfortable silence and said, "Where are we, Adam?"

Foregoing the flippant "in the middle of Italy," Adam was serious when he answered. "In love, but ..." The silence that followed said it all for both.

"Is there any way we can be ourselves and be together?" asked Erin.

"I have to believe there is," said Adam. "Let me finish this job, then we need to make some plans."

Chapter 14

August 16–18, Tuesday thru Thursday

After traveling for more than a week, and now back in his apartment in Arlington, Adam realized he had effectively been off the radar during his absence. Because only a few people knew he had left the country, he was not missed; and thus, no one welcomed him home. He was, however, certain that the President knew he had returned and would be eager to hear news about his trip to Saudi Arabia.

On Wednesday afternoon, Adam called the phone number the President had given him and left a message. President Tripp said that calling this number would connect Adam with a real person who would use her judgment about when to contact the President's personal secretary, who would alert the President, who would then return the call when he could. The President's secretary immediately phoned Adam back and said the President would expect him at the White House the next morning.

Adam sat in a straight-backed wooden chair at the side of the Resolute desk. The President was pressed for time but wanted to get the progress report from Adam in person and not over the phone. Adam told President Tripp about Alia dying just seven years after marrying Ahad and that she had a son just over six years old at the time of her death. Phillip Tripp registered sadness when he heard about her death, but there was no visible reaction indicating special concern when Adam mentioned the son. The news about Ahad was received in a neutral fashion, but the President did offer that he was pleased to hear that Alia had married a nice man. Adam then came to the real meat of the discussion. He described Ahad's concern about his son's activity in Pakistan in a measured way, not emphasizing the need for action, just offering the facts. Adam was successful at this because the President did not seem particularly alarmed nor did he express a need to be involved in the issues involving the Kanaan family. The President did say that Adam's job now was to find out, if he could, the extent of Fathi Kanaan's difficulties in Pakistan, and especially why his father was so worried that he decided to contact the President of the United States. The President told Adam he should take no action on his own. If there was any solid evidence that a real threat was in the works, the President assured Adam he would make sure that appropriate measures were taken.

The President's behavior indicated to Adam that Phillip Tripp believed he was dealing with a public relations problem, nothing more. Adam guessed that the President believed this matter could be managed without consequence if sufficient attention was paid to detail and the timing was right. Adam thought this reaction was overly optimistic, but understandable because he had purposely downplayed the seriousness of the alleged terrorist plot against the U.S. Adam would know more about the situation after talking with Fred Billson and, if justified, he would alert the President. And, based on his reading of the President's reaction, really his non-reaction, when it came to Fathi, Adam would deal with Ahad's concerns about paternity on his own. He would keep the details to himself until he could take the next step.

The situation made Adam feel how he suspected a doctor must feel when deciding how much bad news to tell a patient when trouble was looming and there was nothing the patient could do but worry while the doctor did his best, and both waited for the final results. Where does one draw the distinction between telling the whole truth and only as much information as needed for the benefit of the hearer? How much responsibility should a person in charge of a situation assume in order to relieve the concern in another when the only thing that person being protected can do is fret without effect? Adam had decided that the paternity issue would remain his alone, at least for now, and the potential terrorist threat would remain the focus of his attention.

Adam had decided he would not ask the President if he had had relations with Alia. Anyone who reads newspapers, listens to the news, or watches television crime shows knows about the importance of DNA when it comes to connecting a suspect to a crime scene or biological parents and their children. A complicating factor was that the study of reliable sites on the internet confirmed to Adam that there was more to the process of DNA testing in cases of paternity than in establishing the location of an individual in crime detection. He could get the information easily enough at the NIH, but Adam was concerned about red flags. What if someone connected him to what he was doing for the President and it got out? There would be a storm to end all storms. No matter how much of a long shot the connection would be, there was no point in taking the risk.

Adam was glad to have an excuse to call Erin. When it came to communicating, he didn't mind talking on the phone for factual information, but when it came to lengthy conversations,

Adam was less comfortable. He didn't like discussing feelings and things that were personal and sensitive on the phone. He was a strong believer that seeing a person's reactions when communicating conveyed a message as much as the words themselves, and certainly helped prevent uncertainty and mis-understandings. He missed Erin and wanted to hear her voice, but he didn't want there to be any chance that what he might say could be misinterpreted. He knew this kind of thing was prone to happen when both parties in a relationship were fully invested and anxious about what if and what next. He was in love with her and he didn't want to mess up. In his own mind, he wondered how a person could be as tough as he knew Erin was, and at the same time be someone Adam considered del-icate and vulnerable, someone he wanted to protect from any possible adversity.

"Hi, Adam!" came Erin's cheerful voice. "I was just about to call you. I'm glad you thought enough to spare me the nickel."

This is what Adam hated about the telephone. He would swim across the ocean to see her, and he knew she knew it. Her comment was just a reaction, a relief-valve expression that meant I am so glad you called. *Enough Freud*, Adam thought. "Erin, I miss you. It was so great being with you." These words didn't come close to expressing how he really felt. Just like he sensed it was with Erin, his feelings were so intense it was difficult to sound more than trite or official when deprived of the other's presence. Adam realized that when two people were only talking and robbed of the other four senses as ways to emote and inter-pret they had to take what they could and hope for more when they could finally be together. Then he thought of texting—ugh! Then all senses were gone! "Erin, I have a question."

"Shoot."

"I need some accurate information about DNA paternity testing."

"I can ask around. I am not worried about any disclosure on

my part. I will assign the project to my assistant and there will be enough separation to keep us safe. How do you want to receive the information?"

"If you send me a one-pager, I will supplement it with a Google search, and if I still need more information, I'll let you know." Adam paused, then he said, "Erin, remember that first lunch we had in the Starbucks at Langley, and later the nice restaurant off campus where we had a two-and-a-half-hour lunch, and both regretted, or at least I did, that our time together had to come to an end?" Before Erin had a chance to answer, he continued. "I would like to suggest that we have a dinner date at least once a week as long as we are apart like this."

"Adam, if I didn't know better, I would call you a hopeless romantic. I am all for it but how do you propose we accomplish this?"

"It will go like this. We both prepare a meal that we can eat while sitting in front of our computer. Then we connect with Skype. We can each enjoy our dinner across a table that is five thousand miles wide. And, for my first dinner, I plan to have an encore fettuccini Alfredo."

"Adam, I love the idea and have only one further wish—at every meal we promise that this will only be done until we can be together the way we both want to be."

With this decided, they sketched out a schedule for their upcoming dinners and promised that these would not be the only time they talked.

———————

Thursday morning, Adam was in Fred Billson's office at CIA Headquarters. Fred looked to be in his early fifties. His first words to Adam were, "Have you seen Erin since she left for Rome? We miss her around here."

Adam decided to play it close. There was no need to call unnecessary attention to their relationship. It wasn't a secret. Both the President and Bob Zinsky were fully aware of how they felt, but they were in a different category. And it was personal. "She's a good agent and she brightens up the place," was all Adam felt like contributing.

"You didn't say what you had on your mind when you called," said Billson.

"I don't have much to go on, and my questions might be vague, but I have to start somewhere. Since the person I am inquiring about may be a CIA asset, and a nervous one at that, I am starting here. Erin said if anyone could help, it would be you."

"Fire away, Colonel."

Although Adam was in civilian clothes, his official employer was no secret; and when he made the appointment, he had identified himself as such. "No need for rank. Adam will do. I am seeking information about a possible CIA connection with a man now located in Islamabad. The man's name is Fathi Kanaan. He is from a prominent family in Saudi Arabia. He is an executive in the family's large construction firm currently doing business in Islamabad. He may also be an asset working with an agent in the local CIA office there. Specifically, there is credible evidence that Fathi was approached by Al-Fir, a terrorist organization that is developing a plot that started small but is getting bigger and represents a potential serious threat to the United States. The CIA got wind of this, contacted Fathi, and recruited him to gather and share information about the plot. Concerned about his level of involvement, he consulted with his father, who lives in Jeddah. Both are worried about how far this is going. His father, seeing nowhere else to turn for help, took the initiative to alert someone high in the Administration, but without sharing any details of the plot or the people his son might be involved with. I spoke with Fathi's dad only a few days ago and I believe what he is saying is true. My job now is to confirm that Fathi Kanaan is connected with the CIA—which is why I am talking with you.

"According to Fathi's father, who I have talked with at length, his son is concerned about how far and fast matters are advancing with Al-Fir. Apparently, and I say this with only the slightest of evidence, the CIA agent Fathi has been dealing with in Islamabad, a man named Roland Wallace, is slow walking the terrorist deal and has not offered a plan to extract Fathi, who now believes his life and that of his family could be in danger. Fathi believes the best way to end the plot and get out safely would be for the terrorists to be taken down in Pakistan—soon. According to Fathi, Agent Wallace wants the plot to continue, to the point where the terrorist group is ferried by boat to the U.S. and then is captured when they reach land. To help his son, Ahad Kanaan, agreed to supply a boat to Al-Fir, at first in a ruse to get the terrorists together in one place in Pakistan and make it possible to take them all down at once. But, because of the insistence of the CIA handler, the planning has progressed to the point of ferrying by boat nearly three dozen terrorists to the U.S. The catch-22, if I have it right, is that the asset must continue working full tilt, acting like a terrorist and keeping the plot moving, before he reaches the point when he can safely be extracted. And all signs are that this time will be when the terrorists are apprehended after the boat brings them here to the States. Fathi believes both he and his family will be killed when that happens, and he no longer thinks the CIA agent can protect him. Actually, he is worried that Roland Wallace might be working alone because he has not met any of the other agents in the office."

Fred Billson, who had been listening intently replied, "For a CIA asset, the best way out of the relationship is to say that cover has been compromised. In that case, whatever information has been collected is analyzed, acted on if appropriate, and the asset gets out with any cover that is necessary. If there is reason to believe that the asset is still safe and there is more information to be gotten, we act in the best way to assure the asset's safety until the project is terminated, for whatever reason."

"That makes perfect sense," said Adam.

"Is this asset's cover in danger?" asked Fred.

"His father, who is well-connected, believes so and is highly motivated—actually, near panic—to rectify the situation; which means he could unintentionally expose his son. His panic might be lessened if we could provide a good reason to hold back. The father is also concerned that the CIA agent responsible for his son's life might be carrying this out as a solo project and be in over his head."

"This isn't an easy one, Adam. But are any of them?" Looking past Adam while in deep thought, Billson continued, "I think we can help, but it will take your going to Islamabad and contacting some of our folks there. Your visit should not be heralded, just on the QT."

"You'll notice I am not wearing my dress blues," joked Adam. "I dress down really well."

"Sounds like we can do business, Adam. When can you be in Islamabad?

"I could be in Jeddah by Tuesday, ready to work. And, be in Islamabad by Thursday evening."

"I will contact our people and be back with you by this evening," said Billson before ending the meeting.

"Thanks, Fred." Adam departed, confident that he was making progress.

When he returned to his apartment, a large envelope was waiting for him. He correctly surmised it was the DNA stuff from Erin. Adam read the five pages of detailed material twice. He then got a blank sheet of paper and a yellow number two pencil and started a lesson plan that would be suitable for teaching high school students about DNA testing:

> *Each human has twenty-three gene pairs. A child gets one half of his genetic material from each biological parent. In these genes, there are three billion base pairs that are unique to the individual. In plain English, no two people, other than identical twins, have the same DNA arrangement. This can be said with a level of certainty at the 99.99 percent level.*
>
> *Most paternity testing employing DNA results is called "trio." This procedure includes the mother and two men who are considered possible biological fathers. A tissue sample is needed from each. These samples can be white blood cells, sperm, saliva, a hair follicle, the pulp of teeth, or any body tissue with cellular material that has not degraded. Then, a similar locale on the DNA map from each person to be tested is analyzed.*
>
> *Without exception, all of the DNA characteristics of the child will come from the father, the mother, or both, and nobody else. In order to analyze comparable genetic material, the samples must be taken from a locus on the same genome but where the two possible fathers have different DNA characteristics. When these samples are used for testing, the child will always have the DNA characteristics of both the biological father and biological mother and never have unique DNA characteristics from the male who is not the father. These observations, in some cases, require repeated testing with subsequent specimens to ensure accuracy. Successful DNA paternity testing can be done without the mother's DNA but it is more difficult and time-consuming. In either the trio or motherless testing, it is easier to rule out paternity than to confirm it.*

After reading the information, Adam thought the procedure sounded doable; but it required a sample from the President of the United States, who, based on Adam's observation of Phillip Tripp's response when he heard about Alia's son, gave the impression that he had no reason to think he was the father. This part could be done but it would be painful!

On the last page of the one-pager that had ballooned to five pages was a comment about using blood types for paternity testing. This interested Adam. It was a long shot, but if it worked, it could simplify matters greatly. Like DNA testing, it was easier to rule out than confirm. It was worth a try.

Taking a chance, Adam called the White House to speak with the President's secretary. She was a savvy woman who had been around the White House and had witnessed about all of the shenanigans that could be pulled off. She had also seen Adam in the President's office on numerous occasions and had spoken with him on the phone several times. If she didn't suspect something was up, she would have to be from the moon; Adam knew she wasn't.

When Adam asked if he could have the President's blood type, there was a long pause while she probably wondered if this information was any more confidential than revealing President Tripp's eye color, weight, or shoe size. "It's AB. But you didn't hear it from me."

"Thank you," Adam said, and he ended the call.

Chapter 15

Whenever Fathi Kanaan's presence was required at an Al-Fir meeting, he was contacted by email with a coded message. He received such a message after dinner, informing him that he should travel to Peshawar in the morning. The city, about four hours from Islamabad, was near the Afghan border, in sight of the mountains. He was to meet with Assoud Al Walaki, the supreme leader of the terrorist organization. Fathi suspected they would finalize the details for the big event, and maybe even select a date.

The original plan of assembling three hundred men for a simultaneous suicide assault in New York City, as Mihal had first envisioned, would have been logistically challenging and nearly impossible to pull off. Using thirty suicide bombers, functioning strategically, as first floated by Roland Wallace and then passed onto Al-Fir by Fathi, would be sufficient. Fathi was successful in convincing Assoud Al Walaki and the others that this was a more practical plan.

Mihal had informed Fathi that twenty-two men and five women had been recruited and trained to don suicide vests and blow up the lower levels of One World Trade Center in New

York. Arming the bombs with uranium, another idea from Roland Wallace, would produce dirty bombs that would increase the effectiveness of each. The CIA agent was eager to promise as much as could be sold to the terrorists when it came to wreaking havoc on the United States.

It was decided that a group of thirty, including the handlers, would travel to the United States via boat and then overland by bus to New York City. This was the largest number that could fit comfortably on the boat and enter the lobby of One World Trade Center without causing suspicion. The issue of plausibility continued to plague Fathi, who needed to rein in some of Mihal's extravagant pipe dreams that might not sit well with Assoud. What had finally convinced Mihal to agree to no more than thirty bombers was the phantom group that Fathi promised would be on hand in New York. With this established, Mihal was now fully on board. When Fathi spoke with Assoud, for what he hoped was the last time before the terrorists left the country and headed to America, he would make a convincing argument for the plan, if need be.

In Peshawar and preparing to enter the compound to meet with Assoud, Fathi decided that after this meeting with the terrorists he would demand that Roland Wallace include his supervisor, the station chief, at their next meeting. This would be the time for Fathi to make one final entreaty to arrest the terrorists in Karachi Harbor instead of waiting for them to depart the country.

"Welcome, my friend. It has been far too long that we have been apart," said Assoud Al Walaki, attempting a warm smile that belied his true purpose and deeper motives. This meeting had been called by him as a demand more than a suggestion.

This close to launch, the leader of Al-Fir was eagerly contemplating the events in New York. But at the same time, he was anxious, to the point of being uneasy, because he knew all of the parts, most of which he had no direct control over, must pull together and unfold precisely for the massive operation to be successful. He wanted to make sure everything was ready and then move ahead as quickly as possible with the project he had dubbed "The Big Strike."

"My apologies, Assoud." There were four others around the table, and Fathi was careful to acknowledge them by making eye contact as he spoke. He had seen them at earlier meetings but had never spoken personally with any of them. Since there were no re-introductions and the men obviously knew who Fathi was, he focused his attention and directed his remarks to the leader. "Our lack of communication is no indication of diminished effort dedicated to the project. I will tell you of our plans now, if you are ready."

"Indeed, I am." Assoud then corrected himself. "We are."

Fathi reviewed the plans for the entire operation, leaving nothing out. After an explanation that included exploiting all of the expected lurid details, Fathi was rewarded with five satisfied smiles. It was the first time he had personally gone into such depth with Assoud, but Fathi suspected this session to be no more than a test. Fathi was sure Mihal had told all of this to Assoud in exquisite detail, including every nuance as the plot was building, and that nothing he said today was new information. Instead, the leader was listening carefully to make sure that Fathi's story was consistent with what he had already heard from Mihal.

"That plan sounds very good, Fathi," said a man on Assoud's right. "But how will we assemble the team in America?"

Fathi was encouraged to see this level of interest because he knew his life, and probably his family's, depended on his remaining an indispensable part up to the minute of the attack. "That is an excellent question, and I can finally answer it for you," said Fathi. "I have the team in place and trained as we speak. That includes twenty-two men and five women here in Pakistan. They will travel to the United States, where they will martyr themselves. They will be the ones deployed to the main lobby and the elevator lobbies of the lower seven floors. Two men skilled with explosives have nearly finished constructing twenty-seven vests that will be armed with uranium after they arrive in America. We also have sarin gas in liquid form in a safe and secure location in New York City. This liquid will be aerated for insertion into the building's ventilation system and flammable material will also be added to the plant-watering tanks in the lobby in the building."

"Where are these people?" asked another man at the table.

"The bomb makers and the twenty-seven martyrs are assembled in Islamabad. The team in New York is assembled safely in the city and awaits our arrival. They are ready with the sarin gas, radioactive material, and flammable liquid for the irrigation tanks." Fathi knew he was repeating but it was good they were engaged. "In Islamabad are Mihal and his team, who you know. Two of the men will accompany Mihal to the U.S. to supervise and support the team of martyrs. The entire group will depart Karachi Harbor by boat as soon as a date is set. They will spend about one month traveling to the U.S. During the trip they will complete training and carry out the final steps for individual fitting of the vests. The devices will be made to individual specifications. That will allow more explosive material to be added per person and, since they are individually fitted, the devices will be less noticeable."

Assoud asked Fathi, "Can you tell us more about how the group will travel on the boat to the United States?"

"They will travel in a vessel that has been made available to us by a wealthy benefactor. He shares our determination to destroy the infidel, but he wishes to remain anonymous. In his words 'Allah knows.' The boat he has arranged has traveled across the Atlantic several times. It is an older boat that has been active previously in the waters of the U.S. and Canada. It is registered in the Cayman Islands, but that will not be considered out of the ordinary when the boat enters first Canadian and then U.S. waters through the St. Lawrence Seaway."

"What about Immigration and Customs?" asked the first questioner.

"The boat is large enough so that the passengers can be hidden as a precaution in the unlikely event that Customs agents come aboard for a search. The captain will have a mate and three additional crew. All are sympathetic to our cause. In open water and away from port, our team will be able to assist this crew for some basic tasks if that becomes necessary. We expect no difficulty with Canadian Customs because nobody will be leaving the boat, just passing through Canadian waters on its way to the U.S. Great Lakes. Once at the appointed spot in Lake Michigan, the entire team will disembark in a wilderness area. United States Customs will be cleared at a facility while in Lake Erie.

"The group will disembark and be brought to land in small boats manned by local supporters who are standing by. Our group will immediately board a charter tour bus that will take them to New York City. Tourist buses are common in the United States, as they are here. There are many such buses and this large vehicle will offer plenty of room for our people while arousing no suspicion. The captain and his crew will take the boat to a shipyard in Wisconsin, where it will be docked. This facility has been engaged by a fictitious owner through an untraceable intermediary to extensively refurbish the vessel's interior. The captain will tell the manager of the facility that he will be contacted by the owner in about two weeks. Of course, the boat will never be claimed. It is the donor's wish that the boat's role be eventually discovered and remain as evidence that the infidels will never be safe.

"After leaving the boat, the captain and his crew will travel to New York and meet up with Mihal and his team to return to Pakistan one day before the event. Final supervision will be turned over to the New York team. Those from the New York team that survive will disappear and remain that way for a long time."

"Where exactly will they get off the boat?" asked Assoud.

Fathi welcomed the question. "The boat will unload the team at the shore of Wilderness State Park, at the northwest corner of the top of Michigan's Lower Peninsula. This ten-thousand-acre park is virtually deserted at that time of year. There will be nobody for miles around the drop-off site. Each team member will have suitable credentials, but it is unlikely they will be needed. The tour bus will meet them in the park and transport them to New York. Also, while traveling to the U.S., the team members will have altered their appearances by dying their hair lighter, shaving beards, and wearing more Western-style clothing to call as little attention to themselves as possible when they arrive in New York."

"How long will the boat trip take?" asked another man at the table.

Fathi responded, "Depending on weather and speed, it will take approximately one month. This time will be well spent because the team will follow a regular training schedule."

Assoud spoke. "We are responsible for the term 9/11. The Big Strike will create another day of remembrance for the infidels. We will create a new date of infamy to go along with 9/11. The attack will be in the eleventh month on the seventeenth day of the seventeenth year of the millennium—11/17."

Five people around the table smiled with satisfaction, and the sixth smiled with a sense of relief that the next step in the plan could be set in motion.

Chapter 16

Adam's flight arrived in Jeddah late Tuesday morn-ing. Adam insisted he would take a cab from the airport to Ahad's home but accepted the invitation to dine there. According to Ahad, it would be just his wife, Farah, and Adam for an early dinner. Their two daughters were attending graduate school in England and were not home. After dinner, Adam and Ahad would meet alone.

In the dining room, a large window offered a spectacular unobstructed view of the sun dipping over the Red Sea. The table was covered with a beautiful, white, lace-trimmed cloth decorated with elaborate embroidery in the Middle-Eastern style. The dishes included every type of service piece that seemed possible, and the silver and crystal were elegant. *They are pulling out all the stops*, thought Adam. *The two of them can't possibly dine this way every night.*

Farah was a pleasant and attractive woman in her mid-fifties, at least ten years younger than Ahad. She was tall, with short black hair and was perfectly groomed. Poised and outgoing, she gave the aura of a woman who was both smart and well-taken care of. Farah and Ahad made a gracious host and hostess—comfortable to be with.

The meal was served by two maids; which to Adam seemed too much for only three people dining. Dinner started with a small appetizer that was a triangular pastry with a crab meat filling and a light sauce. The main course was described by his hostess as lamb al-makhtoum. It was three standing double lamb chops with a tomato and garlic sauce. A mixed vegetable side dish called jereesh accompanied the main plate. French bread and butter completed the main course. Dessert was a sweet concoction similar to crème brûlée. In the officially sans-alcohol atmosphere of the country, iced tea, lemonade, and mineral water were available.

The meal was accompanied by a flow of animated talk with absolutely nothing substantive discussed. The three participants seemed happy with this arrangement. The weather was hot, they missed the girls, Adam's trip had been uneventful, and the sunset would be spectacular, as usual. A large part of the conversation, spurred by Adam, centered on the cuisine in Saudi Arabia and North Africa, where both Ahad and Farah had been born. The tradition of cooking a whole goat at home for special occasions was no longer common in the Saudi culture, but they wanted Adam to have the best meat dish possible so they served it tonight. Adam assured them that nothing could have tasted better than the dinner he had just enjoyed.

After dessert, Farah tactfully and accurately said, "Why don't you two men have your coffee on the patio? I know you have a lot to discuss, and I should put some finishing touches on remarks I will be giving tomorrow at the Saudi Women's Society." *A woman's libber*, thought Adam, but he processed it in a positive way, believing women in this country needed it.

On the patio, Adam and Ahad, each with a strong cup of coffee, sat in comfortable chairs that looked out across the expansive lawn to the sea that was now bathed in moonlight.

Adam decided to start the conversation because he wanted to steer it in the right direction as quickly as possible. His guess was that he was the one who had uncovered the most information since they last met. "Ahad, when we last spoke, you had some challenging issues to deal with, and some important questions to be answered. In Washington, I learned some things that I would like to share." With this, Adam explained the process of DNA testing and the difficulty of accomplishing an accurate paternity test without the mother's DNA, and that it was much easier to rule out paternity than it was to positively identify the true biological father.

Breaking what was bordering on an awkward silence, Ahad finally said, "You've done your homework, Adam. Where does this leave us?"

"Ahad, it could be possible for me to answer a question that you might have now, and with confidence."

"How?"

"Can you tell me Fathi's blood type?"

"No, but I am sure Farah can."

"Would you ask her?"

"Yes." Ahad rose and entered the house through the sliding glass patio door. A few seconds later he reappeared with his wife.

Adam knew that Farah, who had joined them, would be seeing her husband in a potentially embarrassing situation but he would have to push on regardless of the circumstances. Directing his question at both of them, Adam said, "Do you know Fathi's blood type?"

"Yes," said Farah. That was all she said as she stood, looking at Adam, who was now also standing. She was obviously not going to give him the answer unless he specifically asked.

"What is it?" Adam said.

"O positive. Why do you ask?" said Farah.

A personal family scene began to transpire in front of Adam

as Ahad, in the clearest and most reassuring way, told his wife about the uncertainty he had lived with for thirty-seven years. As Adam watched, he realized this revelation was not earth-shaking to Farah because whatever happened had occurred a decade before she had even met Ahad. The anguish was Ahad's alone.

Before Ahad finished providing an explanation that was not really necessary, Adam interjected. "Before you go any further, Ahad, let me say that there is absolutely no possibility that Alia was pregnant with the American's baby when she married you. Fathi is your child."

"How do you know?" said Farah, as Ahad stood at her side, speechless.

Adam told them that the President's blood type was AB, which is rare. It was present in just over three percent of the population. "Any child of a person with AB blood would have to have a blood type of either A, B, or AB. It is impossible for an offspring of such a person to have the O blood type," Adam said.

Chapter 17

Both men knew there was a great deal more they wanted to discuss. The night was cool; a welcome respite from the searing heat of the afternoon. Today's high temperature had been over one hundred degrees Fahrenheit, average for this time of year. Adam guessed the temperature was now in the low seventies; it felt like walking in a refrigerator.

When Farah left, Ahad started. "Adam, you deserve to hear an explanation and an apology from me."

Before Ahad could go any further with his mea culpa, Adam interrupted. "Ahad, we both came into this relationship playing our cards close to our chests. Each of us withheld a lot because that seemed to be the right thing to do. But now, with everything on the table, let me start. I think I have less to say, but it is still important." Choosing his words carefully, Adam continued. "Your message to the President was interpreted by him to be a warning and not a threat. Maybe better said, I think he felt it was an opportunity or an obligation for him to play a part in something that was important. His actions were spurred by feelings he had for someone he had cared for deeply a long time ago. The time he spent in the Peace Corps, I suspect, had a profound effect on his life. The note mentioning Alia Fahad prompted him to pursue the issue rather than simply ignore it. I firmly believe that Phillip Tripp was motivated by a sincere and heartfelt concern, and I believe he feared that something bad had befallen a person who he openly described to me as his first true love. The other issue that you and I have discussed was never mentioned."

"What were you asked to do by the President?"

"I was asked to uncover the origin of the note, gain as much information as I could as it related to Alia Fahad, and report back to him. I am officially a member of the United States Army Reserve, operating on temporary active duty. I report to the President and to him only. You are the first person I have revealed this to." *Well, almost*, Adam thought. He had told Erin, but he felt that in his life any separation between Erin and himself had all but ceased to exist.

"How did you end up here, Adam?"

"I went to Khamis Mushait first because that is where Alia told the President she was moving after her marriage, and that is where it was requested a response from the President be sent. It was there where I was able to find information that led me here." Adam paused for a moment and decided he would go further in the explanation. "After you and I met for the first time and I heard about your concerns about Fathi's activities, I returned to Washington. At CIA Headquarters there, I made some inquiries about their field office in Pakistan. As you might suspect, they told me it would not be easy to get information about a possible asset. If Fathi was working with the CIA in the way you described, I was told the people in Islamabad probably would not reveal it to me, and this would be a good thing and mostly for his own safety. That does not mean that this issue isn't on the front burner for them. It only means that the CIA carefully guards the information it holds, especially when it comes to assets in the field. In Fathi's case, this has to be a positive. Knowing that information about Fathi is being kept secret doesn't make our work any easier, but it definitely helps ensure his safety in the long run.

"My next destination will be Islamabad, where I will attempt to find out firsthand the relationship that the CIA has with your son. But, before going there, I wanted to speak with you. I wanted to settle the issue we just talked about and to find out if there was anything else that you could tell me that might help."

"Thank you," said Ahad. "In the spirit of full disclosure, let me tell you my role in all of this and why I am glad my plan, far-fetched as it was, worked in bringing you here." With this said, the expression on Ahad's face became deadly earnest. "Fathi has been dealing with these men for nearly three years and, as they say, the heat is being turned up. With an accelerated time-table, the attack in New York is to be carried out in November, in less than three months. The date selected is the seventeenth, but that could be subject to change. Fathi, at the urging of his CIA contact in Islamabad, has sold the terrorists on a strategy that would employ moving intact a small army to the United States, along with their weapons, consisting of explosives. They will be transported on a boat that I agreed to donate. It will be piloted and crewed by people I have employed. They know exactly what we intend to do but will claim to be sympathetic to the cause of Al-Fir. This fake allegiance is being purchased with double pay and is being assured by withholding half of the money until the terrorists are in custody. The terrorist group will remain together and be under the careful scrutiny of people working for the leaders until the final act. The bombers and the people who will be supervising them will be operating with the expectation of meeting a substantial group of supporters in New York, who will help them complete the act of destruction they are planning. Of course, this group in New York is a total fab-rication, cooked up by Fathi at the urging of his CIA contact. The whole point of this exercise, according to Roland Wallace, is to first lure the terrorists to an isolated spot in the U.S. and then for the FBI to apprehend them as soon as they set foot on U.S. soil. Our preference would be to make the arrests in Pakistan, but the agent has told Fathi that the CIA is committed to capturing the terrorists in the U.S. and subjecting them to your legal system."

"How will this be accomplished?"

Ahad explained the details of the plot as Fathi had shared them with him. Not sure how to process the information, Adam concluded that Ahad and his son were embroiled in a complicated and extremely dangerous business. Could this have been avoided? Yes. Would a plan like this have gone ahead without Fathi? Likely. Will a successful outcome for Fathi's involvement stop carnage in the U.S.? Definitely!

After a moment of silence, Ahad said, "You are the professional, Adam. I am only a hopeless amateur at this kind of thing. What happens next?"

Adam had already processed the answer in detail in his mind, and now it was time to share it candidly with Ahad. "The next thing to be done, Ahad, is for me to get more information from the CIA in Islamabad. I need to find out if they are fully aware of all the details of the plot or, more accurately, are they willing to share? Do they know the timetable? Are the necessary actions being taken to launch a timely response? I hope to get answers to these questions in Islamabad tomorrow. Then, I need to meet again personally with the President to get his permission to widen the scope of the operation. Once I get that, I'll have to meet with the FBI because anyone who steps on U.S. soil, as the terrorists will do when they are delivered by the boat, will be under Federal jurisdiction. We have less than three months until the planned attack, and there is a great deal that must be accomplished. There is absolutely no time to delay. And, because of the time required for passage of the terrorists by boat, movement from Karachi could begin as early as just six weeks from now. This is a scenario that demands immediate action on our part. There is absolutely zero time for delay and no room for error."

The two men talked until well after midnight. They finished their conversation in a more relaxed state than when it had started, but the sense of urgency remained at a high level.

Adam returned to his hotel room around 1:00 a.m. He would have a short night as he had an 8:35 a.m. flight on Saudi Air; arriving in Islamabad at 4:00 p.m. With a promise of not more than three hours of sleep, Adam was glad he had booked a business-class ticket for the almost-six-hour flight. This would be one of those occasions when he would likely get some good sleep on a plane. It would be needed.

Before he climbed into bed, still revved up but at the same time needing sleep, Adam called Fred Billson at Langley. With the nine-hour time difference, Billson's workday would be just ending. Without going into any extra detail, Adam asked Fred if he would give the station in Islamabad a heads up about his arrival and vouch for him, so they could get to the point of his meeting sooner rather than later. Fred said he would contact the office, make a hotel reservation for Adam, and also arrange for an agency car to transport Adam from his hotel to the CIA field office. Fred's secretary would send Adam an email with the details.

"Thanks, above and beyond," Adam said.

"For the team, Adam."

Chapter 18

Adam's flight arrived at Benazir Bhutto Interna-
tional Airport a few minutes after 4:00 p.m. local time. He had
moderate success sleeping for most of the flight. Adam knew
there was no use forcing himself to tackle a problem or to have
clever ideas when he was too tired to give it his all. He could
accomplish more in an hour with a clear mind than in a full
day beating the dead horse that was lack of freshness and little
enthusiasm. Tomorrow would be another day, and it would be
an important one.

One thing Adam did accomplish on the flight from Jeddah
was to learn more about Islamabad from information that was
available in an above-average quality in-flight magazine. He was
glad he took the time to read it and was surprised at how many
interesting facts were revealed. This city of two million was cre-
ated out of a desert steppe in 1960. Located in the northwest
region of the Indian subcontinent, the northern reaches of the
Himalayas are visible from the city as snowcapped peaks. Just
127 kilometers from the city, tourists can ride a series of cable
cars to heights of nearly thirteen thousand feet. Due east was

the northern region of Kashmir. When Britain gave independence to its former colony, India, in 1947, the land was divided. In the south, the population was mostly Hindu and retained the name India. The north and a smaller area in the east, which later became Bangladesh, both primarily Muslim, became Pakistan. The Kashmir region in the far north, which is about two thirds Muslim, was also divided. Pakistan was given the north and India the south. Control of the Kashmir region has been an ongoing dispute between Pakistan and India; even China lays claim to some of the region.

Adam was in his room at the Islamabad Marriott by six thirty, and he was starved. He had not eaten anything substantial since dinner the night before. There was a plus side to this. The hotel featured a fine steakhouse, Jason's, and he knew just what he would be ordering. A big porterhouse would hit the spot. A familiar meal would be just right. Tonight, Adam was not in the mood for exotic or adventuresome cuisine. He needed comfort food: steak and a baked potato, and not mixed up ingredients that required explanation and reassurance.

Adam was also pleased to be greeted by an attractive room with a king-size bed and a mountain view. And the hotel had the advantage of being conveniently located near the CIA's office. Fred's email indicated that an agency car would be there for Adam in the morning at eight thirty to take him to the office. *Nice touch*, thought the traveler.

———————

The agency car was at the hotel entrance promptly at eight thirty. Adam slid into the front seat of the grey Ford Fusion and was greeted by the driver, a clean-cut fellow who looked to be in his mid-twenties. "Good morning, Colonel Grant. I am Andy Grover, Sergeant, but we wear civvies here. Kind of like you." The young man was fresh-faced and enthusiastic. "Your first visit here, Colonel?"

"Yes," said Adam.

"Any questions for me about the city?" After a slight pause, Sergeant Grover continued, "You'll have to wait to talk with the staff to find out what goes on inside the building. That stuff is above my pay grade."

"How long have you been here, Andy?"

"Six months, sir."

"How do you like it?"

"It's been a good gig so far. I don't get the Muslim thing too much, and when I have a beer it is like a stealth operation, but we have our ways. A lot of the people who make a big deal about alcohol, and women for that matter, seem to have a double standard." Then after a slight pause he added, "But that's life, isn't it? The trouble is, here you better not call them on it or you are in big trouble."

After a few more minutes of sparse conversation, they arrived at the CIA's office. Adam saw a two-story, tan-stucco building that was freestanding. From his earlier preparation, he knew he was at 58th Street off Ataturk Avenue. After showing his credentials to a clerk behind a desk just inside the door and going through a metal detector, Adam was told the offices were on the second floor. He was offered the elevator but opted for the stairs instead. Still with him, Andy Grover led him to Room 12. The door was closed and there was no name or other designation on the door. The sergeant knocked.

"Come in," said someone from inside.

Adam entered the room and a tall, gangly, redhead came out from behind the desk and greeted him eagerly, advancing halfway between the desk and the door. "Welcome, Colonel Grant. I'm Roland Wallace. Fred Billson said you would be coming today, but his message was a bit on the mysterious side, so I guess we are starting from scratch."

"Thank you, Mr. Wallace. I guess starting at the beginning is what we are about." He had the feeling Wallace wanted to keep things on a formal setting; and that was fine with Adam. "My reason for being here today has to do with a possible threat that has been raised and, if true, it has serious implications. The origins of this threat are considered to be right here, in Islamabad. They involve a local man who has been described as a friendly, who is embedded in a nasty plot. There is information, not yet substantiated, that he has made connection with someone in this office."

"Any names?" asked Wallace.

"Yes," said Adam, "but this is where we need to have an understanding. If I give you a name and I am off base, I could be creating a lot of trouble for someone. The aims of the person I am referring to are probably laudable, but the person might not be connected here and revealing a name might put that person and the means to deal with the plot in jeopardy. On the other hand, I realize the connection might be here but, for obvious reasons, the CIA contact might not be willing to reveal the identity of an asset. Ring any bells?"

"This could be a tough nut," said Wallace without a hint of optimism or willingness to dig deeper into the issue and move ahead. "Can you give me any details about this purported threat?"

Adam wondered if Wallace had consulted his mental thesaurus and had deliberately chosen the word *purported*, which described a false claim. "It's big. Terror related. And is intended to make a profound statement on our shores, at home. That's about all I can say without overstepping."

"You came a long way, Colonel, to tell me we live in a dangerous world and that Islamabad is one of the more dangerous places." Roland Wallace said this with the expression and tone of a school teacher lecturing a clueless student.

Adam's first impulse was to say what his mother would when she met an uncooperative clerk: May I speak with your supervisor? *Not a good idea*, thought Adam. Or he could act a little ticked off and ask Roland if he recognized they were on the same side. *No, that was another bad idea. Maybe Roland was really okay and was just being careful.* Adam was sure Fred Billson had given Adam a sufficient build-up, but maybe it didn't register with the fellow. *Or did this guy have something to hide?* Roland Wallace did not show anything in his facial expression or behavior to suggest that Fred had vouched for Adam as an authentic colleague who was in the know.

Adam felt he was being treated like a magazine salesman pitching to a person who couldn't read. He had useful information and was not on a wild goose chase. Paradoxically, this brief interchange made what he had heard from Ahad even more credible. These thoughts were processed in a matter of seconds. With a dismissive smile, Adam said, "Maybe what I came here to talk about has been greatly overblown. Well, at least you have been alerted, in case something fishy does turn up."

Relieved that he had parried Adam's main thrust, Roland relaxed and asked Adam, "Do you have any official connections with the Agency?"

Adam thought, *I spent time with the Director of National Intelligence, the Director of the CIA, trained briefly at the Farm, and spent two weeks in North Korea taking down Kim Il-un.* He answered, "Not officially. I am on TDY, serving the government but without any clout, just as an information gatherer." *That was lame*, thought Adam, but he felt he had to say something. Since he wasn't going to get anywhere with this fellow, there was nothing to be gained by confronting Wallace and possibly causing him to do something rash that could upset the plans put in motion by Adam and his team.

"Sorry, I couldn't be of more help, Colonel." With that, the non-conversation was at an end.

Even though the meeting didn't yield much, it was not a total loss. Adam had plenty of information to share with the President and, if the President agreed, Adam would have another meeting with Bob Zinsky.

Chapter 19

August 31, Wednesday

President Tripp started their meeting. "Adam, you have been a busy man this month. I want you to know how much I appreciate your keeping me up to date. But first, I wonder why you were curious about my blood type."

Oh, heck. Vera told her boss, thought Adam. *How should I respond?* Then he remembered: tell the truth and the truth will set you free (John 8:32). "That was going to be part of my report today," Adam replied. "It is as simple as this: Ahad Kanaan knows he married Alia Fahad only a few weeks after you left. Soon after the wedding, the couple moved to Khamis Mushait, and in nine months Fathi was born. According to Ahad, even though he loved Alia and wanted to marry her, their union had all of the trappings of a shotgun wedding. When Alia announced she was pregnant three months later and the baby was born weighing over seven pounds, precisely nine months after the wedding, Ahad wondered."

Adam was ready to continue, but he saw a big smile come across the President's face, which quickly developed into hearty laughter. When he had finished a good belly laugh, the President said to Adam, "This issue could have been settled with a simple question to me."

Adam, now relieved, said, "I know that, sir. But I thought that question was, to put it mildly, indelicate. And I noted your response when I mentioned her son. You didn't look like a man in doubt. I saw less reaction when I mentioned the son than I saw at the news of Alia's death. Based on that, I concluded there was no way the child could be connected to you. I was right."

"Now, tell me about the blood type."

Adam explained the impossibility of a person with type AB blood, which the President had, having a child with type O blood.

As Adam was preparing to move onto a different subject, President Tripp interrupted him. "Adam, you still didn't ask me."

Reluctantly, Adam asked, "Did you?"

"No," offered the President. "And not because I didn't want to! But Alia had definite ideas on the subject." After another chuckle, he continued. "Now, with that settled to the satisfaction of Ahad Kanaan, not on my word but with the blood type, I get the feeling there is more behind his message to me—possibly a lot more."

Relieved that the President was a guy who gets it, Adam proceeded with an explanation. He quickly summarized Fathi Kanaan's multi-year involvement with Al-Fir while acting as an asset for a CIA agent stationed in Islamabad; how he involved his father, Ahad; and the fact that he believed they were dealing with a credible, imminent threat to the United States, specifically directed at One World Trade Center. Adam emphasized that he thought Fathi Kanaan was credible and almost certainly a person with good intentions.

"How convinced are you that this threat is real?"

"I am convinced to the point I believe it should be followed up thoroughly by a responsible officer," said Adam.

"Do you have any recommendations on how we should proceed?" asked the President.

"I don't think I am the best person to answer that, Mr. President. My experience with the CIA is limited and I don't have the right connections to pursue this in the way that it needs to be done." Then, to add a little levity to a serious discussion, Adam said, "But, I do have a girlfriend who is a CIA Station Chief."

Phillip Tripp smiled as he was once again reminded of why he liked this soldier. "Let me say, Adam, I highly approve of your selection when it comes to CIA operatives! And, by the way, how is Erin doing in Rome?"

"She is doing well, sir, and working hard, as you can imagine. I actually saw her on my way home from Saudi Arabia on my first trip. She helped me with CIA contacts in preparation for my visit to Islamabad, with no questions asked, of course." Adam didn't feel it was necessary to mention the paternity testing issue they had discussed. That book was closed. He also didn't think he had to mention their three wonderful days at Lake Como.

"Colonel Grant, you have had an unusual career in Washington D.C. You have worked with the Chairman of the Joint Chiefs of Staff, the Director of the CIA, the Director of National Intelligence, and the President of the United States—all in your first year. At that rate, I expect you will be dealing with the Chief Justice if you get a parking ticket."

This must be beltway humor, thought Adam, *but pretty cool coming from POTUS.*

"I can see no reason to remove you from this assignment," continued President Tripp. "My recommendation is that you tell Bob Zinsky exactly what you told me, the second part that is, nothing about the paternity issue. That does not need to be shared with anyone. He is the best person to deal with the terrorist threat. He will need help, of course, but he knows where to find it. As for you, I want you front and center in whatever comes of this. I will make that clear to the Director, but I don't think that is necessary. In case you don't know, Director Zinsky is a big fan of yours."

"Thank you, sir. That's good to hear."

"I will contact Bob Zinsky today. After that, he will contact you and I expect it will be soon. I will tell Bob I will be receiving regular briefings from you, but also I expect to hear from him any time he thinks it is necessary. You and I have been able to communicate effectively Adam, and I want you to know that I appreciate your candor and your initiative. We seem to have made a pretty good team, with you doing all the work, that is."

"Thank you, sir," said Adam. "I will report to you as soon as we have news."

As he left the building, Adam thought, *Hot damn, this thing has legs.*

Chapter 20

Tuesday morning, after a long Labor Day weekend, the Director of the CIA listened attentively as Adam told him essentially what he had told the President.

"Do you believe this is a credible threat?" asked the Director.

"Yes!" Adam answered emphatically. He wanted to leave no doubt in the Director's mind where he stood on the issue.

"I get the impression you have more confidence in the father's version of events than you do of the CIA's in Islamabad," said Bob Zinsky.

"That is correct, sir."

"Why is that?"

"First, I had the distinct impression that my visit to the office was not wanted, even to the point of deflection, despite an introduction, really an endorsement, provided by one of your own, Fred Billson. I don't blame Roland Wallace for not sharing details with me, a stranger, especially when it involved the fruits of his labor, but there was more reticence, even dismissal, than I expected. After all, Fred vouched for me and I wasn't asking for details, just some sort of recognition that I was there on legitimate business, even if it was regarding a matter he didn't want to discuss. Because Wallace was stonewalling, I decided the best strategy was to quit the meeting without tipping my hand to him and regroup here, in D.C."

With a grim look, Director Zinsky responded. "I think you made the right decision to back off, at least for now. Meeting the father and then speaking with Agent Wallace means you have dealt with both sides of the equation. I believe that puts you in a good position to decide who is dealing with us openly, and to make recommendations for the next steps we take." After a pause, the Director continued. "Adam, what you have described has two components that must be weighed carefully before we proceed. First, we must ask if the threat is legitimate. I believe it is, but let's say we have doubts. Could it be a hoax? If it is real, is it likely to be of much less consequence than we've been led to believe? Then, whatever the intended scope of the plot, what is the chance of it even happening? When presented with something like this, our response must weigh the magnitude of threat against the likelihood of it even happening. From what we know, a worst-case scenario would result in the murder of 4,000 innocent people while lying waste to One World Trade Center. That is such a horrific consequence, if there is any possibility of this happening, it tips the scale toward our doing whatever it takes to confirm this threat and to destroy it. My recommendation is we begin full-scale plans for those steps now. That means we gather the best information in the shortest possible time frame and then, based on what we learn, do whatever needs to be done. Adam, with your knowledge of the situation and the people involved, you are the ideal, and by that I mean *only* person to be carrying the ball."

"May I comment?" Adam asked.

"Absolutely."

"Based on my second meeting with Ahad Kanaan, it is clear that Fathi first shared information with him two years ago. This was a year after his son was first approached by Al-Fir and shortly after that recruited by the CIA. During these two years, Fathi told his father that he was losing confidence in Roland Wallace because the man kept changing plans while allowing the plot to move ahead, despite having enough information to take it down. I believe that Ahad knows a great deal; maybe all the details of the plot. He has been kept informed at every step as his son continues to cooperate with the terrorists. He believes the only way Fathi and his family can be kept safe is by his son cooperating with Al-Fir until the CIA stops the terrorists. I am convinced Fathi was initially drawn into this web innocently. He only pretended to be complicit because of Roland Wallace, and now he does so because he is afraid. The only safe exit strategy for Fathi is to have the plot crushed by the authorities, using the information he has been supplying to Roland Wallace. Instead of this happening, Wallace continues to tell Fathi the CIA is holding off any action to see how far the plot will progress. Their rationale, Fathi said, was to let the plot move ahead so that even more of the terrorists could be rounded up and neutralized.

"Both Fathi and Ahad believe the situation is out of hand. With the plot growing and the exact time of the attack set, Fathi has continued to urge his CIA handler in Islamabad to act, but he gets no satisfaction. Ahad sent a message to the President in desperation. He told me that was the only way he could think of to call enough attention to prompt action that would protect his son. That message is how I became involved."

"Sounds like we are dealing with a couple of pretty good guys who are in way over their heads, and they could use our help," said the Director.

"That's a good way of putting it. I don't think Fathi or Ahad are in any way at fault when it comes to the origin of the threat. I believe Al-Fir would have proceeded with the plan regardless of who they recruited to help. And the CIA sought out Fathi, not the other way around. A scheme of this size will bring together a lot of bad guys. Rounding them up and identifying them, alive or dead, will be easier if they are together in one group. The challenge for us is to decide how far to let the plot develop before springing the trap. To be honest, sir, I suspect the weak link is the CIA in Islamabad; and possibly, at this point, the best plan may be to herd all of the terrorists onto the boat, monitor their travels closely, and capture them here."

"You could be right, Adam. But what is our next step?"

"In my opinion, we need to get our team together. Each of us should be forthcoming with information we have and the operational capability we can offer. I am convinced we can establish cooperation and support for what I believe will be a complicated and dangerous operation. If we do our jobs right, we can take this thing down without it causing any harm."

"Who are the people we should gather together? And where?"

"My suggestion is that Kanaan Construction finds a legitimate reason to call Fathi home to Jeddah. If that ploy is too suspicious, then Fathi could be called home with the excuse that his mother is ill. This should be properly staged to remove any suspicion on the part of Al-Fir. Once Fathi is in Jeddah, I will meet with Ahad and him, and with anyone else you suggest, to get fully up to date on the progress of the terrorists' plan and the Kanaans' involvement. Once we have this information, we can formalize a plan for neutralizing the plot in the safest and most efficient way."

"Are you comfortable taking this next step on your own?" asked the Director.

"Yes, sir. I think it is the best way since we are running out of time. I believe I have Ahad's trust, and that will go a long way toward gaining Fathi's. My goal will be to assemble information that I will share with your team of professionals. I will stay with the project in any way that I can be useful and as long as I am needed."

"And, the President?"

"The President has already heard everything I told you. I would be more comfortable if you were the one who kept the President informed of our progress. I am still learning when it comes to the details of communication within the government. I appreciate the confidence everyone has shown in me, but I am sure you can see why I think it is important to respect the chain of command."

"That sounds good, Adam. To sum up our discussion, we have just ten weeks until the attack is scheduled, and we have a lot of work to do. I agree the next step is for you to meet with Fathi and Ahad Kanaan and find out everything they know. Then I suggest we get a team from here, with the most important being the FBI, because before this deal is finished, we will be acting on U.S. soil. Thank you, Adam. Let's meet again in about a week, after you return from Jeddah."

Chapter 21

September 8, Thursday

Adam bounded out of the cab in front of the now familiar Kanaan home. He carried a small overnight bag that he had kept with him in the backseat during the ride from Abdul Aziz Airport. Adam saw the front door open and a man who greeted him with a friendly, "Hello, Colonel Grant! We have been expecting you." The man was of moderate height and appeared to be close to Adam's age. He had a well-trimmed full beard, close-cropped hair, and wore casual Western-style clothes. He was the person Adam had seen in the photograph, albeit without the beard, on his last visit with Ahad. As Adam, mounted the three steps leading to the entry, the man said, "My name is Fathi Kanaan. My father and I have been looking forward to your visit. Welcome."

Adam immediately experienced positive vibes about the prospects for today's visit. He had no preconceived notions about who he would be dealing with in Ahad's son, but the warm greeting from Fathi was reassuring. Adam's first impression spawned instant and welcome relief. They only had one day to work and there was a lot to accomplish; they needed to be in sync immediately.

"Would you like to put your bag in your room before we get started, Colonel?" asked Fathi.

"Yes, that would be fine. And, you can call me Adam." Fathi led Adam to a guest bedroom; a few minutes later, Adam met his host in the hallway.

"Would you like something to drink before we get started?"

Adam answered in the affirmative. He selected coffee, black; Fathi did the same.

With a mug in hand, the two men entered the veranda where Adam and Ahad had had their long and meaningful talk. Ahad Kanaan, who had been seated, rose to offer Adam a friendly greeting, after which the three sat down, observing each other expectantly while waiting for someone to speak. Adam believed Ahad should talk first because it was his house, he was the senior member, and he was the one who had involved Adam by extension with his message sent to the President of the United States. Fulfilling Adam's expectations, Ahad said, "Adam, we all have a lot to say, and there will be time for each, but in light of your recent time in Washington, I suspect that hearing what you have to say will be the best way for us to get started."

This was exactly what Adam had hoped to hear. Before starting, Adam studied the elder Kanaan and was pleased to observe a subtle change in Ahad's demeanor. He seemed to be more relaxed, but he remained focused; a man who was in control of his emotions but also able to take charge. Adam's discourse would not be brief. It would involve details, timing, and surmises that required explanation. And, for the best effect, the information would be delivered without repetition and verbosity. He had rehearsed what he would say in his mind and it came out a dozen different ways on the long plane ride from the U.S. But, as so often had happened in the past, the words that came out today were not any of the canned speeches he had assembled in his mind. Rehearsed but modified to suit the time, the place, and the company, Adam's words were exactly what he wanted to say. Adam began. "Fathi, I assume your father has filled you in on what he and I have discussed already. I also expect that he explained why I came here initially so, unless you have questions, I will move on and assume that we are all up to date about what we will be discussing today."

A subtle nod of assent from both Ahad and Fathi confirmed that Adam's statement was founded. He continued. "I had two important meetings in Washington. The first was with President Phillip Tripp and the second was with the Director of the CIA, Robert Zinsky. Before that, I met with the CIA officer in charge of central administrative coordination of covert activities in the Middle East; and before I returned to Washington, I visited with Roland Wallace, the agent you have been meeting." Adam noticed Fathi grimace at the mention of his visit to the CIA office in Islamabad.

Adam continued. "When the President heard the backstory that provoked the message you sent, Ahad, he listened attentively. Based on what he heard, the President has agreed to take the necessary steps to help you and Fathi deal with Al-Fir. He asked me to proceed cautiously and to do so without calling any attention to my actions. For that reason, he asked me to meet privately with the Director of the Central Intelligence Agency, Robert Zinsky. I have no official connection with the CIA, but I worked with them as a consultant for several months earlier this year and I am functioning as a representative of the Agency now.

"Director Zinsky heard the full story of the plot and the part both of you play in it as you explained it to me. The President accepted it as a credible threat and authorized me to begin a process to sort out further details and then report back to him. He promised the full support of the CIA, and since the action could reach the U.S., we are also working with the FBI. He promised to deal with whatever *could* occur with a full and all-out effort on the part of the U.S. government. I hope you realize that what is certain in your minds, based on three years of exposure to the plot, is coming on as a sudden rush for the people I have been talking to in our government. I think it is commendable that Director Zinsky has reacted quickly and is amenable to responding in an all-out way. Fathi, I know most of the story, but I want to hear from you, in your own words, how you became involved."

With a wistful look going past Adam's shoulder and avoiding his father's gaze, Fathi Kanaan took a deep breath and began his story. "I moved to Islamabad three years ago with my wife and our two girls, Badia and Maha, who were eight and ten years old. The girls were excited about the move, but my wife, Lila, was not at first. She eventually adjusted to the new society as we developed a few friends in the community. The girls are enrolled at St. Paul School. This Catholic school has classes that are conducted entirely in English and has excellent academic standards. My wife has been active in parent groups with the school.

"My job in Islamabad, at first, was supervising the completion of an airport runway project. When this was completed, we began a residential building program in the city. This involved mostly apartments, condominiums, and then a few single-family dwellings; all built on contract. The residential part was a new venture for Kanaan Construction. Islamabad is a new city. In less than fifty years, it has been transformed from a near desert steppe to a metropolis of two million; with a growing need for more housing. Our expertise is in concrete forming and that is the way building is done in a place where lumber for construction is lacking. This venture, to date, has been successful, but as you have heard, life here has had an unexpected dark side.

"While doing business, I deal with many people, ranging from banking and finance, to real estate sales, subcontractors, and customers. I am a builder, but anyone who is in business like us must be part salesman, so I did my best to connect with the people I met, who I thought could be prospects for new business. Nearly all the people I encountered were local and they were different from those I was used to working with in Saudi Arabia and England. The people in Islamabad live in a new city and in a new country, both built on top of an ancient society that dates back thousands of years. The population is made up of many different ethnic groups—but they have two very powerful things in common: their religion and a hate of India. One focus of discontent with India is in Kashmir, but it is not limited to this area. The feeling of the Pakistanis is a pervading attitude of dislike and dissatisfaction with a lot that, for me, defies explanation. There is almost a national paranoia.

"My main outlet away from work turned out to be not just a way to keep in shape but it was an opportunity to meet new people. I started playing squash again. This is very nearly the national sport in Pakistan, at least in terms of participation, and second only to cricket. I play well enough to allow me to compete with some of the better players, and I was asked to play by some regulars who wanted to improve their game by seeking stiffer competition. After participating for a few months, one of the average players invited me to lunch. He didn't offer a particular reason, so I just assumed he wanted to expand our relationship to something more than being opponents on the squash court."

Ahad, who had not spoken since his first remarks, asked Fathi, "Looking back, was there anything about this fellow that led you to suspect what he would say to you?"

"Absolutely not," said Fathi.

"I am sorry to interrupt, go ahead," said Ahad.

This exchange led Adam to think that some of what Fathi would say today would be heard by Ahad for the first time.

Fathi took up his story. "When we met, Fadel, the name of the man who I was having lunch with, began talking about how frustrated he was that his country continued to be involved in what was essentially a proxy war in Afghanistan as well as all of the terrorist activities that were associated. He blamed it on two things: the imperial behavior of the United States and the antipathy he felt all Christians and Jews had for his own Muslim religion. He especially blamed those in the United States, with a feeling that amounted to hatred. At that point, I made what was in retrospect a big mistake—I simply listened. When I didn't outwardly object to what he was saying, he became animated and even zealous. Before I could get myself out of what was becoming an uncomfortable situation, he told me that he was involved in an organization that was patriotic, effective, and had important plans. What he was saying sounded dangerous, but not threatening to me personally. I assumed he was speaking to me as a friend and confidant. Before lunch ended, we talked about other things, so I wrote off his comments as an aberration, something he had said just to get it off his chest.

"Then, a few weeks later, he invited me to a meeting with some of his friends, who he said were interested in talking with me about some construction issues that I could maybe help them with. Once again, using what I have to now believe was bad judgment, I agreed to the meeting. I met three rough-looking men wearing traditional garb. They quizzed me about the construction of multistory buildings. During this conversation, it became clear to me that they were more interested in how a tall building could be destroyed rather than how it was built. I wasn't sure what they wanted to destroy, but it sounded like it was something big. I spoke around the issue, without really saying anything. The meeting ended without incident, it just stopped. They had evidently heard enough."

"Did you suspect anything at that time, Fathi?" asked Adam.

Fathi answered, "To be perfectly honest with you, Adam, now it is impossible to reconstruct my feelings. At that time, I had to be totally clueless and hopelessly naive to have missed their true intent. I just wrote them off as being nut cases, and I decided to steer clear of Fadel. And then, a couple weeks later, I received a call from a man who said he was from the U.S. government and connected with the consular office at the embassy dealing with immigration. He asked to meet with me. I didn't connect this call with the earlier events I described, so I agreed to meet him. He told me that he was just seeking information; that I might be of help answering some questions he had. He assured me that the meeting had nothing to do with me personally. A few days after the call, we met at a small restaurant that he chose.

"At lunch, the man, who identified himself as Roland Wallace, told me he was from the Central Intelligence Agency and not immigration. He apologized for the deception and said he avoided identifying himself as CIA because he didn't want to scare me off. He asked if I was aware I had met with members of a known terrorist cell. When I heard this, I nearly had to pick myself off the floor. My answer, obviously, was no. This meeting changed my life, and I don't have to tell you how upset I am that it ever happened. Now, there is nothing I can do but finish what I have started."

It was obvious to Adam that Roland Wallace had recruited Fathi, and it was no wonder that Roland refused to answer any of Adam's questions.

Farah Fahad walked onto the veranda and announced that lunch was ready. The three men were famished.

Chapter 22

Lunch started with fresh mushroom soup, followed by assorted cheeses, rice crackers, salsa, hummus, and dates. There was also a small lettuce salad. The meal was finished with a perfectly ripe half mango in its shell. Iced tea and lemonade were the beverages. With this menu, Adam's first thought was he must be at a ladies' luncheon, then he realized that Ahad's wife had made a smart move. She had provided a light lunch because she knew the men would be embroiled in a heavy discussion for the remainder of the afternoon. They would all be better off if they didn't have to fight drowsiness that could be the aftermath of a heavy midday meal.

When the men returned to the veranda, Adam began with the obvious question, and it was directed at Fathi. "How did your dealings with the CIA proceed?"

"Agent Wallace said that what I had heard at the meeting could be something that was only being dreamed about or it could be a project the group was seriously considering. It was probably the first, he said, but in cases like this it was better to err on the safe side. He told me the CIA had been watching this group, called Al-Fir, for more than a year. It was an ultra-violent offshoot of al-Qaeda, and it had carried out several especially vicious attacks in Pakistan in the past year. Then, contradicting his first statement, he said word was filtering out about the possibility that they might be in the throes of planning a huge attack in the United States, and it would be a sequel to 9/11; with greater loss of life and it would employ a novel approach."

Adam asked, "Did Agent Wallace attempt to recruit you?"

"Yes."

"Did he succeed?"

"Yes, he did. I am now sorry to say."

"Were you offered anything?"

"The agent started that conversation, but I stopped him and said that the only things I wanted were to do the right thing, to remain anonymous, and for my family to remain safe."

"What happened then?" asked Adam.

"Agent Wallace told me that if I cooperated, he and the agency would take every measure possible to ensure my safety and the safety of my family. He told me they had done this sort of thing before and they knew what to do and when to do it. He was very reassuring. After we reached this agreement, he helped me formulate a plan to gain Fadel's confidence and let events unfold from there."

"Then, what happened?"

"Agent Wallace made the point that it was important for me to have patience and not to be in a hurry to push any of my ideas onto the group. Even more important, he said I should be convincing and remain consistent in expressing my interest and enthusiasm for the project. The plan was that I shouldn't come on as a rabid ideologue who hated the United States—a Muslim fanatic. Instead I should assume the demeanor of a ruthless, self-serving, greedy, but also calculating, opportunist. I should convince them I would benefit personally and financially from any victory achieved over the United States. I should also make it clear to them that I would be more useful to their cause if I continued to engage in my usual business activities. As a successful businessman, I could retain my position in the community and use this as leverage to convince other like-minded leaders to contribute to the Al-Fir cause, especially with money. In short, I would use both my position in the business community and my unique expertise with construction to help further their cause."

Adam listened carefully, trying to get into the heads of the terrorists. "Were you convincing with this approach? Did the members of Al-Fir seem to value your input?"

"Yes and no. Using my social and business position was an effective way for me to work my way into the heart of the plot, but I soon got the feeling that they were just using me. Once they had everything they needed, I would end up being another one of their victims. I am afraid that is where I am now. I think my usefulness has almost come to an end."

"When did the real planning start?" asked Adam, as both he and Ahad leaned forward, eager to hear more.

Fathi continued. "It took six months after Fadel first said all the weird stuff and the meeting with the three men before Fadel brought up the subject again. By that time, I had decided I had totally misunderstood him and that the men he asked me to meet were neither serious nor effective, and that they were all talk. But then Fadel said another group of men wanted to meet with me, but only if I was interested. I remembered the advice of the CIA agent, who I had not met with again, and indicated I was willing but didn't act too eager. I agreed to a meeting, but in an offhand way. After I agreed to this meeting, Fadel said he would make the arrangements and let me know where and when it would take place.

"In a week, he offered me a date for the meeting, and I agreed with the time. He picked me up at my office and we drove to a rundown apartment building in an old neighborhood. There I met five rough-looking people. The man who did all the talking and was the apparent leader made vague reference to an activity that would be taking place in another part of the world, and that their final planning would benefit from someone with my connections and who had experience in construction. They asked if I would be willing to help. The meeting ended without them exacting a firm answer from me. These people appeared to be very patient."

"Were you put off by this vagueness?"

"No. Instead I decided to call the number that Roland Wallace left with me at our first meeting, and we made arrangements to meet again. When I told him what had happened, Agent Wallace said these people were acting as he predicted, and I had to agree he was right. At this second meeting, we settled on a scheme we had worked out at our first meeting, and we arranged to meet in three weeks. He told me he was encouraged at my report. He also said the bigger the threat, the longer it would take to work out plans and, based on what I had told him, he suspected that was why they were working deliberately. He also told me that since nothing bad had happened in the last six months, I must have convinced them I was the real thing."

"How often did you communicate with Agent Wallace after this?" asked Adam.

"Using drops, actually cryptic notices in the paper and pre-planned locations, we met two or three times in the first eight months and only as needed after that," said Fathi. "Maybe a dozen times in all."

"What did you talk about?"

"I told him what I had heard at the Al-Fir meetings and, with time, it was clear to both of us the group was up to something big. He seemed excited and I was beginning to be sorry I had gotten myself into this thing. As the meetings with Al-Fir continued, they started sharing more details with me. As they did this, their confidence in me seemed to grow, or maybe it would be more accurate to say they let their guard down and started treating me more like a brother. They listened to my advice and even accepted some of the plans I came up with."

"When did Agent Wallace become alarmed and bring up the possibility of busting up this enterprise?" asked Adam.

"He never did. He just urged me to play along and let the plot get as big as it could as long as it was doing no real harm. He promised me that before anything bad happened, the CIA would move in. He said that the longer we waited the greater effect our intervention would have."

Ahad broke his silence. "This is where I come in, Adam. Fathi told me about the progress that had been made, including the fact that it had been decided to assemble the entire team in Pakistan. Over time, a scheme was devised to deliver the terrorists by boat to the U.S. The idea for the boat came from Roland Wallace. There didn't need to be an actual boat, he said, but the *promise* of having one would make it easier to capture the entire team in one spot. After this, the CIA continued to find reasons to put off any action until the plan moved further along.

"We, I say 'we' because by now I was a co-conspirator with Fathi, were beginning to believe that Agent Wallace had even bigger ideas. This was confirmed when he said the capture would take place after the boat delivered the team to the U.S. Now it was clear he was talking about a real boat! He said capture of the terrorists on U.S. soil would make a bigger splash and subject them to the U.S. legal system. It would be a big deal in the national and international news and, although it would be necessary to involve the FBI and possibly some others, the credit for the bust would go to the CIA, and mostly to the agents in Islamabad. It now seemed to both of us that Agent Wallace wanted the credit. With this, we began to seriously question his motives. Adam, I now pose a direct question to you. Am I being too cynical with the assessment I just gave?"

Adam suspected that he knew the answer, but he felt like he should at least give the impression there was a plausible explanation for the CIA man's behavior. It wouldn't be easy to come up with one, but he would try. "Ahad, people have different jobs, come from diverse cultures, and have their own motives. I can't speak for someone else. It is all I can do to deal with my own actions—but having said this, it is entirely possible that Agent Wallace has managed this in a reasonable way but one that would benefit him most. Also, we don't know how deeply involved the Agency is. I know that it has not reached Langley, but how far short of that must be determined. I do know that succeeding at a major operation like this would put the agent responsible in line for special recognition and possibly a big promotion—and that could be Agent Wallace's strategy."

Ahad said, "I can see the logic of your answer, but I don't think something like this would happen with a person like you."

Adam did not respond to Ahad's comment. The best thing for him to do now was move ahead and deal with conditions as they were. "I suggest we spend the rest of the afternoon writing down the specific actions and the time frame for what is being planned by Al-Fir. There should be just one copy and, if you agree, I will take it to the Director of the CIA. I can't speak for Director Zinsky, but I am confident he will treat this as a credible threat and, as such, will mobilize all of the resources he has available. Fathi, I agree with your dad that Agent Wallace is not handling the matter in the most professional way, and I will also discuss this with Director Zinsky. So, gentlemen, after we test our best penmanship and get the notes from this meeting summarized, I would like to hear more about this boat that you have reluctantly mobilized for action."

"Adam," said Ahad, "I can do better than that. After we finish here, let's take a drive up to the harbor. The boat is there, undergoing an overhaul on the diesel engines, replacement of the pumps, and some other small projects mostly related to performance. The inside is in pretty rough shape but by the time the mechanics finish their work, the boat will be fast, seaworthy, and suitably fitted for the trip to America. The boat has a relatively narrow beam, and it is not stabilized, but it can cruise at twenty-five knots. We are adding an extra fuel tank to make it possible to reach the entrance to the St. Lawrence Seaway after fueling in Portugal without having to slow down for reasons of fuel consumption."

"Have you chosen a captain?" asked Adam.

"Yes," said Ahad. "He is an interesting fellow who agreed to make the delivery, but with the provision he receives double pay. He could care less about the mission. He just wants the money and he told me that he was eager to see the Great Lakes. He will leave the boat at a maintenance yard in Wisconsin after making the delivery and will be out of the country and on his way home before whatever the passengers are up to is revealed. He has not been told the intent of the people onboard, and he hasn't asked. He does know there will be explosives brought on board and he wants them locked up. He must have suspicions, but he wants to keep things the way they are. After the terrorists are captured, we will make sure the authorities know the captain was working with us and in no way complicit."

Adam was amazed at how far this family had become embroiled in this dangerous plot.

———————

The next morning, Adam sat on the plane, studying the action plan that the three had assembled for dealing with this bizarre terror plot. Before he contacted Bob Zinsky, Adam would organize all the facts and put the material into good order for his meeting with the Director. He wondered if Fathi and Ahad were selfless patriots in service of humanity, or were they hapless victims of a misadventure they had become embroiled in through a series of unintentional but very serious missteps? Adam had to view them on the kinder side and think of them as special people who screwed up and were now taking significant risks to do the right thing. At this point, it was his responsibility to do everything he could to keep these two good men and their families safe.

Chapter 23

Fathi was back in Islamabad. The meeting with his father and Adam only intensified his feelings of urgency and dread. Procrastination, or more likely deliberate delay, on the part of Roland Wallace had allowed the plot and Fathi's role in it to reach a dangerous point. He could now only get out safely if the leaders were captured or killed. Hearing Adam Grant say that the President of the United States and the Director of the CIA, and soon the FBI, would be involved was reassuring, but how far the plan had progressed suddenly cast a new light on this affair and Fathi wanted it to be over with soon. He wanted to get out—especially after a phone call from Assoud Al Walaki summoned Fathi to Peshawar the following day.

"Hello, my friend," was Assoud's mellifluous greeting to Fathi as he entered the room at the Peshawar compound. Assoud was alone. "The reason I have asked you to come today is to discuss a very important part of our plan. It deals with actions that have been organized by you alone. I am sure you realize that we are depending almost entirely on you for moving our army to the United States aboard a boat and, after that, having them join with a team you have organized in New York. I need to know if the arrangements are completed."

"Yes, Assoud, they are."

"And, *they* are what, specifically?" *He is making me drag this out of him,* thought Assoud. *That's okay, because I will not have to put up with this much longer.*

"I have arranged for a 117-foot boat. It is being refitted in Jeddah as we speak. We are adding an extra fuel tank and making sure the engines are in top shape for the trip. It will arrive in Karachi around October first. The vessel will be manned by four people, a Captain, his Mate, and two deck hands. It will have adequate provisions for all the passengers. Their accommodations will be spartan but serviceable. The boat will have sufficient space and some equipment for the bomb makers to complete their work on the customized vests, but they will be asked to bring along any special tools and other equipment that they need to complete their task.

"The boat will also have a configuration below deck making it possible for the passengers to be hidden for a short time in case a Customs search is carried out. The boat will have a neglected external appearance, and the condition of the inside will justify the need for a total re-do of the interior. This appearance serves a dual purpose. It saves money for the donor and it makes the purpose of the trip, to a boatyard in Wisconsin, entirely believable.

"In contrast to the cosmetics, the propulsion, navigation, and safety systems will be in perfect condition. The boat is capable of sustained speeds of twenty-five knots. The trip should be completed in less than a month, including an initial trip from Jeddah to Karachi and back to pick up the passengers. I checked the boat personally when I was in Jeddah to see my mother, who was ill. Final preparations for the engines and other parts are nearly complete."

Noting the satisfied look on Assoud's face, Fathi continued. "The generous gift from the donor includes paying for the crew plus all maintenance and provisions. His donation will be worth well over four million dollars." This was a number Fathi came up with as he spoke, but it was probably not far off. "The boat will not be returned. It will essentially be abandoned by the crew after they leave it at the boatyard in Wisconsin, but this will not become apparent until well after the attack has occurred. When it is recovered in the U.S., any attempts to identify the donor will be shrouded in confidentiality and secrecy by the multiple layers of transactions that have taken place in the Caribbean Islands, where the boat is registered."

This information satisfied Assoud. "From what you have just told me, we have no responsibilities other than delivering the team and special supplies to the boat in Karachi during the first week of October."

You mean martyrs and bombs, thought Fathi.

"Are there any possible complications that we can anticipate, work we should be doing to keep them from happening, or obvious things we should be avoiding?"

Yes, thought Fathi. *You can anticipate having the whole operation taken down the minute people reach the staging point in the United States, and you can avoid all of this by abandoning this crazy plot.* His answer was simply, "No."

"Thank you, Fathi. You are a loyal soldier for the cause. I hope this is not the last time we work together." *Not true,* thought Assoud, *but how else to end the meeting and to soothe any fears Fathi might be harboring about his future?*

"It has been an honor to be part of such an important action against the infidels," said Fathi, for whom lies like these had become all too easy to spout.

OPERATION THUNDERSTRUCK | 135

After Fathi left, Assoud summoned his associate who was in the next room behind a closed door. When the man, who was senior to Assoud but remained unknown to any but the highest levels in the organization, entered, Assoud asked him, "Did you hear all of that?"

"Yes," the man said.

"Are you satisfied?"

"Yes."

"Immediately after the boat leaves Karachi, we will be ready to silence him," said Assoud. "By that, I mean we will watch him closely and monitor all of his communications. We may even find the need to closet him with force. There is a chance that the people in New York will try to contact him, and for that reason, we should keep him alive, but very close at hand, until the attack has actually begun."

"What about his family?" asked the man.

"They will be watched closely by our men in Jeddah. After our job is done, they will also be dealt with. They all know too much and will no longer be of any use after our work in New York is completed. If they remain alive, they will only represent a continuing danger to our cause."

"And the other issue?" Assoud's visitor asked.

Assoud was sure his questioner already knew the answer. The group was aware that the CIA had been making inquiries and probably had established contacts with people who had some knowledge about the actions they were taking, even some who had been fed misinformation, but they did not know who they were. In this business, there would always be traitors who turned on their own people if the price was right. But the action they would take now would both scare any traitors and eliminate the person they were dealing with. Assoud responded, "The CIA man, Roland Wallace, will be taken care of immediately. We are reasonably sure he has kept what he knows or suspects to himself. We have been told he intends to take full credit for stopping us. He has told no one in his organization, but this silence can last only so long. He will eventually need help. He could start talking at any time, so we can't afford to delay. There is always the possibility he could begin enlisting the aid of his colleagues or at least give some hints that could reveal his intentions."

"Will his death be connected with us in any way?"

"Not as long as he hasn't told anybody about us," replied Assoud.

"Good," said his companion, who left the room, tacitly leaving the responsibility for elimination of the CIA agent in the hands of Assoud Al Walaki.

This meeting with Assoud, which reeked of ominous undertones, convinced Fathi that it was time to get his family out of Pakistan. He expected his wife, and to some extent his daughters, would be happy to hear they were returning to Jeddah. They had come here with the understanding that it would be a temporary move. The business he had started in Islamabad could now be managed by local employees. With Fathi supervising from headquarters in Jeddah, the business had every chance of prospering under the direction of Prem Salam, a Pakistani who Fathi had carefully hired and trained with the intention of him eventually taking over as general manager of the operation.

He was sure Lila would be eager to return home. He would also tell his wife he had been working with the CIA and the reason why. This would be a tough thing to do, and it would not make her happy. Actually, she probably would be furious with Fathi and ask him how he could become involved in something so irresponsible and dangerous while putting his family at risk, etc., etc. The worst part was that she would be absolutely right.

Lila and Fathi were alone in their kitchen. "Lila," he said, "I have to tell you about something I have been doing. I kept it from you because I didn't want you to worry." Pretty lame, thought Fathi. "It is important that you know about it now because it means our time here will be coming to an end soon."

"I call that good news, but what else do you want to tell me? What is going on that I haven't been told?" said Lila.

"You have heard me speak of Fadel?"

"Yes."

"Not long after we moved here, he introduced me to some men who he said were interested in construction. It sounded like it would be a good business contact, so I agreed to meet with them. The men were kind of weird and rough-looking, but there are many people like that here, so I wasn't put off by their appearance or actions. I thought I should be open-minded."

"And then what happened?"

"After several contacts with these people, I learned they were actually terrorists. You can ask me why I didn't realize this sooner, and I wouldn't blame you. I have asked myself that same question a dozen times. I don't have an answer for myself and I don't have one for you. The man who told me the people I met with were terrorists said he was from the CIA, here in Islamabad. He asked me if I would be willing to continue meeting with these men and provide him with information that would help him stop any plot that they might be hatching. He said there would be no danger for me or my family. He told me that they get information from many sources and there was no way what I was doing could be traced."

"How long has this been going on?"

"Three years."

"Oh, my God!"

Before his wife could say any more, Fathi said, "Anyway, now things are getting out of control. I told my father …"

Not letting her husband go further, Lila interrupted. "When?"

"He has known about this for almost two years."

"Fathi, you tell your father and not me? What did he say?"

"At first he wasn't convinced that this would amount to anything. He just told me to continue providing information as long as it wouldn't come back to bite me, but he said I should get out of the arrangement as soon as possible."

Gaining more control of her emotions, Lila continued. "Your dad is a smart guy. Were you able to do what he advised?"

"I tried, but the CIA agent kept turning up the heat on the whole thing and now it has developed into a plot to attack the New World Trade Center in New York City on a scale that will surpass the death toll of 9/11."

"Fathi, this is terrible … unbelievable, how could you …?"

"Lila, this is where we are now. The terrorists will be transported to the United States on a boat. Once there, they will be captured, and this will be before they can do any harm. At the same time, all of the people involved in the plot, including the leaders here in Pakistan, will be captured and we will be done with this awful mess."

"What does your father think about this now?"

"Lila, my dad is a man of action. He contacted the President of the United States and this led the U.S. government to mobilize an effort to stop the terrorists' attack. My dad's crazy action was effective! We are now working with a personal envoy of the President of the United States and part of the overall plan is the move we are making now, getting the family back to Jeddah."

"What about you?"

"I will be staying in Islamabad for a few more weeks. During that time, I will be under the protection of the local authorities and the U.S. government, so I will be safe. When this is all over, I will join you and the girls in Jeddah, and probably never see this place again." After dropping this bombshell, Fathi tried to sum up as the tension lessened. "Lila, I got involved and before I even knew what I was doing, I became an informant for the CIA. I never intended to do anything like this, but I did, and I can't get out of it until the whole thing is dealt with in the right way. I got into it but we have to pull together as a family to get out."

The two stood in the kitchen, looking at each other, waiting for the next words that would be spoken. Lila Kanaan decided she would talk. "Fathi, it is not so important now to talk about how this came about. We can do that later, and I promise we will. The important thing is that we do the right thing now and do it fast. Your plan to move us away from here is a good start. We should be safe in Jeddah. My question to you is, are you sure you can get yourself out of this situation?"

"I am working on that, believe me. My role started innocently as an advisor on construction and design, but it soon became clear to me that my dealing with them would have nothing to do with our business. Almost before I even knew what was happening, it became apparent their real purpose was to launch a terrorist plot against the United States. Following the lead of the CIA agent, my job was to sell the terrorists on a plan. This plan would make it possible for the authorities to capture the whole group, stop the plot before anyone got hurt, and at the same time eliminate the possibility of anyone knowing I was involved. I could have gotten out in the beginning, maybe, but I didn't. Instead, I agreed to continue working with the CIA. He assured me that when the time was right, the CIA would take over and I would not be involved in any way, and that their intention was to take down the terrorists in one swipe, which would mean there would be nobody left to come after me."

"You mean us," said Lila.

Fathi didn't respond.

Lila suddenly felt weak and spent. She sat down on a chair, completely drained. Fathi knew he had let down his wife and their daughters. He had entered into this awful mess slowly, and the awful implications had become clear so gradually, that it was hard for him to say just when he had reached the point of no return. He bent down and put his arm around his wife to comfort her; she stood and tried to comfort her husband in turn.

"We'll get through this," she said.

Fathi was relieved and thankful. He wondered how he could have been so lucky to have the wife he had. Lila could have railed at him, and she would have had every right. Instead, she was smart enough to know that this was a big deal and screaming recriminations was not the way to solve anything now.

Chapter 24

September 11 – 12, Sunday thru Monday

Fathi Kanaan checked the Personals section in the *Pakistani International News*, an act that had become a daily ritual. He found the notice he had been waiting for. It indicated, in code, the time and place for tomorrow's rendezvous with Roland Wallace. The announcement described a lost male Yorkshire terrier, about seven pounds, with black and tan markings. A small reward was offered. He had seen similar notices before, and each conveyed a special meaning. Fathi looked at the log Roland had given him when the project first started. The next entry on the list was for just such an animal, and the message was clear: Roland wanted to meet at 9:00 a.m. the next day at the usual place.

These meetings were held in the apartment of a woman who Roland saw on a regular basis. Roland always arrived after she had gone to work, and they lasted only an hour at most. The entry to the apartment was private. No one saw the men and the woman never asked what the meetings were about. Based on what transpired the last time they met, Fathi expected the CIA man would be asking about the final plans for the boat.

Fathi was looking forward to meeting with Roland, reinforced with support and additional information he had gained after talking with his father and Adam Grant. Roland would learn that people in high places in Washington D.C. were now aware of the plot. It was no longer something that involved just the two of them. Fathi feared there would be a confrontation but considering the dire consequences if the plot wasn't stopped, there was no time for delay. Fathi would urge Roland to capture the terrorists and stop the plot in Pakistan. The boat could be there in sight, but its position at the dock in Karachi would mean that it was only a marshaling point. The bombers would be captured before they departed for the United States.

In the slum area of the city, Katchl Abedis Mansur admired his latest creation. It was the size of three bagels stacked on top of each other. He had been busy these last few weeks assembling other similar devices. Those units were for a special event that would occur soon in the United States. They would fit snuggly side-by-side in form-fitting vests to be worn by martyrs who would be expressing ultimate devotion to the cause. Or, as Katchl, who very much enjoyed being alive, questioned, was it stupidity they were demonstrating? These martyrs would soon be on a journey by boat nearly halfway around the world. Their trip would end in glory, at least that was their intent. Katchl would also be on that boat, to complete final adjustments on the vests. The difference for him was that he would be returning home, alive.

Today's job was simple and straightforward. Sometime after midnight he would go to the Al Guhrair Apartments, located in DHA Defence 2, and leave the small present he was working on for one of the tenants. The landmark building was seven stories of what were called luxury apartments, but he had heard they were nothing special. What an irony, Katchl thought, the sales brochure touted the apartments were within walking distance of a mosque and a large sign in the parking lot said: "We love our children. Please drive slow." The truth was, most of the apartments were occupied by foreigners, not Muslim, and few had children.

For Katchl, the best part of the set-up for this job was that the parking lot was separated from the building by a large, well-landscaped green space that was well-lighted, while the parking lot was not. He would be looking for a grey Ford Fusion that belonged to an unlucky fellow who would be sleeping in one of those so-called luxury apartments. He hoped this man had an especially good night's sleep because it would be his last.

———————

Roland Wallace clicked off the alarm fifteen minutes before it was set to ring at 6:30 a.m. This ritual was repeated daily, except for weekends and vacations. Roland didn't know why he set his alarm every night. He was always awake before it went off. He hated the sound of the alarm—*really* hated it and could think of little worse than starting the day with that hideous sound in his head. On the rare occasion when it rang, he had to make a conscious effort to work off the crummy start to his day.

As he was putting on the slacks to his brown suit, rumpled in the seat from sitting at his desk for days on end, Roland thought about wearing his other suit. No, it was too late to bother changing. He already had the pants on and he didn't want to make the effort to take them off and find his grey suit in the closet. It had been months since he had the brown suit cleaned. He would wear it one more day and then take it to the cleaners.

Roland Wallace had developed a habit of checking out where he was in life while getting dressed and eating his small breakfast, alone. It was not difficult to take inventory. He was divorced, and it was mostly his fault. His wife had put up with his job, including the travel, long separations, and the hours—but she drew the line at his dalliance with a young filing clerk from the office. It was by no means the first, just the one she fixated on. Maybe she was just looking for an excuse to do something she had been thinking about for a long time. He didn't even know why he had affairs. When his wife confronted him, he wasn't repentant. He just wondered why she chose to finally start bitching. He never did know for sure what was on her mind, although when she remarried quickly, he had his suspicions.

As Roland thought about his actions, he had to admit that fooling around didn't bring him that much pleasure. Maybe the reason he acted the way he did was because he was bored. He needed more excitement than he was getting at his desk job. The routine at work had become deadly and it was almost more than he could deal with. All he could do this morning was what he did every morning. He told himself there were no do-overs. What he had already done was done and he should move on. There was still time to put some excitement back into his job and he was working on that. His wife was history. His children, a son and daughter, were both in college. Thank God, they were paying in-state tuition. He helped his children as much as he could, but they would both end up with some serious debt. They never told him how much, but he expected it would be considerable because both had cars and lived in decent apartments—their problem. All Roland had was his job, and it was up to him to make the most of it; which was exactly what he was about to do.

When Roland was growing up, his family routinely used the phrase "middle management" as one of derision. His father was president of a small bank and his brothers were professionals, a doctor and a lawyer. When his two brothers were described around his home, they were called the "Jewish mother's dream," even though the family was Episcopalian.

Roland had chosen a different path. While he was completing

his undergraduate work at a prestigious liberal arts college, majoring in political science and economics, he was recruited by the CIA. His family was impressed, and Roland was proud. He was embarking on an exciting and patriotic career and this made him, at least for a brief time, the darling of the family. The excitement lasted for a while; then the job turned into not much more than shuffling papers and talking on the phone. Without knowing exactly when, Roland realized he was mired in that terrible zone of middle management. He was getting older and was being passed in the Agency by men, and even women, who were smart, ambitious, and on their way up. When his divorce was final, the posting in Islamabad was a welcome change—and opportunity. A lot was happening in the Middle East. Maybe this would be his chance to escape the dreaded work-related trap that was only exacerbated on those rare occasions when he got together with his brothers. Not only was Roland's family blasé with his CIA job, Roland was now bored with it himself.

Three years ago, when an informant identified Fathi Kanaan as having met with a suspected terrorist cell, things changed. Roland Wallace saw the opportunity for something big, maybe even very big. The hint of a plot that Fathi Kannan first described to the CIA agent had the potential to be a dream come true. It could be career changing, even a life-changing opportunity for Roland if he managed this chance properly. From his last meeting with Fathi, it was clear to Roland the time for action was getting close. Today's meeting could be when the CIA agent called a halt to just watching and waiting and made plans to move ahead. He was glad Al-Fir had agreed to the plan he had come up with for a boat to carry the bombers to the United States. This part of the plot, for Roland, had been a huge break-through. It would lead to results that for him could be the best of both worlds. Even if there were problems with the boat, which he hoped wouldn't happen, it still could be used to get the group together in one spot and capture them in Karachi. But this was not the best option, because he wasn't sure he could depend on the Pakistani locals. He had purposely not told anyone in the CIA about this yet, but maybe after today, with the trap ready to be sprung, he could at least let the Field Director in on things. With all he had accomplished, Roland was sure he would still be able to get major credit for what he believed he deserved. Either way, this was going to be a good day.

Roland Wallace approached his car with a little more spring than usual in his step. Regardless of what transpired at the meeting, he would play a key role in representing the interests of the United States in stopping an encore of 9/11—he would be lauded a hero and could even become a legend in the Agency. As Roland slid into the front seat, depressed the brake pedal, and inserted the key into the ignition, Katchl Mansur watched from the edge of the lot and dialed. His phone repeated faint sounds as he entered the numbers before depressing the send button, starting an irreversible climactic chain of events. The instant the phone rang, the car he was watching lifted three feet in the air with a violent fireball that ejected the four doors before settling back to the charred pavement. The entire scene was clothed in a veil of black smoke and spewing yellow flames. *He must have had a full tank of gas, mused the bomber.* The careful driver had secured his seat belt before starting the car, so his charred body was now fused to the seat frame that cradled it.

———————

When Lila saw the news alert on TV, she knew there had to be a connection. Just a day ago Fathi had told her about the CIA agent, and now this. Her husband would not be at his office yet, but he was never without his cell phone. She called him immediately.

The first words he said were, "Lila, I heard."

Chapter 25

Back home in his apartment, Adam looked forward to his third Skype-assisted dinner date with Erin. It was Sunday, so the six-hour time difference had to be dealt with. Erin would eat at a fashionable eight thirty in the evening, and for Adam it would be two thirty in the afternoon.

These two hours they spent together were the foundation for the superstructure that was the two shorter calls they made each week to catch up. As special as this time together was, it only emphasized to Adam that he needed to decide what would be next for them. Though Adam saw Erin on the screen and heard her voice, she was still 4,500 flight miles away. He longed to feel her touch. Adam knew that she too was not satisfied to have their lives play out this way, as parallel paths separated by space and engulfed in the responsibility of mutually exclusive job situations.

Director Zinsky told Adam that Fred Billson would be expecting him at his office by 9:00 a.m. Adam looked forward to talking with Fred again, especially with all that had happened since they last met. Fred Billson seemed like a good guy and the information he had given Adam turned out to be both accurate and useful.

Fred Billson was pleased when the director told him to be ready to meet with Adam Grant. Billson's knowledge of Pakistan, gained from a prior posting, and news he was expecting to hear from Adam, gave him hope that important things could be moving forward. All of this would depend on what Adam took away from his meeting with Roland Wallace at the CIA Islamabad field office. And, more important for the desk-bound Billson, was the chance he would be taking part in what he had reason to believe would be momentous events unfolding soon in Pakistan.

As Adam made the short drive to Langley from his apartment, he organized his thoughts. He purposefully turned off the radio in his affordable blue Hyundai on mornings like this because it provided quiet to think and plan his day. Adam's main questions for Fred would be about Roland Wallace. Had Wallace shared information about the plot with others in the CIA or was he acting solo? If the answer was the latter, they would all have some catching up to do.

After an elevator ride to the third floor and a short walk down the hall to enter Fred Billson's area, a somber-faced young woman ushered Adam into the boss's office. It looked to Adam as though she had been crying. As Adam entered, Fred Billson sat motionless behind his desk. He did not stand up to greet his visitor. The man looked devastated.

"What's going on?" asked Adam flippantly. "Not that happy to see me?" As soon as the words were out of his mouth, he was sorry.

Taking a breath and collecting himself, Fred stood, shook

Adam's hand, motioned for Adam to take a seat, and said, "Sadly, your visit today is well-timed. You are exactly who I should be seeing now. Let me explain ..." After sharing the barest essentials of the assassination of a fellow agent, Fred Billson, now fully professional and under control continued. "His death is harsh news, but what is disconcerting is the information the station chief found in Roland's apartment, on his computer, and in several of his office files. It corroborates what you told me a couple weeks ago. He found a set of files that meticulously document a log of multiple meetings, over a period of three years, all dealing with Roland's management of Fathi Kanaan. Nobody else in that office, or elsewhere in the CIA, had any knowledge of this operation. We are all reeling. I hope you and I can share what we know and find a way to move fast and act on what we can learn from these files before it's too late."

"I am terribly sorry about the loss of your agent," was Adam's sincere condolence. "Of course, you and I are on the same page, but when it comes to this assassination, I can do nothing but believe the terrorists were on to him, which makes me wonder if they are also on to Fathi. Even if they are, the difference is, they need Fathi, at least for now. Can you confirm my hunch that the terrorists Fathi is working with are also the people who killed Roland, or do you have other ideas about who and why?"

"Not yet. But before I say more, can you bring me up to date?"

"Roland Wallace effectively shut me out," said Adam. "Our conversation ended before it even started. I decided not to push him because I didn't know how he would react."

"What you have just told me answers some questions, but there are still some unknowns and, of course, the inexplicable. Roland Wallace broke one of the most important rules we have in the Agency when he didn't share a word, not even a morsel of information, about his contact with Fathi Kanaan and what he knew about Al-Fir's plot. When the station chief searched

Roland's apartment, he found notes that covered eleven meetings with Kanaan. They record a steadily building plan to attack One World Trade Center. It corroborates everything that Fathi and Ahad told you. From what we can piece together, Roland was going to spring this on us and, when he did, we would be running around like chickens with our heads cut off, putting things together in a mad rush to catch these guys."

"Any idea why Wallace did what he did?" asked Adam.

After a thoughtful delay, Fred Billson said, "His station chief said the guy was a loner. He had been there for more than three years, and from his unshared records, his contact with Kanaan began shortly after Wallace arrived. This seemed to be his main activity, but he kept it quiet and had just enough other action going to keep people from wondering what he did with his time. He was divorced and not close to his family. We know of no other people or close associates he had. My guess is that he wanted to make a big bust and get people to notice him in a positive light. This is a good example of why we are told the CIA is not a place to try and act like the Lone Ranger."

"That makes sense," said Adam. "My main concern and question now is what happens to Fathi and his family? Fathi Kanaan is a smart guy, but he knows who the bad guys are, and where they are. He has shared all that with his dad and me, and I am sure most of it with Roland Wallace. I want to believe the terrorists think Fathi is still loyal to the cause and to the success of the attack in New York. They were obviously watching Roland, who was probably nothing more than a thorn in their side, so they eliminated him. I have to believe they are planning the same fate for Fathi, but only later."

Billson's mood lightened somewhat, now that he could start making solid plans going forward. "First, we organize our team here while we coordinate with the office in Islamabad. I am not sure the folks there can do much more than monitor Fathi Kanaan and his family to keep them safe, but whatever they do has to be done quietly so as not to raise any suspicion. The Islamabad office should do nothing that will give the terrorists any hint that we are on to them. When the terrorists are corralled and the Kanaan family is safe, the rules of engagement will change. When that happens, the office in Islamabad will need all the support we can give them. We will eventually need assistance from local Pakistani law enforcement to round up the leaders, and the FBI should be on board ASAP for what is likely to happen here if the boat really delivers the terrorists on our soil. I know there will be a lot more, but for now, is there anything else you can think of that I have left out?"

"I agree with all of this," said Adam. "I will be returning to Jeddah soon, to check on the progress of the repairs on the boat with Ahad and Fathi. It would be great if Eddie Freeman, from your shop, could travel there and install surveillance and tracking equipment on the boat. We worked together earlier this year, and he is good. If anyone can, he will find a way to install devices that won't be found."

"That's a great idea," said Fred. "I'll contact Eddie myself. If you and I work together, I am optimistic we can stop this before anyone else gets hurt. Bob Zinsky wants you and me to partner on this project. I suggest we share daily progress reports until this comes to an end."

Adam agreed wholeheartedly. The meeting ended with both men intent on the tasks ahead.

Chapter 26

———————————

There was no doubt in Fathi's mind about who was responsible for the horrific act this morning. It was done by the people he would be meeting with in a few hours. He was certain. Their message was clear: time for action was running out. How much longer could he keep himself and, more importantly, his family safe while these murderers were free?

"Good afternoon, my dear friend," was the sharp greeting from Mihal, the leader of the motley group seated around the familiar table. "No doubt you have heard about the explosion this morning. Too bad for that CIA fellow, but he brought it on himself. He was nosing around and asking questions. He was sniffing too close to our plan, but I don't think he learned anything that can harm us. The way we took care of him will be a warning for others to keep their lips sealed, at least for now. Then, in a month, everyone will know because we will have won."

Marshaling every resource he could, Fathi maintained a neutral, disinterested look as he listened to Mihal. How much of this bravado was directed at Fathi? Did they know he had been meeting with Roland? Probably not, but they knew Fathi was not one of them. They didn't like him or trust him. Fathi knew, now more than ever, that his life would be spared only as long as he was a vital part of the plot. He knew he would no longer be of value the minute the attack was launched. When that happened, he would be eliminated; and in their ruthless craze, they would probably kill his entire family too. When Assoud had said at their last meeting that he looked forward to working with Fathi on future projects, it was pure deceit—a lie. His performance at today's meeting was crucial.

"I am sure you had good reasons for doing what you did," said Fathi. "I agree, this should quiet some, but it might arouse others. What will the CIA do in response?" Talking like this helped Fathi keep his emotions in check. He was playing defense by going on the offense the only way he could. Challenging Mihal by implying that his audacious actions could possibly endanger others in the group was done to add to his standing and to help ensure his safety and that of his family, at least for now.

"I make the strategy and direct the planning," said Mihal. His comment was met by nods of agreement from the three others at the table. "You come up with tactics that are useful in making our plans work, my friend. We will make the plans and you stick to your part. It is only together that we accomplish the deed. Now, we must discuss where we are with the grand plan and decide what is next for us to do."

With this exchange, Fathi felt like he had weathered the storm. With everyone's attention on him, he began. "The pieces of the operation are falling into place nicely. The maintenance work and upgrades on the boat are almost complete. Our bene-factor is bringing in an expert to make sure all of the electronics and navigation systems are in order. He has only been told that the boat is to make a transatlantic crossing and must be seawor-thy and safe."

"Will the boat have a sufficiently skilled captain and crew?" asked Mihal, who had never been at sea and was concerned for his own safety.

This question had been asked earlier, and Fathi had avoided providing details. Now he had a satisfactory answer and was happy to provide information that this group wallowed in. Because of the danger and secrecy of the mission, a regular captain and crew for hire would not do. Most people skilled enough to be a ship's captain would be likely to ask questions and eventually uncover the real purpose. Fortunately, Al-Fir had no members or connections that were even remotely suited to captain a ship; Fathi had free rein for this and once again called on his father for help.

"A captain and three crew members have been hired. They are sympathetic to our cause and can be trusted. They are currently in Jeddah, where they will remain with the boat."

"When do we get to see this mystery boat?" asked Mihal.

"As I said earlier, the boat will be in Karachi Harbor the first week of October. I can be no more specific than that." Fathi then showed them a black-and-white photo of the boat taken with his phone and printed for just this occasion. He had erased the image and continued his practice to never bring his phone with him to meetings like this. The men around the table were impressed. With a secure hold on their attention, Fathi continued. "Another important detail is that for safety reasons, the explosive devices will not be armed until the boat reaches its destination in America. The captain has warned that otherwise, if they hit severe weather, all could be lost." This was an exaggeration, but the group was impressed at Fathi's concern for their safety. "The boat will have a secure hold for the explosives, and the captain requested that he keep the key to the lock in a secure place."

"Isn't that giving the captain too much control?" asked Mihal, who was loath to relinquish any of his authority.

"No," said Fathi. "It is just being wise with how we manage our investment. If it will make you feel better, you can discuss this with the captain personally, in Karachi, before the boat departs. He is a good man. I am sure he will also give you a tour before the team boards the boat, if that is your wish."

"I am not questioning your selection of the captain and crew. I just want to be sure everything comes off as we have planned," replied Mihal. He wanted to avoid crossing Fathi now because there was still a great deal of important work to be done by him, especially with managing the team in New York.

"Mihal, I fully understand your concerns, and I appreciate all of the effort you are putting into this project. You know I am as eager as you are for us to succeed. I truly believe in our cause or I wouldn't be doing this." Fathi was convinced that Mihal's final solution for him was already decided, which is why Fathi would say and do whatever it took to ensure that Mihal kept him around until November 17.

"What about the team?" asked Mihal.

"The bomb makers you have enlisted will board the boat with the rest of the team in Karachi Harbor," said Fathi. "It will be up to you to decide how and when they are delivered to the boat."

"We will take care of that. We have made all of the arrangements. Bribes have been paid to the port authorities so that what and who we load on the boat will not be questioned. The people we are dealing with are sympathetic, but not so much that they will forgo the coin they can earn by looking the other way and forgetting that they did." *Maybe I have been too harsh in my opinion of this businessman who is not one of us, even if he tries to act like it,* thought Mihal. But he dismissed his thoughts almost immediately. Mihal was glad Fathi would be dealt with when the time was right.

Fathi left the meeting in frenzy. All he wanted to do was see his family, hold them close, and get them safely to Jeddah. His parents' house had plenty of room for Lila and the girls to stay as long as necessary. They would pack tonight and leave early tomorrow morning. For now, he could pass off this departure as simply a trip to see the grandparents. After a quick trip to deliver Lila and the girls, and to meet briefly with Adam and his father, Fathi would return to Islamabad. He would remain there, alone, until the boat reached its destination in the U.S. and the group, including Mihal, was captured. As soon as that happened, Assoud and his cronies in Peshawar, and Moham-mad in Islamabad, would also be arrested. The charade would be ended and Al-Fir would fold. Then, he promised himself, he would leave Pakistan forever. It couldn't happen too soon.

Chapter 27

September 15, Thursday

For Adam, the trip from D.C. to Jeddah was turn-ing into a milk run. This time he chose to fly Emirates, which offered a nonstop flight. It took twelve hours, but Bob Zinsky insisted that Adam fly business class. This wasn't just for convenience and comfort. The Director knew the travel was putting wear and tear on his main man. He wanted Adam as fresh as possible for the work he had to do when he arrived, and a comfortable seat and more leg room would help.

Time was short and the stakes were high. Adam didn't have the luxury to lay low for even a day to get over his jet lag. He had to be sharp the minute he arrived in Jeddah. He was eager to see the progress Ahad's team had made with the boat. "The boat" was how everyone referred to the vessel. Because of what it was being used for, there was no personal attachment or pride of ownership. The boat had a name, Adam was sure, but he had never heard it used.

Adam was pleasantly surprised when Fathi Kanaan met his flight at the King Abdul Aziz Airport. "Welcome, Adam. Nice to see you again," was the greeting he received.

Fathi looked like a different man. His once cheerful and confident demeanor had been replaced by a countenance that registered pain, concern, and frustration. This came as no surprise to Adam. The CIA agent Fathi had been working with had been murdered; no doubt at the hands of Al-Fir. There was every reason for Fathi to believe that would also be his fate if the terrorists had their way. Adam knew Fathi had moved his family to his parents' house, and that he would be returning to Islamabad soon to make his actions appear as normal as possible.

As they walked to the parking garage, Fathi began, "Adam, I wanted to have this chance to speak with you alone, before we got to the house. I suppose you know my wife, Lila, and our two daughters are here in Jeddah, staying with my folks. After the murder of Roland Wallace, I knew my family was in danger. I didn't want to take any chances. They are safe here, and they will not be returning to Pakistan. I will go back tomorrow. I am reasonably sure of my safety while preparations are still in progress and Al-Fir is depending on me to coordinate activities of the team they are convinced is poised in New York. Once they are confident that the team is in place and I am no longer needed, possibly even before the actual event, they will eliminate me and, I expect, my family too. That is the way these people operate. They do not like loose ends, which is what I will soon be. I'd like to ask you to please do *all* you can to keep these bastards from getting to my family."

"Of course, we will," said Adam. "The United States owes a great deal to you and your dad." This promise by Adam was absolute and uncompromising. He and his team would do all in their power to back up that promise.

As they parked in front of the house, Fathi said, "Enough of this conversation for now. I have to lighten up, especially around the kids. Lila knows the seriousness of the situation, but we have to be thinking of the girls and not let them get scared. They are not stupid. They sense something is amiss, but they are also kids and they rely on us and trust that we will do the right thing. Now my job is to live up to the confidence they have in me."

Ahad met them at the door and offered Adam a hearty greeting. Seeing the small bag Adam was carrying Ahad said, "Still traveling light, Adam."

"Yes," his guest responded. "Every day that I avoid the luggage carousel is a good day for me."

Visibly eager to move on with the day's schedule, Ahad said, "Is there anything you need to do before we go to the boatyard?"

"Nothing other than to stow my bag and hit the head."

With apology, Ahad said, "As Fathi must have told you, we have his family with us now so you will be staying in the service quarters. I am sorry for any inconvenience."

"Nonsense. That's just fine with me, Ahad."

As the three men drove to the boatyard, Ahad brought them up to date. "The minor overhaul on the boat's engines has gone smoothly and will be completed in a few days. The other smaller jobs are also going well. Fortunately, there have been no surprises. You will see what we have accomplished when we get to the marina. Your man, Freeman, arrived yesterday and he has been busy installing communication and surveillance equipment."

"I am eager to see the progress you have made," said Adam. "Ahad, tell me again how you found the boat."

"I located the boat in Egypt. It was built in 2003, in an Italian yard. It has an aluminum hull, good power, and cruises at twenty-five knots, and displaces 225 tons. The owner became ill soon after he purchased the boat, and used it very little himself. His family put it out for charter after that. Over the years, the boat has had some hard use and suffered a lot of cosmetic wear and tear; this allowed me to purchase a pretty substantial boat at a very good price."

"If you don't mind, Ahad, in addition to the price of the boat, how much will it cost for the repairs, wages for the crew, dockage, and anything else that is needed? I am not trying to get into your business, but I will do what I can to have our government reimburse you. If I can speak for our government, the cost of the boat will be minuscule compared to the lives saved."

"I think you will be surprised, and pleased, to hear that I paid only one and a half million dollars for the boat, a bargain. I am not sure about the cost of the overhaul and repairs, but I expect it will not be cheap. The captain will receive $50,000 and he will decide how much of it will go to his crew. Fathi told the terrorists a significantly higher number for the total cost. I don't know which of us will end up being correct, but I am sure you know that no price will be too high when it comes to the safety of our family." As they turned into the yard, they saw a bustling work dock and a sizable yacht. "Let's look inside," said Ahad.

As the men boarded, the description that Ahad had offered proved to be accurate. "This is perfect," said Fathi. "It's pretty much a mess but I am sure the people I am dealing with will consider this clean and inviting."

Ahad began the tour. The top deck was spacious and primarily open. It had full controls and a wide, unobstructed space. As part of Ahad's re-fit, heavy vinyl drop curtains were installed to protect the forward bridge deck from the weather. "October in the north Atlantic could be cold," said Ahad.

The main deck, located below the upper bridge deck, had a secondary forward steering station and a mostly open plan with a lounge, dining room, a couple of heads, and an owner's stateroom. They proceeded to the lower deck that had the original crews' quarters that would now be used for the passengers, galley, and ample storage space. The engines and other mechanical equipment were aft. Ahad pointed to a large object just forward of the hatch to the engine room. "This plastic tank was added specifically for this trip. It holds six thousand gallons of diesel fuel, almost doubling the boat's original capacity. This will provide sufficient range to leave the Mediterranean and enter the St. Lawrence Seaway with a reasonable margin of safety while the boat travels at a sustained speed of over twenty knots. It is important for the success of this plan to keep the boat away from fuel docks and prying eyes.

"The two diesel engines total 2,285 horsepower. With only 2,200 hours since their last overhaul, they have a lot of life left in them. Actually, most of the engine maintenance we had to do was because the engines were used too little, not too much. Two generators will supply sufficient electricity and the boat has a desalination system to supply fresh water. There is enough room for general supplies and there will be sufficient food for the trip, some of which will be kept in an extra freezer we added. The mainstay of the food will be dried because this saves weight and space and makes best use of the water that can be replenished."

Adam was amazed by the care and concern Ahad had shown for the project. He was preparing the boat with the same attention to detail he would if he were traveling himself. *That was a measure of the man,* thought Adam. "How about the crew?" Adam asked. "Where did you find them?"

"That took some doing," said Ahad, "but I got it done. The captain is Egyptian. He knows what we are up to. He has been around the block, as they say. He agreed to do it but only at double pay. The captain enlisted three additional crew for the trip. The total cost, as you were told, will be $50,000. The captain will be given $25,000 up front and the remainder will be given to him when he returns home. He will keep what he decides is his share and dole it out to his helpers as he sees fit. It will be the captain's first visit to the Great Lakes. He is excited to be in those waters that he has heard so much about. That is one reason he agreed to do this."

"What does the captain think about all of this?" asked Adam.

"He knows that the attack will never take place, and was definite when he told me he would not have accepted such a job if the attack were to really happen. He will tell his crew whatever he feels they need to know. The fact that his bonus depends on his reaching the destination and discharging the passengers is plenty of incentive for him to succeed," Ahad responded.

"If it makes the captain feel any better," said Adam, "tell him the boat will be shadowed by a U.S. Navy vessel during the entire passage. If the need arises, he can contact the Navy vessel at any time he feels it's necessary. He can count on help being on the scene in less than an hour."

The familiar figure of Eddie Freeman popped through the stout hatch closing off the engine room. "How are things going, Eddie?" asked Adam.

"Great, Adam. It's a lot easier doing this work than fitting radios in your ears, belt buckles, and rings." Eddie was referring to the project he had worked on with Adam earlier in the year. "It was disappointing that none of that ever got used. I am glad that the equipment I am installing here will be."

"Tell us what you've done."

"I have installed cameras in all the living areas of the boat, including the heads. Everything that goes on can be monitored at headquarters. A panic button is installed at each helm station, and an extra-large radar deflector is stationed higher than usual to enhance the boat's radar reflection. This will make it possible for the shadowing vessel to keep the boat in sight at all times without any concerns about atmospheric conditions, including fog. The navigation system and radio capability will be routine maritime. A special radio, for use by the captain and mate only, will remain on the bridge and will stay on the designated channel to contact the following vessel."

"Sounds good. Do you want to go along for the trip as a riding mechanic?" joked Adam.

"That would be a *no*, Colonel."

Eddie returned to his task, while Ahad, Fathi, and Adam continued their inspection. "What's the next step?" asked Adam.

Fathi spoke first. "The traveling team and their equipment will be in Karachi by the first of October. A private dock has been arranged, and the necessary bribes have been handed out to allow a four-hour window for the boat to load and depart. During this time period, nobody will be taking official notice and no cameras will be in action. Well, except for what I hope will be about a dozen CIA operatives watching from every angle they can negotiate."

"That goes without saying," said Adam.

Fathi continued. "Adam, once everyone and everything is onboard, the boat will leave and the operation will be turned over to the captain. I am sure he will be very much comforted by the surveillance you have arranged. I will be in Islamabad, but I plan to clear out as soon as I hear that the terrorists have been taken into custody."

This all sounded good to Adam. "As soon as you return to Islamabad, our people will contact you, and you will be under their discreet but effective surveillance and protection fulltime. Mohammad, Assoud, and the others will also be watched constantly."

Ahad spoke. "My job ends sooner. When the boat departs for Karachi in a week, I will be effectively on the sidelines."

Adam said, "I will be returning to Washington for joint meetings with the CIA, FBI, and the Navy. I will also meet with Homeland Security, Customs, the Coast Guard, and a representative of the Emmet County Sheriff's Department in Michigan. That's where the terrorists will be landing on U.S. soil. Of course, the three of us should remain in close contact from here on."

Mihal phoned Assoud Al Walaki. "He has gone to Jeddah, and has taken his family with him. They packed lightly, so I don't know if this is simply a visit or if he is moving his family."

"That is not unexpected," was Assoud's reply.

"How should we deal with this?"

Assoud did some quick mental calculations and offered a plan, wanting to make it clear that he was in charge and calling the shots. "When Fathi returns to Islamabad, we will have men watching him around the clock. More important, we will have a similar team, only bigger, watching the family in Jeddah. As long as we can use his family as leverage, we can be certain Fathi will comply with our wishes and carry out the plan as he promised. With the distance separating them, there is no way he can protect his family before we do something that he wants to avoid at all costs. Right now, Fathi's cooperation is essential for our success. What we can do with his family if he gets out of line in any way gives us sufficient leverage to make sure he delivers." After a slight pause, Assoud continued. "I know Fathi is worried, but that is to be expected after what we did to the CIA man. But, until our team is landed and we have made contact with the group in New York, we need him. Only he has the details for the entry into the U.S. and the means to transport the team to New York, and, of course, the team he has arranged to meet our people there. Maybe we are depending too much on this man, but we can't change that now. We will deal with him as we have planned, but only when our task is completed. In the meantime, we should manage his family in any way necessary to make sure he delivers his end of the bargain. Once this is over, we will disappear into the hills for a while. The only person who has seen and talked with us is Fathi. I have no objection to killing his family, but we need them alive, either in his father's house or in our custody, until this is over. I will decide."

The call ended.

Chapter 28

"Thank you for this thorough briefing, Adam," Robert Zinsky said after listening to a carefully organized twenty-minute update. "What you just told me and what I heard from Fred Billson gives a good description of the unauthorized practice that Roland Wallace was involved in for the last three years. He was doing the wrong thing, that's clear, but why did he do it? What was the man thinking? It's clear now that he was killed by the people Fathi Kanaan is working with, but we can still hope that the terrorists haven't made the connection between those two. Because Fathi is still alive, I think that's the case. Wallace must have been successful maintaining cover for his asset, but it's clear the terrorists were tipped to something Wallace knew about the plot and it got him killed."

The unspoken thoughts of Robert Zinsky, Director of the Central Intelligence Agency, were: The man is dead. He was one of us. I don't want to be too hard on him, but what he did was unacceptable. Roland Wallace recruited Fathi Kanaan and received information from him about a terrorist plot against the United States. He then urged the man, now an asset, to become involved deeper in the plot, while giving the impression that the operation was being guided by the CIA—the organization not just him alone. Instead of sharing the information with the Agency, Roland Wallace kept it to himself. It could only be assumed that Wallace wanted to take this entire plot down on his own so that he would receive all the credit.

Adam had arrived in D.C. only yesterday. Now, meeting one on one with the CIA Director, he was eager to nail down the many loose ends. Director Zinsky was a key factor when it came to any hope of success with their efforts to thwart the planned attack on One World Trade Center. Bob Zinsky knew and had considerable influence with all the players at the highest levels whose help would be needed, and he had their respect. Adam was glad to have his trust.

Robert Zinsky continued. "We only have two months until this thing is scheduled to go down. We can't waste a damn minute. The team has to start moving now and doing it right. If we screw this up, it's on us. We did the right thing to keep things in our shop while we gathered enough information to *know* what to do, but now it's time to get all hands on deck and *do* what we know needs to be done. All the big guns should be fully on board—all of them." The planning process was racing in the Director's mind. He was leaping ahead mentally, but he was the kind of man who could remain focused and in control in circumstances like this. He knew this was not the time for undisciplined behavior.

Adam said, "Thanks to the information provided by Fathi and Ahad Kanaan, we can stop this, but our starting blocks are awfully close to the finish line. We're beginning a 200-meter dash only twenty meters from the finish line. Events are rushing at us and we need to get up to speed pronto if we plan to get to the wire first—and we must. On the other hand, if we mess up with the capture in Michigan, we will miss an opportunity to show the world, including future terrorists, what we are capable of. Most of all, we have a responsibility to keep the Kanaan family safe from harm. We are close to the wire, but there is time, not much, but still time. You are absolutely right when you say we need to share what we know with the right people and enlist their aid by asking them to hop onto a fast-moving train."

Bob Zinsky said, "As a start, Adam, we need to get all of the players in one room and devise a scheme that can be carried out seamlessly. There is no time for separate meetings, memos, private conferences, or anything that could cause a delay. And there is no time for posturing or grandstanding either. Any credit will be shared. The winners will be the people in our country and the world, who may be able to live under a reduced terror threat. I'll make a list of people I think should be involved and you tell me if you have any ideas about who else should be added, or for that matter, dropped from the list."

Adam sensed how serious Zinsky was and recognized the amount of responsibility he was being given. *This means an "A" game performance on my part, nothing less,* he thought, *so I better get on it.*

The Director continued. "The way I see it, these are the main players: FBI Director Phil Stark, Director of National Intelligence Orville McPherson, and Chairman of the Joint Chiefs of Staff Paul Lippmann. Homeland Security and Justice also need to be there. It will be our job to convince them we have one objective and that we are all on the same team."

"What next?" asked Adam, who was excited at the prospect of some significant movement in the process.

"I will set up a meeting. I think it will be best to have it here. I will warn you now, you will be the one leading the briefing. I am sure there will be lots of questions and, in some cases, skepticism. We need to convince these people with the first go around, so be ready. We have known about this for a while. You'll have to remember these guys will be hearing about it for the first time and it will take some convincing on your part. I know you will do your best."

Chapter 29

The conference room was small and unadorned. With these high-level participants gathered in such an unassuming space, Adam felt like he was looking under the hood of a Ford Focus and seeing a 660-horse power engine. The funny thing was, Adam already knew four of the top people in the room. They were DNI Orville McPherson, who he had met during his North Korean assignment; General Paul Lippmann, Chairman of the Joint Chiefs of Staff; and, of course, Robert Zinsky and FBI Director Phil Stark. Adam was meeting the others, including the directors of Homeland Security and TSA for the first time.

Robert Zinsky took care of the introductions. The others knew or were familiar with each other, but the CIA Director went through the process to make sure everyone knew who Adam was and, especially, to explain Adam's role in the project. With everyone's attention on him, Adam began a careful and detailed explanation, starting with the cryptic message Ahad had sent to the President. He told the group about his trips to Jeddah, his meetings with Ahad and Fathi, the death of Roland Wallace, and the personal and unshared office files that revealed

Roland's involvement in the project. Although they had all heard about the assassination of a CIA agent in Islamabad, they were hearing for the first time that this was not random terror, but instead was part of a bigger and more dangerous plot. When Adam finished his presentation, he invited questions.

"Colonel Grant, do you believe what you have heard from the Saudis, Ahad and Fathi Kanaan?" asked General Lippmann.

Adam, who perceived a mild put-down in the way Lippmann said *Saudis*, answered unequivocally. "Yes. They are intelligent and well-intentioned businessmen who are demonstrating courage, despite the danger to themselves and their families."

"Why would an experienced CIA agent like Roland Wallace keep such valuable information hidden, endangering both an asset and himself, and not share it with the appropriate people in the Agency?" asked the DNI.

Robert Zinsky fielded this question about his agency. He said he had no ready answer and admitted he would probably never have one that satisfied him. He said the Agency was conducting a thorough investigation but had found nothing yet that he could share. He assured the group that his agency would continue to study this failure in the days to come and would take measures to ensure that it didn't happen again.

"Who came up with the idea of the boat?" asked the FBI director.

Adam explained it was originally Roland Wallace's idea, as a way to capture the terrorists in one batch. "Fathi was willing to go along with the idea to herd the bombers in one spot, but he did not think it was necessary to actually transport them to the U.S. He felt the capture could occur in Karachi Harbor. However, the group became fixated on the idea of a boat delivering the team to America and they scrapped the plans for sending the bombers individually or in pairs, ramped up the plan to include more bombers and explosives, and rejoiced as they plotted an even bigger attack. With this decided, there was no turning back."

"Do you think using the boat is a good idea?" continued FBI Director Stark.

Adam looked at Robert Zinsky, who nodded to indicate that Adam should answer. "When I first heard about there being an actual boat, I thought it was a crazy idea, but by then plans were so far along it was too late to make any changes. It didn't make any difference what I thought. We had to deal with the boat as a given. Then, after I gave it more thought, this does provide a way for us to have what amounts to complete control of the operation. We could apprehend the terrorists on U.S. soil and prosecute them for intentions not deeds. At the same time, as the bombers are captured in Michigan, we can get Assoud Al Walaki and his cronies in Pakistan."

"Are there any other issues that you haven't brought up?" asked McPherson.

"Yes, one," said Adam. "Fathi Kanaan has moved his wife and two daughters back to Jeddah. They are staying with his parents in their home. After Roland Wallace was assassinated, Fathi wanted to move them to a safer location because he is worried about them being threatened as a way for the terrorists to ensure that he will remain committed to the plot. He has returned to Islamabad and will remain there until the terrorists are taken down. We have people closely watching Fathi and his family. If the terrorists were willing to kill Wallace, which I am sure they did, Fathi and his family are also in real danger." All of this seemed to register with the group, so Adam added, "For now, Fathi should be safe because Al-Fir needs him alive to carry out their plan. But once the attack is completed, we are sure they intend to kill the entire Kanaan family."

Phil Stark said, "You made no mention of what will happen after the boat reaches Northern Michigan and the terrorists are captured. Does that mean there is no possibility of anything happening in New York?"

Adam was pleased that he would have a chance to answer

this question. He had covered it in his initial explanation, but the attack Al-Fir had planned was so horrific that it was good to be able to once again offer assurance to the group. "Correct. Beyond what I have described with the landings in Michigan, there is nothing happening in the United States. The team in New York does not exist, it is only phantom bait. Everything they have been told about assistance in New York has been entirely fabricated. Our plan is for the operation to end with the FBI taking over, in force, in Wilderness State Park, in the State of Michigan. The minute the boat unloads the terrorists, they will be placed in custody."

"It sounds like you have done an excellent job so far," said General Lippmann. "I know why Bill Wieland thought so much of you. If I may, though, I would like to offer what I think needs to be added to make the right things happen in the scenario you have laid out. I know you have thought of most of what I am going to say, but I would like to say what I see as our role to get the next part of the process rolling." Addressing the group, General Lippmann said, "Taking the last part first, the Kanaan family needs protection. This could be touchy. It is likely there are people watching them, both in Jeddah and Islamabad. We need to have assets in both places to neutralize any threats before they are carried out but not let the bad guys know we are on to them. If they find out, the whole thing may fail. And we need to be ready to get the bad guys in Pakistan quickly, and that will take cooperation with the locals. The Navy should shadow the boat as it crosses the Atlantic, and we need to have someone monitoring the actions on the boat with the gear that you told us Eddie Freeman installed. And, finally, we need to have a pretty big team in place to meet the boat in Michigan."

They don't just give those four stars away, thought Adam. "You heard this for the first time only a few minutes ago, General, and you came up with just about everything we decided would be needed. Thank you. Are there any other thoughts?"

Orville McPherson said, "I don't know the exact strategy to employ, but I do know we will have our hands full deciding who needs to know what and when as this intercept rolls out. When this plot is thwarted, the terrorists will know what we have done and how we did it. If Al-Fir is as small as we think it is, it won't be just the bombers who will be captured; we could wipe out the whole organization in Pakistan. A bonus of this plan is that it could have the effect of dissuading others to join Al-Fir. How much the public should know is another issue—it is something we will have to take up with the administration."

Phil Stark, the FBI Director said, "I see this as being a big operation at the point of takedown. Actually, I was in that park as a boy. I camped there with my dad and brothers when I was a kid. We drove up from Detroit, and when we got there we thought we were in heaven. From what I remember, it will be an easy spot to control. I endorse the place and the timing. There are not many people in the area, especially in November. We can establish a diversion by saying that a training exercise is being carried out. This will allow us to get a sufficient-sized force in there without raising alarm. Since the terrorists will be coming in on a big boat, they will have to be brought ashore using smaller vessels because the water is pretty shallow for a half mile or more. As a logistical plus, Pellston Airport is only thirty minutes away; we could have a C-130 transport in and out as needed."

"I didn't get into that much detail," said Adam. "We have equipped the boat with inflatables sufficient to ferry all of the terrorists to shore, which was our original plan, but then we thought better of it and decided to bring the people and supplies off the big boat using our own small boats. They will be launched from the shore and manned by our people. This will make it easier for us to maintain control of the terrorists' movements after they have left the boat. Al-Fir has been told the martyrs and the handlers will be met by a charter bus and a van to take the people and the supplies to New York. Just the first part of this will happen. There will be a bus and a van, but the bus will be taking the terrorists to Pellston Airport, and from there they will be flown to a federal detention center. The explosives will be transferred in the van to a federal facility for disposal."

"Not to get in the weeds," said the FBI Director, "but will there be any Customs or Immigration issues?"

Adam responded. "The boat's papers will indicate only a captain and a crew of three. The thirty-two terrorists will not be acknowledged. The passengers will not be an issue until the boat enters Canadian waters at the St. Lawrence Seaway. At that time, they will be hidden in engine room space and other closed lockers for a brief time if needed. The boat is ostensibly on its way to a shipyard in Sturgeon Bay for refitting. Its papers will indicate that."

"Will the need for a refitting be obvious?"

The question was from someone who came in after the introductions, did not identify herself, and who Adam didn't know. He responded, "The interior of the boat is run down. I have seen it and its condition speaks for itself. The boat will clear U.S. Customs in Cleveland and the Customs officers there will be alerted in advance so there will be no problem. The officer will conduct a cursory pass while onboard that will appear thorough enough to avoid arousing suspicion. We will take similar precautions with the Canadians. They have agreed to cooperate. Once the boat enters freshwater, it will be shadowed by a series of medium-sized and innocent-looking pleasure craft manned by our Coast Guard out of uniform. They will be able to stay within sight of the boat without raising suspicions because they will simply be traveling in the same direction. Once the boat is on Lake Michigan and ready to be unloaded, two Coast Guard craft will be standing by from the waterside, while the FBI and whatever reinforcements they choose, including locals, will be ready on land."

Chapter 30

When Assoud Al Walaki saw the men enter the room, he greeted them with the cordial demeanor of a person who was going to ask a favor. "Welcome, gentlemen."

When did we become gentlemen? mused Mihal. *He wants something.*

Assoud did not wait for a response. "The boat will arrive in Karachi in three days," he started. "To be safe from prying eyes, we will have only a few hours to load it. Are you ready?"

"Yes." They all registered assent.

"Good. The boat should arrive in the afternoon, according to Fathi Kanaan, who so far has delivered on his promises. The people and supplies will be loaded beginning at midnight. For safety, I understand that you have arranged for this to be done unobserved between midnight and 3:00 a.m. Can you get the job done in that time? The maximum time window we have allowed for is four hours, but the added hour is only to make sure we have sufficient dock availability."

"Yes," said Mihal, making clear he was the spokesman for the group. This would require some quick work on their part, but he was eager to please the leader. He wouldn't tell Assoud that he had also spoken to some of the men on the dock and had extracted a similar pledge of secrecy.

Assoud explained that the boat had departed two days ago, for what he had been told would be a five-day journey. After the boat was loaded in Karachi, it would return to Jeddah to be refueled and additional provisions would be added. It would be a brief stop. From there, the boat would take the North Atlantic route to North America. That trip across the Atlantic was expected to take about ten days. The boat would then proceed through the St. Lawrence Seaway to the Great Lakes, where it would be met by the team that Fathi Kanaan had arranged.

"No disrespect, sir," said Mihal. "Are you sure he can be trusted?"

Assoud responded, "I understand your reservations, but you must realize that his motives are not exactly as yours. He is a follower of the Prophet, but his main reason for joining us is his wish to bring our culture back to the state of glory that it once had. His aims are more social and economic than religious, but nonetheless, they are real." With a pause he added, "Just to be sure, Mihal, we will keep a very close eye on Fathi and his family in Jeddah, and that includes his parents, who he is very close to. We know he has taken his wife and daughters back home, for what has been described as a 'family visit with his parents.' Strange they waited until the first week of their children's school term to make this trip. Please know, my friends, we are taking the appropriate steps to ensure his loyalty until our aims have been achieved. After that, we will do what is necessary to attain our ultimate goals. You can be sure of that."

This seemed to satisfy the men, and Mihal was especially pleased with the intentions Assoud had expressed.

"Now, I must ask you to make another contribution to a cause that you have already given so much for. I need three of you to join the team on the trip to America. You will not be asked to commit the final and ultimate act. We want you to come back to us. You are too useful to the cause to lose. There is so much more that only men with your experience can do. Your role on the boat would be to keep the team encouraged and motivated and to supervise their activities onboard, including anything necessary to complete their training. I have no doubt they will have questions. You will also be there to help the two bomb makers, who will arm the devices after the team leaves the boat and begins travel to New York on the bus."

The four looked at Assoud in stunned silence until one muttered, "But, our families?"

"We have thought of that," said Assoud. "They will be taken care of while you are gone. There will be no need for you to worry."

"We realize that we are needed back here to do more work," said Fazeez, who was a concrete thinker and practical fellow. "But, how do we get home?"

"We have arranged for that," said Assoud. "You will have credentials and a plane ticket to leave New York departing the day before the attack. We realize that it would give you pleasure to see the results firsthand, on the ground, but it will be impossible for you to travel safely after we have completed our work. When we are finished, the country will go on high alert, as it did after 9/11, and travel will be curtailed. I am sure you understand."

The four huddled briefly to discuss the request for only three of them to travel. The spokesman, Mihal, answered. "We are honored. I will do it gladly, along with Abdul and Fazeez. Mohammad will stay home."

After their morning meeting with Assoud in Peshawar, the men were back in Islamabad that afternoon. The first task for each of them was to meet with their families. In each case, the men were greeted by wives who already knew about the plans. Assoud Al Walaki had contacted the women beforehand to extract a promise from each to support their husbands in this quest. Making his request more palatable was his promise of a gift of 200,000 rupees each. Mohammad's wife got an extra bonus, the money and her husband. Being a practical man, Assoud also suggested that the women pack suitably for their husband's one-month trip because the time would be short. They all agreed.

Chapter 31

Captain Ilyas Cham was pleased that Hamid was turning out to be a capable mate. He was impressed by how Hamid used the radio expertly to request information from the port captain's office about the dock where they were to tie up at Karachi Harbor. This was completed well ahead of time, as the boat prepared for the initial passage to the Harbor entrance channel. Using the directions relayed by his mate, Captain Cham eased the boat northeast through the narrow entrance, moving slowly with just enough way to enable steerage. The captain knew there were two crucial factors when it came to boating mishaps in close quarters, such as in a harbor. These possible miscues were an errant course that would put the boat in the wrong place, and excess speed, which caused exponential damage, and a costly exacerbation of the embarrassment resulting from a boating mishap. Moving slowly would be a mitigating factor in case he miscalculated at his first visit to this tight harbor, and he knew that nobody received bad marks for being cautious. He had been told before leaving Jeddah that they would have a reserved spot for the boat to tie up. There would be no waiting, and the dock chosen for them would be especially suited for their special but unstated purpose. As with the other arrangements, this happened thanks to a considerable bribe given to the port director by the terrorists.

Hamid was told the boat should proceed to a starboard mooring at the first dock, A, on the east wharf. A quick look at the Google land map informed Hamid that this dock would be served directly by the East Wharf Road, an ideal situation for the loading of their secret cargo. The two deckhands did a capable job managing the boat's lines and were served well by a competent dock gang. By 4:00 p.m. the boat was secured and ready for fuel and fresh water. They would begin loading their cargo around midnight, in eight hours.

As directed, Captain Cham used one of two cell phones he had been provided, each with diametrically opposite purposes, and called the number he had been given. When Assoud answered, Captain Cham informed him that the boat was at the dock and ready. Assoud, who had already been informed of the boat's arrival by people who were watching the dock, told the captain to begin refueling immediately and do whatever else he needed before heading back to Jeddah. The time for loading would be, as promised, just after midnight, and would be completed in less than three hours. Assoud told the captain that as soon as loading was completed, he should depart. The boat should not linger as a temptation for prying eyes. This conversation, as every utterance from the boat for the next month, was received and logged at CIA Headquarters by one of the analysts who functioned as part of a team that served the Agency around the clock and around the calendar.

When Assoud called Mihal to tell him the boat had arrived and it would be ready for loading tonight, a tingle of excitement stirred the usually taciturn man. After hearing this, Mihal told Fazeez and Abdul that the moment was at hand and they should prepare to move. The first thing for them to do was to assemble the twenty-seven martyrs that were camped out in the rambling but decaying compound where the group conducted its regular business. As part of their instructions, the martyrs carried with them sleeping gear and clothes appropriate for the long, cold voyage. They were told that toilet articles would be available on the boat and they would receive suitable Western-style clothes when they landed in America, to put on before they arrived in New York.

When they were assembled in the reception hall, the biggest room in the building, Mihal told them they would be leaving tonight, within hours. Sundown would be coming soon, and he suggested that they pray together as a group to demonstrate their solidarity and commitment to the noble cause. After prayers, they would assemble their gear and get ready for transport.

He wouldn't tell them until it was time to board the vehicles, but Mihal had decided on transporting the team and supplies in covered trucks. Even with the "no-eyes-on precaution for the departure" promised by Assoud, covered trucks would seem much more natural on the dock rather than a large bus. The passengers would have some discomfort but the added security would be worth it.

————————————

Fathi was expecting a call from Mihal. It came at 8:00 p.m., four hours after Adam had called Fathi to let him know the boat had docked in Karachi Harbor. Mihal said the boat would be loaded at midnight and depart Karachi before 4:00 a.m. to retrace its journey back to Jeddah for more supplies and fuel and then depart for the United States. Trying to sound pleased at receiving the news, Fathi agreed to a meeting at 9:00 p.m. He was leading a triple life, playing both sides of the terrorist plot while carrying on a normal life directing the Kanaan Construction Company and caring for his family. Pursuing his role as a convincing accomplice for the terrorists while at the same time assisting the U.S. government was still working, but for how long? For the other part, he had built a solid team at Kanaan Construction, but he would be leaving the job and the country soon. That would mean depending on his staff even more than they knew.

Every part of this trifurcated life was difficult, but the part that trumped all else was the responsibility he felt for the safety of his family. Moving them to Jeddah was a good start, but they would never be truly safe while Al-Fir remained in operation. Adam had promised he would do everything in his power to keep his family safe, but Fathi knew the ruthless behavior of the terrorists he was dealing with and what they were capable of doing. He was worried.

At the meeting with Mihal, Fathi listened to the conspirator explain the details of the trip that Fathi knew much more about, especially the ending. The most galling words from Mihal were the mendacious comments about how they would all meet back in Peshawar and celebrate a job well done in a little over a month. Fathi knew the celebration would include elimination of him and maybe his whole family. Undeterred, Fathi offered his own words that were equally insincere. "Mihal, you have done an excellent job so far, and I also know you are uneasy about making this ocean voyage. Let me assure you, a boat capable of completing the passage from Jeddah successfully in five days is both fast and seaworthy. It will take you to America to complete your sacred mission while under the caring eyes of Allah."

Mihal, with his brow furrowed in great interest and concentration said, "Tell me again, Fathi, what can the team expect when we arrive at the top of Michigan?" Fathi was sure Mihal knew the plan as well as he did, but needed reassurance. He dutifully recited what he had told him several times before. When Fathi had finished, Mihal must have felt it was his duty to ask a question to justify his request. "What part of the plan do you worry about most when it comes to something that could go wrong?"

Fathi answered the best way he could, and it was one of his first honest statements, but the significance was known only to him. "Mihal, I worry that everything and anything that *could* go wrong *will* go wrong if anyone fails to play his part to perfection. Everyone who I have worked with at my end is competent and dedicated. I mean no offense to your team, but the people who I have organized are capable of functioning independently. They are dedicated and reliable. Like you, they plan to live in a better world when we are finished." As he said these words, Fathi realized that what he had just said was true. The only catch was that he was describing the team assembled by Adam Grant and not a group of home-grown terrorists bent on killing their own countrymen. How can you do this? thought Fathi.

———————

Once the three trucks arrived at the dock, the loading was completed in less than two hours. Mihal heaved a great sigh of relief as he saw the lines freed and felt the boat slowly swing 180 degrees to head southwest out of the harbor it had entered only hours earlier. This was the first tangible step forward. So far, events had been carried out to perfection. With some pride, that he thought was well-deserved, Mihal credited this success to his close oversight of the project. His dedication and hands-on involvement were key, he thought. They would be recognized, and he would be rewarded. The next crucial steps, though, caused him worry.

Success of the operation depended on the actions of a man who was highly skilled and supremely capable at what he did. He was smooth-talking and convincing—but could he be trusted? At this point, Mihal could retain equanimity only by believing that Fathi was indeed trustworthy, and he tried to believe this. Even so, he was glad Assoud had decided to employ the most effective leverage possible to keep Fathi from doing something rash, like have a change of heart that could threaten the successful completion of the project. Assoud would employ a team in Jeddah to monitor the Kanaan family and to act if there was any sign of wavering commitment on Fathi's part. *It was about time for this,* Mihal thought.

A nagging concern lingered with Mihal. Could Fathi somehow have been connected to the dead CIA agent? The lack of response from the CIA after the explosion was encouraging, but was it enough? Mihal was glad he met with Fathi today. This man talked a good game, and Mihal wanted to believe him, but …

With the captain and his mate at the helm on the top deck, Mihal and his charges were on the main and lower decks below. All of this space was for their use, except for what had been the owner's stateroom. It was now re-configured with four bunks to accommodate the professional crew. Mihal was impressed with the calm demeanor of the captain and the businesslike approach of his crew. His brief contacts, mostly with the captain, had been formal, useful, and had built confidence. Their common purpose was implied not stated. Mihal was confident that things would go well, and he was equally confident there would be nobody left to tell the tale but him and his trusted companions, Abdul, Fazeez, and the two bomb makers. The captain and crew would meet their fate, one way or another, in time, but that would be Assoud's decision.

On the first morning at sea, after everyone had gotten a few hours of fitful sleep and selected a place to stow their sleeping bags and meager belongings, Mihal called a meeting. Because his nautical experience consisted of nothing more than a few short excursions in a small fishing boat, he was pleased when Hafeez, one of the deckhands, offered to give brief instructions about safety. This was not an activity that Hafeez was used to, but the captain had asked him to do it. He had heard it delivered so many times by others, he felt he could do an adequate job.

His first instructions dealt with the use of life preservers. On a bigger boat, this would be followed by a lifeboat drill, but this practice would not be carried out today. Hafeez told the attentive group that it was unlikely they would be needed, but on command from the captain or a member of the crew, each person was to don a flotation device immediately. The preservers were secured at the ceiling of both decks and could be easily accessed. But, they were to be left in place and taken down only when specific orders to do so were given. The usual drill was to have the passengers practice putting them on, but Hafeez decided to not go to the trouble. He then told them that inflatable rafts sufficient to hold all of the passengers and crew in the event they were needed were onboard. In case of an emergency, the rafts would be made ready by the crew; they were not to be handled by anyone else.

Finished with the safety aspect, he told the group that any sea sickness they might encounter would be temporary. There was no mention of preventive medication or of anything available if a person did become sick. Hafeez assured them that they would suffer only one episode, if they were afflicted at all. This was not true, but he said it anyway. The weather report for the crossing was generally good, so he didn't anticipate much in the way of difficulties with motion sickness. The passengers were told that the boat had the capacity to make freshwater from the saltwater they were in. This would continually re-supply the large tank of freshwater already onboard. Even with this capability, they were told to be careful in their use of water. For bathing, they could use saltwater initially but should dry thoroughly and then have a brief freshwater rinse. Looking at the group, his impression was that personal hygiene was not a high priority. He asked if there were any questions. There were none. Relieved that this was the case, and with his mission accomplished, Hafeez re-joined the other crew on the deck above.

With the group still assembled, Mihal, flanked by his two comrades, spoke to the group. "We asked all of you to leave your cell phones at home," he began. "In case any of you forgot, I would like for you to give them to me now." At first, there was no movement. Then, one man sheepishly came forward, and he was followed by three others. "Is this all?" asked Mihal. When he got no more responses, he handed the phones to Abdul, who deftly removed the chips and returned the phones to their owners, more as a symbol, because they would never be using them again. Mihal continued, "Cell phones have GPS devices and any active phone onboard could reveal our location—and that would not be good for our cause. Praise Allah.

"We have sufficient rations onboard to feed everybody for the next thirty days. For the first ten days or so, we will be able to have fresh fruit and vegetables. Then, for the remainder of the trip, we will eat mostly dehydrated food, and once each day you will have a hot meal available from a variety of frozen dinners that we have stocked on the boat. The food will be nutritious. We have done our best to select things that are also tasty. You are all dedicated soldiers, so we know that if we don't have your favorites, you are willing to make any necessary small adjustments when it comes to food."

These comments were well received, and Mihal continued. "I am looking for three volunteers to oversee the cooking and food distribution. There are four microwaves; I expect that they will be used extensively. Two extra-large freezers have been added, but they will be locked." Not sure how accurate the count had been, Mihal could have added "as long as the food lasts," but he decided not to. "If there is a kind of meal not available now, please let us know and we will do our best to add it when we re-supply in Jeddah."

Two women and a man raised their hands to volunteer. Mihal said, "I will show the three of you the galley and the food stores. Meals will be served at the same time each day and will be available for one hour. Access to food in the kitchen will be limited to the cooks and anyone who they specifically designate. A variety of foods like crackers, nuts, dates, soft drinks, and water will be out and available at all times between meals."

Mihal said all of this at the advice of the men and women who had been active in the recruiting process. They told Mihal that these martyrs were looking forward to meeting their rewards in heaven but, in the meantime, they expected to be treated with respect and live a life free of hardship since they had committed their lives to the cause. Paradoxically the decision they had made was both selfless and selfish.

At the back of the gathering listening to Mihal, two young men exchanged glances, no doubt thinking about what was ahead of them. Something very special, outside of the original plan, was in store for one. He had made his own plans, and he had shared them with no one. Was he alone in thinking this way? It didn't make any difference. He would finally be doing what he had been planning for months. It would take shape the minute he set foot in America. This young man had questioned Mihal, innocently enough, during the last stages of training, about where the boat would be landing. At first reluctantly, and then with some pride at the cleverness of the plan, Mihal told the young man that the boat would be landing in a wilderness area at the top of Michigan.

With this information, the young man would separate from the group and travel on foot southward to meet his cousin, who he had contacted the minute he knew where the boat would land. Their plans had been made with the help of letters they had traded over the last month. His cousin would drive north from the City of Dearborn. They would meet at a dead-end road near the drop-off site, which, based on the size of the park, would likely be not more than two miles, easy walking distance. In the confusion that was bound to be present at the landing, it would be possible for the young man to slip away from the group, join his American relative, and be on his way to the Detroit area before he was even missed.

With this first instructional meeting, Mihal was satisfied that they had accomplished an excellent start. For added peace of mind, he decided that at least two of his team should be awake at all times. Each person would pick an eight-hour shift to be completely off duty for sleeping. A second person would be available on-call if needed, and the third would be fully active and functioning.

Adam Grant was viewing the live feed. He wouldn't be monitoring the action in real time every moment of the trip, but somebody would. The start of the voyage, for Adam, was a pretty big deal and he wanted to see it as the events unfolded. Adam was eager to observe this group. It was almost a morbid curiosity. The people he was watching had discarded the primeval need for survival in favor of the promise of a reward in heaven achieved by offering their own life in the process of killing the infidel. Were they acting to express devotion to the prophet or was it the sensual reward that they truly believed awaited them?

After giving his musings a moment's thought, Adam decided

against sharing them with the analyst who was part of the twenty-four-hour observation team. Instead Adam avoided profundity in favor of the obvious. "It is weird listening to a man address the mundane issues of diet, hygiene, and preserving freshwater when the people he is speaking to plan to blow themselves to bits in a month."

"Makes me sick," said Marilyn, a twenty-four-year-old beginning her career as a counter-terrorism analyst.

"Look at the bright side, Marilyn," said Adam. "In a few weeks, we are going to give them a second chance at life. Like it or not, that is what we will be doing when we apprehend them on the beach at Wilderness State Park. I suspect that once they are off the hook, their willingness to re-enlist to the bomb squad will be close to zero."

They listened as Mihal continued with housekeeping details.

"I get the impression this dude is auditioning for a job with Crystal Cruise Line, but he had better not use this particular experience on his résumé," was Adam's contribution of gallows humor to the others in the monitoring room. He was mostly ignored.

"Can you connect with the shadowing boat?" asked Adam, directing his question at Marilyn, who seemed to be the most adept at managing the multitude of dials on display.

She referred to the log and identified the boat as the *Monsoon* out of Bahrain. She raised them on the phone, spoke with the radio operator, and asked to speak with the skipper. "Colonel Adam Grant calling regarding Operation Thunderstruck," she said.

After a short pause they heard, "Lieutenant Commander Eikenberry, the *Monsoon*."

"Commander, this is Colonel Adam Grant on special assignment with the CIA and coordinator of Operation Thunderstruck. How is your progress with the shadowing operation?"

"We are one mile dead astern, traveling at twenty-two knots, maintaining our designated separation. If the professionals onboard were worried about being followed, we would be hanging back much farther, but I have been told that the crew are friendlies and are happy with us being this close. There is little, if any, chance that the passengers will be aware of us, and it is my understanding that they will not be allowed on the bridge or be able to view the radar screen, which already has available on-deck equipment that can be deployed as needed for blockage of the reflection for the twenty degrees dead aft."

"You will be on them until the Suez?" asked Adam.

"That is affirmative," responded Lieutenant Commander Eikenberry.

"Thank you, Commander," said Adam. "We are maintaining continuous twenty-four-hour monitoring of voice communication and have surveillance cameras on the boat you are following. If it becomes necessary for you to approach the craft, contact us. We can assure that none of the explosive materials they are transporting are fused and that to the best of our knowledge no one onboard is armed."

"Roger that."

Chapter 32

Assoud received the call he had been eagerly awaiting. It was from Mihal. The boat had completed the first leg of the journey, traveling from Karachi back to Jeddah. In a few hours, it would be on its way to America. Assoud was satisfied with the report that all was going well. Mihal commented that having everyone together in close quarters made it easier to keep a careful watch over the group. He even told Assoud that someone had brought a domino set and that the game was providing amusement for several who were becoming avid players. The biggest problems the group would face were boredom and being sure of the direction of Mecca at prayer time.

Mihal was calling from a public phone at the dockside in Jeddah, where they had refueled, added water, and procured additional supplies, including some special food items that had been requested. The men that Assoud had arranged to be on hand to meet them were helpful. This made it possible to complete the task of re-supplying in a day.

Assoud asked, "Mihal, did you see anyone around who appeared to have a special interest in the boat, besides the team of our men that met you?"

"No, I have not. Should I be looking for anything special?" asked Mihal.

"I can't tell you anything more than this person, or people, might be better dressed than the average person you would see under the circumstances. They would simply be watching and, in general, look out of place on a busy commercial dock," explained Assoud.

"I can assure you that I did not see anybody like that. Are you worried?"

"No, Mihal, I am just being careful. What you tell me is reassuring and I am pleased with what you and your team, Abdul and Fazeez, have done so far. I am sure that with this excellent start, in a month we will achieve something that will change the world."

"Thank you, Assoud," said Mihal, who was not happy having to share recognition with his companions, who Mihal was beginning to deal with as underlings.

"Then, I bid you a safe journey. I expect to hear from you next when you come ashore in the United States. Your idea to have no cell phones onboard was brilliant. It is inconvenient to be out of communication, but it is a small price to pay compared to the value of avoiding someone tracking the location of the boat." The leader abruptly ended the conversation.

Mihal was happy that he had at least been singled out for his idea to eliminate the cell phone risk. It was good that this strategy was acknowledged by Assoud.

Assoud was content that Mihal was doing as he hoped he would and that the first half of the plan was being executed flawlessly. He only wished he was equally confident about the second half. The final events would be taking place five thousand miles away, and would be carried out by surrogates who he had no control over, or for that matter even knew. He hoped these people would live up to the praise that Fathi had heaped on them—and that he could trust Fathi.

Assoud was glad he had taken the precaution to have the Kanaan home in Jeddah watched. It would be done by the same team that had met the boat and managed the re-supply process. They were perfect for the job. They were smart and tough and, being Saudi nationals, they could move around freely without raising suspicion. They were said to be flexible and willing to do just about anything if the pay was right. Like Mihal, they had reported nothing unusual or worrisome during the brief time the boat was in port. Now that their responsibility at the port was finished, they would shift their operation to the Kanaan household and watch for any unusual activities, and report to Assoud daily.

———————

Captain Ilyas Cham, at the helm, was looking forward to a pleasant voyage to America. Before the trip was over, he would have taken the boat more than one thousand miles into the freshwater between Canada and the United States. From studying the charts and what he had heard from others, he knew the Great Lakes were deep and the scenery would be close at hand, a pleasant change from the endless grey landscape that accompanied a North Atlantic passage in late October.

After the salty mix at the beginning of the St. Lawrence Seaway in Canada, they would be in sweet water for nearly four days. The boat would pass through several locks, with the most interesting being the eight-lock series of the Welland Canal. This system of locks would lift the boat more than three hundred and twenty-six feet over a thirty-two-mile span from Lake Ontario to Lake Erie. It was one of the largest vertical lifts by a lock system in the world. For the trip through the Welland, even experienced seamen benefited from employing a lock captain whose role was mostly to negotiate the lock masters. However, given the nature of the group he was transporting, Captain Cham would forgo this option and manage the trip through the locks without seeking outside help.

At some time during the voyage, the captain would receive instructions on how his passengers would be leaving the boat. He already had the GPS coordinates for the drop-off point. Should he feel guilty that he would be turning them over to the U.S. authorities? No, he decided. In exchange for their incarceration, possibly for only a brief time, he would be saving these people from a certain death of their own choosing. He wondered if they truly understood what they were doing. He had his doubts. He wanted to think he would be giving twenty-seven human beings their lives back and a chance to reconsider their priorities. He believed these men and women had been brainwashed by zealots and convinced to give up their lives for Allah—while the ones doing the convincing would live. How could this make sense to anyone recruited for this awful fate?

Satisfied that he was doing a good thing, and would be paid double for his effort, Captain Ilyas Cham believed this job had more in its favor than against. He was a happy man.

Saad, a Saudi citizen who made a living doing odd jobs, was heading the team hired to watch the Kanaan family. The Kanaan home on the Red Sea was not Saad's usual stomping ground. It was far more upscale than his life afforded. The properties were large and the homes were separated by expansive yards. The scheme that Saad had devised was to rent a small panel van and affix a magnetic sign indicating that it was a home maintenance service. In this case, it could be serving any one of the residents in the area. The van would be alternated with a car to avoid being too obvious. The good thing was that the Kanaan property had a single access from the main road in front. A drawback was that the house was so far from the public road and had such full landscaping in front that the house itself could not be seen from where the van would be stationed. And, there was another concern.

A boat dock was situated behind the house, and next to the dock, in a hoist, was a powerboat that could take its occupants anywhere along the shore in minutes, and to the port of Jeddah in less than an hour. Saad, and his team of Ruhi and Talal, would use the computer in the van to access a Google Earth map that would tell them in real time if there was any activity at the boat dock. It wasn't perfect, but it was a way to watch a place that was not high risk. Saad could have employed a boat to watch the dock and house from slightly offshore, but he decided that could be too obvious, overkill, or both.

The Kanaan family, minus the two daughters attending university in England and Fathi, would be, for the most part, in the house under the watchful eyes of Saad's team. The people in the house included Ahad and Farah Kanaan, Fathi's wife, Lila, and her two daughters. Each morning, Ahad left the house with a driver. He went directly to the company office and did not leave the building until he returned home about five o'clock in the afternoon. Either Talal or Ruhi followed the car at a discreet distance and waited outside the building until Ahad left for the return trip home. They were confident that Ahad Kanaan was simply conducting his day-to-day business. Saad considered Ahad's activity reassuring because it suggested he was not worried about the immediate safety of his family. There was nothing for them to worry about.

When one of the other family members left the home to go to a local shopping center or other nearby businesses, they were followed discreetly. This was a matter of some concern, but Saad could think of nothing to solve that problem. It had now been three days and the only one leaving for more than a brief trip was Ahad. Since there was no activity that was alarming at the Kanaan home or Ahad's office, there was no need to report to Assoud in Peshawar beyond the one daily call to check in.

———————

Adam was glad he had requested that two men be stationed inside the house with the Kanaan family. Fred Billson had made the arrangements and assured Adam that the men, armed and capable, would remain in regular contact. The surveillance team on the outside had already spotted Saad and his team, and reported this to Langley. So far, Ahad had been going to the office every day with an armed driver who was a Saudi security officer made available by the local CIA team. It was decided that Ahad should continue his usual work routine to avoid giving the impression that the family was suspicious or in hiding. The slight risk to Ahad, as he drove to and from work, was considered an acceptable trade-off to the suspicion that would result from him not leaving the house at all.

The women and young girls made occasional trips away from the house, but they were routine and explainable, like getting their hair done or going shopping. During these excursions, they were kept under observation by one of the surveillance teams assigned to watch them. These men also noticed Saad's team of less skillful operatives and saw nothing that concerned them. The women knew they were being watched but gave no indication of this, as they were instructed. Adam reassured Farah Kanaan that the people working for the terrorists were in turn being watched by Adam's team and that her family was in no danger. It was not easy for the family to act normally under the circumstances, but they had no choice.

The CIA team was under Adam's orders to react only if someone was in danger. They were to do nothing that would provoke suspicion or alarm. Any action on their part could endanger Fathi in Islamabad, where he was alone and vulnerable.

So far so good, thought Adam.

Chapter 33

Assoud and Fathi had not spoken since the boat departed from Jeddah; it had been more than a week This lack of communication alarmed Assoud, so he decided it was time to take action. What he was planning to do might be extreme and unnecessary, but considering the high stakes, he would do it. He called Saad.

"There is a slight change in plans," said Assoud.

"What is it?" said Saad.

Assoud hoped Saad would not balk at this request. There would be violence and it was not something that had been discussed when he hired Saad for a surveillance job, but the possibility was always implied. Details behind the task Saad had agreed to were never explained to him, but that was the way he wanted it. Saad told Assoud he was a contract worker and made it clear from the beginning he had no desire to be involved in a process that he could not control. What Assoud would be asking the man would put Saad fully in control.

"Saad, I have decided that having Ahad Kanaan unwatched for so many hours each day is a chance we can no longer take. More important, our watching the family will have no effect on their son, Fathi, in Islamabad, if he doesn't know we are watching them. It is essential that we do everything in our power to keep Fathi from losing heart and letting us down this late in the process. He must remain committed to the plan; something that can be guaranteed only if we maintain control over him. If he were to become weak in any way and decide to reveal our plans to the authorities, three years of work would be undone and our own lives would be in danger. If we can use his father's safety, or his life, as a bargaining chip, that will make me much more confident that we can keep Fathi in line."

Hearing nothing to stop him from going further, even after saying more about the plot than he wanted to, Assoud continued. "To ensure that our plan is carried out without interference, and for our own safety, I need you to abduct Ahad Kanaan the next time he leaves the house. You are to subdue him and deliver him to a place where he can be kept under your control, out of sight, and without the ability to communicate until the project is completed. Once we have him, and have let the family know the consequences that will result from any action on their part, there will be no more need for us to be concerned about their seeking help. Fathi will follow through with the plan if he knows any failure on his part could mean his father's life. When our plan is successfully completed, as we expect it will, Ahad will be released, or at least that is what we will tell Fathi. Until that time, Fathi will remain true to the cause because he will want to keep his family safe and his father alive. When we are finished with our job, it will be necessary to deal with Fathi Kanaan and his family, but that is for another day. Who knows, they might suffer an unfortunate accident?" At this point, Assoud could only revel in the thought of the entire Kanaan family going the way that the CIA man did.

Assoud was relieved when Saad said, "It is not necessary for me to hear any more about your plan. I will limit my activity to what you are requesting. This is doable, Assoud. We are doing our best to keep a careful watch, but as it is now, there are too many things about the family's movements that we have no control over. We should have no difficulty getting the father when he leaves. We will take him tomorrow morning on his way to work and will keep him safe and out of sight until we hear from you. And, my friend, I am sure you will agree to adjust our fee, as you promised, if it was necessary for us to do something more than we had agreed to originally. Tripling the amount originally agreed on would be sufficient—plus expenses."

"Of course," said Assoud, who was happy he was dealing with the right kind of people for the job. He wasn't sure about the pay though. He wouldn't have any extra money while he was up in the hills, but the good part was that the bill collector wouldn't be able to find him there either.

Chapter 34

Ahad awakened at the usual time. He was satisfied that his family was safe and thankful that the CIA had provided people to be with them inside the house and others to follow them on the rare occasions when they went out. This arrangement was confining for them, but it was for their safety, and it wouldn't be for long. Their ordeal would be over soon. The men guarding the family inside the house were well-qualified Saudi nationals employed by the CIA. To be on the safe side, Ahad remained in close contact with Adam in Washington and also with the local authorities. If needed, assistance would be at the house within minutes of a call that would be placed to a special number. Ahad was confident the house, with its thick concrete walls, heavy shutters, and stout doors would hold off any intruders until help arrived. If he hadn't had this confidence he would never have left his family.

The black Mercedes S600, with Ahad in the backseat behind lightly tinted standard automobile windows, turned north out of the driveway to begin the forty-minute drive to Kanaan Construction. Once in his office, Ahad and Fathi would speak with each other on special cell phones exclusively for this purpose, as they had been doing daily. Ahad communicated using code words to tell his son that everything was fine at home and that Fathi should continue to maintain his usual routine. Ahad knew that he, too, needed to behave in a way that would put the terrorists at ease and confident that arrangements for their operation were in place and functioning.

Ahad's driver was new. His usual driver, whose skill was *driving*, had been replaced by a Saudi bodyguard who knew how to drive and was an experienced security guard. Like the man inside the house, his service had been arranged by the CIA. While he drove, a loaded and chambered 9mm Glock automatic weapon lay on the seat beside him.

As the car picked up speed, a white van with a home maintenance service sign on its side kept pace just a few hundred yards behind. Ahad's driver had noticed it but was not yet alarmed. A few seconds later, a large delivery truck traveling toward them suddenly swung to the left across the centerline in front of the Mercedes, blocking the way. Ahad's driver stabbed the brakes in a panic stop to avoid hitting the truck. In an instant, when the Mercedes had come to a full stop, the van pulled up on the driver's side and a rifle protruding from the passenger side of the van's window shot out the glass in the driver's side door. With nothing between the muzzle and the target, the full force of the second shot mangled the driver's head. His lifeless body slumped toward the passenger seat, a bloody and tangled mass above his shoulders.

Two men jumped out of the van. One reached through the shattered glass of the driver's door and hit the switch to unlock all the car's doors. The second man opened the back door and grabbed Ahad Kanaan, who was clutching his face in pain. In seconds, he was dragged to the van and both the truck and van sped off. Thirty minutes later, the van was parked in front of a small warehouse at the edge of what looked like a mostly deserted industrial park. Ahad, who was in obvious pain with a bleeding wound on the left side of his face, was taken from the van into a squat, rundown, corrugated-metal building on the edge of the complex. Ahad Kanaan, with his hand over his left eye, was pushed into a small partitioned office and seated on a straight-back wooden chair. Plastic cuffs were placed around his ankles and grey duct tape secured his chest to the back of the chair. His hands would remain free as long as he was being watched. Saad pulled Ahad's hand away from his face and saw what looked like a scrape of the skin that began at his forehead and extended down to the middle of his cheek, traversing the lids of his left eye. Even though there was only a small amount of blood, the man's eyes were clamped shut in response to pain and fright.

Saad decided the wound was from a shard of glass. It was unfortunate. The obvious discomfort would only add to any difficulty they might have when it came to dealing with their captive. It was hard to determine the extent of the injury, but it did not look good for the man's eye. There was some clotting blood on Ahad's left eyelids, which were tightly closed. When Saad pried the left eye open, he saw a slimy black spot oozing from the center of a cut in the clear part at the front of the eyeball. Saad knew this was called the cornea. His girlfriend used contact lenses and she was constantly talking about her cornea that hurt when she wore her lenses too long. His prisoner's eye looked nasty, so Saad took out his not too clean handkerchief, put it over the eye, and secured it with a piece of duct tape. The man needed a doctor, but that was not going to happen. *At least he had another eye he could use*, thought Saad. With some pride at this accomplishment and thinking about the increased fee he would be receiving, Saad called Assoud and told him that his team had successfully completed the job. He did not mention the eye.

Assoud then called Fathi and told him that he shouldn't worry when he heard news about his father. He told Fathi that while he trusted him, some in the organization were concerned that with his family recently returning to Jeddah they might do something that would upset the plans for the project in New York. "You are a loyal soldier and faithful to the cause," said Assoud, "but we are not sure that your father fully shares your dedication." Without going into detail, Assoud told Fathi that for insurance, his father was now a guest of Al-Fir. He assured Fathi that his father was safe and comfortable and would remain so until the mission was completed. "When our work is done, your father will be returned to the family unharmed. Having your father with us is just a precaution. It was ordered by one of my superiors. It was not my idea at all," he lied. "I am only doing as I am told. We are grateful to you for your demanding work and now for this sacrifice. All of this will end soon. Continue to have faith. Allahu Akbar."

Fathi detested Assoud even more. The regret he felt for his actions crushed him. How could he have let this horrible thing happen? How could he atone to his family for all the heartache he had caused them? Regaining his composure, Fathi realized that he could start repaying them now by being resolute. He would adhere to the plan and do everything, no matter how difficult, to cooperate with Assoud. He fully realized that since it was almost certain they would capture the bombers before they had done anything more than set foot in America, the only harm that could come from this entire process would be to his family. Protecting them now was his main job.

Fathi immediately called his mother using the phone Adam had provided. Farah Kanaan told her son she had already been informed that Ahad's car and his dead driver had been found. Doing his best to remain calm and in control, Fathi told her that he had been told that Ahad was all right; that he had been taken and was being held for insurance. Trying to convince himself as much as his mother, Fathi said he had been assured that nothing bad would happen to the man who was her husband and his father. He told her the people who had ordered Ahad's abduction said he would be set free when they were satisfied their other plans were completed. Fathi told his mother that as long as he was the key to the plot, Ahad and the family would be safe. Her husband would be freed by the CIA and Saudi authorities, and the terrorists would be taken down soon. She must keep her faith. With her husband kidnapped and his driver dead, Farah looked to the CIA protector, the stout walls of the house, and Fathi's promises as her only hope.

Adam heard about the abduction from the CIA agent who was guarding the Kanaan home. Shortly after that, Fathi called Adam. It was only slightly consoling to Fathi to learn from Adam that his father was wearing an Eddie Freeman ring with a chip enabling GPS tracking. They knew where Ahad was being held captive and were confident he would be safe until the terrorists were apprehended in Michigan. Adam told Fathi that the best way to keep his father safe was to continue cooperating with Assoud and for his family to keep to their normal activities as much as possible. As long as the plot progressed and Assoud was dependent on the team in New York, that only Fathi controlled, Ahad and the rest of the family would be safe.

Adam told Fathi that another CIA agent would be added to watch his parents' home from the outside and a team of Saudi national police with a CIA contingent would be watching the building where the GPS signal indicated Ahad was being held.

It would be a long siege for the Kanaans because they could do nothing. In contrast, the time would fly by for Adam and his team, who were assembling a precision operation with many moving parts and thousands of miles in between. The gloves were coming off. It was a match of wits between Adam's team and the terrorists. They were in a deadly game where winning depended on sound planning, stealth, and staying power. Adam was confident his team continued to have the upper hand. They knew all the cards in the enemy's hand. But even though Adam had all the high cards and they were hidden, they would win only if they played them perfectly. To do this, they had to avoid panicking the terrorists, who could still commit a kamikaze attack if they thought all was lost. In that case, Adam's team would still win but it would be a hollow victory if there were casualties on their side; and he knew if there were any, it would be the Kanaan family, people who he truly liked and respected.

Adam was sorry that Fathi and his family were paying such a high price and enduring what had to be unspeakable mental anguish. A big part of this was the fact that even though they knew where Ahad was being held and were watching his location constantly, they could not rescue him yet. Adam knew if Ahad were freed, Fathi would be dead. If Fathi failed to remain convincing, the whole family would be at risk of being killed. The successful conclusion for this mission required near simultaneous take-down of the terrorist team in Michigan, the plotters in Pakistan, and the kidnappers in Jeddah. Nothing short of precision could offer even a chance of total success.

Chapter 35

October 12, Wednesday

In the minutes before Adam would be briefing his team about the final push for Operation Thunderstruck, he organized his thoughts. Much had happened in the last two months, and his job was to explain the issues clearly, answer any remaining questions, and highlight the courageous efforts of two men, one in Saudi Arabia and the other in Pakistan. This morning he would explain the detailed interdepartmental plan that was moving ahead; an action that demanded equal parts precision and speed to achieve the successful capture of the terrorists who had been planning a repeat of 9/11 for the last three years. The chilling scenario Adam would be outlining would encourage the team to do everything in its power to ensure that what happened sixteen years ago would not happen again. The example they would be setting by snuffing out Al-Fir before any harm was done on U.S. soil would be a powerful demonstration of the will of the United States in the fight against international terrorism.

Since Ahad's kidnapping, Adam knew the time for subterfuge was over. The standoff was no longer a matter of posturing and waiting. On the plus side, the result of an action like this most often broke in favor of the participant with the better plan. Adam remembered the admonishment of a stockbroker his dad had done business: "The man with a plan beats the man without a plan every time." Adam believed his team had a plan and that it was the better plan.

A thorough appraisal of the situation convinced Adam that his side had more information about the terrorists' intentions than they had about his team's plans to stop them. He believed when the terrorists silenced Roland Wallace, they were convinced the CIA had been stonewalled. Fathi told Adam that Wallace had not shared information about this plan with other informants. Since these people knew nothing about Al-Fir's plans for One World Trade Center, there could be no leaks. Adam was confident the bombers, those directing them, and the bomb makers who they were monitoring constantly on the boat would be apprehended in Michigan. Soon after that, Assoud Al Walaki and the other leaders of Al-Fir-would be captured in Peshawar. But for Adam, the operation would only truly be successful when the Kanaan family in Jeddah and Fathi in Islamabad were rescued unharmed.

Adam's thoughts, as he looked at the room filling in front of him, were: The rat is the problem. We know his whereabouts and intentions. We have both the bait and the trap. With this advantage we will prevail every time but must find a way to keep the rat from biting us before we kill it. There are people with awesome power and responsibility assembled here today. They will be charged with studying the behavior of the rat they know, using the bait that has already been prepared, and then springing the trap we have built to kill the rat.

While the participants were assembling, Bob Zinsky called Adam aside. He told Adam that he had just spoken with the President and assured him that plans were moving ahead and according to schedule. The President, he said, was pleased with what they were doing but he was sorry that the Kanaan family was in such a bad spot. "I told him we were doing everything in our power to take down the plot, keep the family safe, and rescue the father," said Zinsky. "He was encouraged when I told him you said we would have a window of opportunity to rescue Ahad."

"Thank you for letting me know," said Adam.

"Adam, the group today will be pretty big, and there will be more brass than you've seen together in one place in a while, maybe ever. You have come through with flying colors at everything I have seen you attempt so far, and I don't think today will be an exception. Just remember, all of these people are just like you. They put their pants on one leg at a time," said the director trying to help Adam relax.

"I'll do my best," was all Adam could say.

The group was meeting in a small auditorium at CIA Headquarters. It would be an impressive array of men and women. Adam was glad to see it was not just another old boys' club. The number of powerful leaders in the government he would be speaking to would be over two dozen. Adam had been briefed ahead of time about which department heads and higher-ups would be attending. As he looked at those in the room, several were familiar faces from the last briefing, but the group had swelled in size. It was apparent that each of the leaders had brought along two or three aides. Adam took this as a positive sign. Getting buy-in from the heads was important. Their bringing staff confirmed that this meeting and the threat it was dealing with was being taken seriously. It was likely the staff in attendance today would be doing much of the work to achieve the crucial actions that would be decided at the meeting.

The session started with Bob Zinsky introducing Adam Grant to the group. The Director was sorely pained that he couldn't credit Adam for his role in the recent take-down of Kim Il-un, an operation that thwarted a near-certain nuclear attack against the U.S. Instead of crediting the real hero, it had been necessary, for reasons of international policy, for the government to attribute stopping the nuclear threat to a popular uprising by the North Korean people, leading to the overthrow of a dynastic dictatorship which, it was hoped, would be followed by a new democratic government.

As Adam surveyed the crowd, he recognized Phil Stark, the Director of the FBI; Orville McPherson, the Director of the National Intelligence Agency; General Paul Lippmann, the Chairman of the Joint Chiefs, who succeeded Adam's late boss General Wieland; the Director of Homeland Security; and the Commandant of the Coast Guard. Several others Adam didn't know personally, including an Admiral representing the Commander of the Fifth Fleet, the Secretary of Homeland Security, and the National Security Advisor representing the Administration. There were several members of the CIA Directorate, who would be working closely with their boss, and TSA and Customs and Immigration were also represented.

Adam explained that they were assembled to develop final plans for containing and taking down a plot by the terrorist cell known as Al-Fir, whose intent was to attack One World Trade Center. Because of early and effective action, the terrorists wouldn't get close to New York; instead they would be captured the minute they stepped onto U.S. soil. Adam did not tell them how the plot originally came to light. That was not necessary now, and likely never would be. Adam told them he was representing the Central Intelligence Agency. He did not mention the President's role and didn't emphasize Roland Wallace's actions either. In doing this, he left out nothing he thought was important for this group to know now. When he finished, Adam invited Director Zinsky to comment on anything that he might have missed or that should be added.

Bob Zinsky stood, and in the presence of this larger group, he silently thanked Adam for soft pedaling the disaster inside the CIA that was so closely tied to the series of events they now faced. This black mark on the organization would be dealt with in due time. "Thank you, Adam," began the Director. "I really have nothing to add except to re-state that this is a real threat to the United States. We have every opportunity to deal with this problem successfully, but it will take a coordinated effort on the part of all the entities represented in this room for us to achieve success. Now, Colonel Grant, let's hear the plan for taking down this organization, with what we are now calling 'Operation Thunderstruck.'"

Adam used six PowerPoint slides to demonstrate the three-pronged approach he proposed. He had considered a handout, but later discarded the idea because even with a sophisticated audience, it would be too easy for one of the papers to get into the wrong hands. The slides made it possible for everyone to focus on the same thing as he was talking. If they understood, that would be good. Even if they didn't, or had other ideas, there would be common ground for basing an opinion and an appropriate point of departure for discussion and resolution.

On the left side of the screen, as seen by the audience, and the westernmost point of the action on the world map, was a ship. Adam described it. "This is the boat that is transporting thirty-two terrorists and a crew of four to the United States. The captain and his three crew are in our employ and are effectively delivering the quarry to us. The terrorists include twenty-seven suicide bombers, two bomb makers, and three supervisors. They are members or recruits of Al-Fir, whose leader is Assoud Al Walaki, a terrorist who is currently directing the operation from Peshawar in Pakistan."

Adam drew the group's attention to Northern Pakistan on the right side of the screen. "This is where Assoud is located now and where he will remain until the plan he is masterminding is completed. He has a few trusted people with him. They operate independently and are supported mostly by wealthy, like-minded donors. That may be the reason why they were so susceptible to the offering of the CIA asset who suggested an anonymous donor for the boat and crew, and promised to provide support for the attack using sympathizers already in the U.S. The Al-Fir leaders organizing the plot are implicated in the death, by car bombing, of a CIA agent in Islamabad. They are ruthless and violent. They have kidnapped the father of the CIA asset in Jeddah. It is our belief that they will kill both the asset and his father, and possibly the entire family in Jeddah, when the attack they have planned in New York is completed. Of course, the attack in New York will never happen, but vengeance against the Kanaan family is nearly certain if we fail to protect them. We must protect them," Adam quickly added.

Everyone was attentive and quiet. There were no hands raised and no questions voiced. Pointing to the center of the screen, Adam continued. "Here we have an acute problem. The family of Fathi Kanaan, the asset, is now living in Jeddah. Fathi's wife, two daughters, and his mother are virtual captives in their own home under the protection of the United States and with cooperation from Saudi authorities. Unfortunately, as I said, Fathi's father, Ahad Kanaan, was abducted last week and is being held hostage elsewhere in the city by the terrorists in an attempt, we believe, to ensure that his son fulfills his promise of fielding a second terrorist team in New York. We are not sure whether Assoud Al Walaki knows that Ahad is the anonymous donor of the boat, but he is definitely using him as insurance when it comes to dealing with his son."

Adam saw looks of concern, but he did not discern any lack of understanding or puzzled faces. He knew there was at least one nagging question he should preempt; he decided to do just that. "It would be natural for you to ask if we are taking any special precautions for New York and One World Trade Center. The answer is no—because there are no terrorists engaged in this plot in New York or anywhere else that we know of, except for the three places I have just pointed out. Everything that was promised, when it comes to involvement here in the United States, is false—a ruse. None of this was officially planned or known to the CIA stateside. It was developed by an individual CIA agent, and his intentions, though likely well meaning, were done outside the normal boundaries of the organization and were learned of only after the agent's death. We are convinced that the only way to save the Kanaan family is to continue the deception. In a near-simultaneous operation, we will capture the bombers in Northern Michigan, secure the safety of the Kanaan family in Jeddah and Islamabad, and capture the terrorists in Peshawar. The capture of the bombers on U.S. soil before they can do any harm should be a giant step in our continuing war on terrorism. It will send a strong message to the leaders and it could go a long way in discouraging recruitment. We look on this as both a challenge and an opportunity."

Adam's mention of the anomalous behavior of a CIA agent was necessary, but he believed that in the context of this presentation and with the serious nature of the problem at hand, the people he was talking to would remain focused on the task at hand. The CIA would get a pass for now. "The question is, how do we behead this three-headed dragon?" As he showed the next slide, Adam hoped he hadn't overdone it. Possibly inspired by *Game of Thrones*, it depicted a dragon with three heads. One held a boat in its jaws, the second the Kanaan family, and the third, Assoud with Fathi on a leash.

Moving to the next slide, it showed a boat at the top of Michigan. "Taking the intended threat first, we propose meeting the boat with force as it arrives in the upper Great Lakes. We chose this place because it is a large state park that is deserted this time of year. This makes it an ideal place for assembling a force to capture the entire group, as well as their explosives and other paraphernalia. There will be no danger of accidental detonation because the fuses were not to be installed until the group reached New York—*which they never will*." The latter was said with emphasis. He went on to explain that this capture would be a combined effort of the FBI, Homeland Security, and local law enforcement. The captives would be taken to a federal facility by U.S. Marshals, to be dealt with in our legal system.

Adam next turned his attention to a detail from the middle of the first frame. It depicted a hostage and a house full of females. "The minute the terrorists are in custody, action to free Ahad Kanaan from the men detaining him will be carried out and the terrorists' surveillance team that is watching the Kanaan home will be neutralized. Local Saudi security forces and the CIA will complete this action." In the next diagram, Northern Pakistan was shown. "Working in both Islamabad and Peshawar, a special Marine task force that has been embedded in the U.S. Embassy will work with local Pakistani officials and the CIA to secure the safety of Fathi Kanaan and to capture Assoud Al Walaki and any accomplices who are with him, including at least one other operative that has remained in Islamabad."

For the finale, Adam showed a rendition of the three-headed dragon that emphasized if only one or two heads were removed, there would be the possibility of the beast spewing fire and wreaking havoc, which would greatly degrade the value of the results even as the beast was dying. "For this reason," he stressed, "the operation must be coordinated with all three actions occurring nearly simultaneously." Then, to be sure his message was understood, he added, "We must completely cut off each head before the next one becomes aware and has time to act."

Everyone nodded in assent.

To conclude, Adam said, "The U.S. Navy is currently shadowing the boat that is transporting the terrorists. This is being done in a relay fashion. The first shadowing boat was a coastal patrol that monitored the boat's progress between Karachi and the Suez Canal. The boat carrying the terrorists is passing through the Canal now. We are in contact with Egyptian authorities, who will inform us if there are any irregularities during the fifteen hours when we will not be directly observing movement of the boat. After that, a destroyer will follow the boat through the Mediterranean. Then, a second destroyer will follow the boat until it reaches Canada. From there, it will be shadowed by the Coast Guard until it reaches upper Lake Michigan, where it will be watched by local authorities and the Coast Guard. When the group finally comes ashore at Wilderness State Park, they will immediately be taken into custody by the FBI."

"Thank you, Colonel Grant," said the CIA Director. "Over the next several weeks, Colonel Grant, myself, and the rest of the CIA team will be working with each of you as we carry out the plans we have outlined here this morning. The way this operation has been planned, there will be no threat of actual harm to our country. We intend to use this action as a lesson and a deterrent. Beginning now, our main activity is to complete this job successfully, and for that we need the help of everyone in this room."

With no questions from the audience, the Director ended the meeting, confident that everyone in attendance was on board.

Chapter 36

The watch schedule Captain Cham implemented was working well. Either he or Hamid were at the helm, in eight-hour shifts, and at least one deckhand was available. The boat's autopilot had proven to be reliable, taking much of the strain off the helmsman. Of course, Captain Cham was always available should a need arise.

The unusual circumstances surrounding this assignment meant he would not be returning to Pakistan or Saudi Arabia anytime soon, but he had no compelling reason to go to either of those countries anyway. There was plenty for him to do at home, in Egypt. The captain's role in the terrorists' debacle would be known to only a few, including the people in the United States government who were directing the operation. The small number in Saudi Arabia and Pakistan who were involved in planning the attack had only met him on the boat and assumed he understood the true intent of the mission. They did not know to what extent he or his crew had been involved, and the captain intended to keep it that way. Moreover, the captain and his three crew had been offered protection by the U.S. government. They were promised transportation back to their homes in Egypt, and there would be no official mention of their involvement when the plot was discussed later. If the subject of the crew did come up, they would be described as unwitting participants or they had gotten away.

The fact that he was not taking these people to slaughter was a relief, but Captain Cham harbored an uncomfortable feeling. The people he was transporting didn't realize he was rescuing them from impending, self-imposed death. He considered them to be loaded guns with the safety on, for now, but that could change at any time. Even though his actions would alter the outcome, Ilyas couldn't change the fact that twenty-seven of the people onboard fully believed they were being delivered to a certain death. The fact that he was part of a plan that would offer them the possibility of being rehabilitated did little to make him feel different about them or how they might feel toward him. To ease his mind, Ilyas tried to concentrate on the fact that, with proper help, these people might come to their senses and live out their lives in a productive way.

During the run from Karachi Harbor back to Jeddah, Ilyas took down the aft radar blocker to see if he could locate the boat that was following them. The signal was set for the maximum twenty-five miles. Because of the earth's curvature, that was about as far as radar would be effective. The first time he checked, he was able to confirm the blip produced by the *Monsoon*, which was well inside the twenty-mile range. This separation remained the same for over an hour. According to the instructions from Mr. Kanaan, his employer, Captain Cham radioed the *Monsoon* to confirm what the radar had reported. The response was affirmative. The *Monsoon's* captain said he was keeping Cham's boat on their radar and further radio communication would only occur in the case of an emergency or when the *Monsoon* handed over the job of shadowing to the next vessel assigned to the task.

Below the navigation deck, Mihal wondered what he could do to remain productive. He couldn't think of much that demanded his attention. His two underlings, Abdul and Fazeez, were managing the day-to-day issues and the people he was supervising were self-reliant. This left him with time to incessantly go over everything imaginable in his mind, repeating the mantra *What am I missing?* The problem was that he kept returning to the fact he was uncomfortable being in such close quarters on a daily basis with the martyrs-to-be. It was one thing to recruit and train them. At those times, emotions were at their peak and everyone involved was focused on the imminent deed ahead. On this long journey, Mihal wondered how their feelings of suicide reconciled with their caring about the meals they were fed, the satisfaction of winning a game of dominoes, or getting a good night's sleep. How could these issues even matter when you were planning on blowing yourself up? Mihal had observed, *they do!*

Because of the emotions he witnessed, Mihal was happy it had been decided to delay putting fuses in the explosives, and that they were locked up. There was no doubt the bomb makers would be busy arming the devices in the van as they were transported from Wilderness State Park to New York City. This deadline could put a strain on the operation but, on reflection, Mihal was more comfortable doing it this way. After all, who knew if during the long ocean voyage some of these men might decide to go to their reward sooner? It was comforting to know the explosives were secure.

Mihal was disappointed but not surprised that his feelings toward these people had changed. He was uncomfortable and wanted it to be over with. Would he do this again? He didn't know.

———————

The boat had few private spots, but Habib and Jawad, two of the male martyrs, found a few minutes alone at the aft rail of the navigation deck. It was ten o'clock at night. Most of the others were on the lower deck, talking and playing dominoes, or simply staring into space. Some were sleeping. Habib, who was handsome, young, and outgoing viewed his fellow passengers on the boat as being not much more than zombies. He said to Jawad, "What else could a person be but deranged if he decided the most productive thing he can do with his life is to strap on a bomb, squeeze a trigger to ready the fuse, relax his grip at the proposed time, and get blown to bits? Seventy-two virgins? Nuts!"

Based on his companion's behavior during prayers, Habib assumed Jawad was a practical fellow like him and not a religious zealot. Habib thought it was very likely that Jawad too had second thoughts. As Habib vented, Jawad just listened. After a few more minutes, Habib stopped talking and they both proceeded to the lower deck, and found their sleeping bags.

———————

On the bridge, Ilyas could see the entrance of the Suez Canal. The cost of the boat's trip through the canal, a hefty $56,000, had been paid in advance, so it was only necessary to call the authorities and identify the craft to gain entrance. The passage connecting the Red Sea and the Mediterranean, built in 1869, was just over one hundred miles long. Near its center was a large natural body of water called Bitter Lake. It constituted about half of the passage. Taking advantage of a natural body of water like this was a strategy used a half century later by the developers of the Panama Canal, which runs through Miraflores Lake.

Viewed from above and depicted schematically, the Suez Canal looks like a python that just swallowed a goat—a long tube with a bulge in the middle. Except for regular maintenance and minor upgrades, the Canal has changed little from when it was built more than 150 years ago. Probably the biggest change was political and not physical. The Egyptians took over the Canal in 1956, under the leadership of President Gamal Abdul Nassar with help from the Russians. The Israelis, French, and British started a small war opposing this action but quickly withdrew amid rebuke from their traditional allies, including the United States, which was not informed of the action ahead of time.

The Suez Canal has a depth of at least twenty-five feet near the edges and it increases to seventy-five feet at the center. Unlike the Panama Canal, the Suez has no locks, a feature that allows for quicker passage. With the imposed speed limit, the Canal was normally traversed in eleven to fifteen hours. Since large ships could not pass each other traveling in different directions, one-way passages were staggered, with two eight-hour periods northbound and one southbound each day. It was said the Canal was undergoing a multibillion-dollar upgrade to allow for increased traffic, including two-way passages for some larger vessels and the promise of reduced travel time, but this activity was not apparent to the captain whose attention was focused straight ahead.

For this trip through the Canal, which demanded close attention and skill, Ilyas steered most of the way. According to the rules of the canal company, a pilot was onboard, but on his twenty-first passage through, Captain Cham was qualified and relished the challenge. In this narrow strip of water, it was impossible to get lost, but the churning water from the other boats and the sometimes fierce and changeable desert winds made steering the boat straight for one hundred miles a challenge.

Mihal was pleased when the boat finally left the Canal and entered the Mediterranean. It would have been difficult for him to explain to anyone, but the Canal was a claustrophobic experience. The wide-open space of the Mediterranean was a great relief. Mihal was also happy that the captain had approached him with an offer to at least once each day, for about fifteen minutes, update Mihal on their progress and answer any questions that Mihal might have. Since this was a unique experience for Mihal, there was much for him to learn before he could even make a stab at answering the many questions that were put to him each day by those he was leading.

"Thank you for meeting with me, Captain Ilyas," said Mihal. "The trip has been very smooth so far. All of us appreciate the excellent job you and the crew are doing."

"Thank you," said the captain. "I am glad that we have been experiencing such fine weather and, from the forecasts available, it should remain this way for the next few days. Our trip through the Mediterranean should be smooth. This weather is a safe way to initiate passengers who are doing something like this the first time. I can't promise the same for the North Atlantic. We'll just have to wait and see."

"The trip through the Canal was interesting, but I am glad to be in the open sea again," admitted Mihal. "This is the farthest I have been from home, and the sights are very interesting. I suspect they will be even more so before we reach our destination." As soon as he had said this, he was sorry. He had no intention of divulging such personal and flowery thoughts.

"I had better get back to work," said the captain, who was also pleased that he had agreed to have a meeting each day with the leader of the group. He knew Mihal would live to see another day. And the man appeared to be reasonably well-grounded, so he should be able to maintain things below in proper order.

Mihal remembered that Jawad had asked to speak with him. Mihal had approached Jawad the first day out, asking him to be his eyes and ears by keeping track of the inner workings and private conversations of the people on the boat. These people would be giving their lives for the cause. To do this required continued and unwavering devotion to Allah and the spirit of the Jihad. One bad apple could spoil the whole barrel, which simply couldn't be allowed to happen on this long voyage. It took some convincing, but appealing to Jawad's dedication and pride, helped Mihal get the young man to agree to report anything that he thought the leader should know.

Mihal would find him now and get it over with. Jawad was one of the few martyrs Mihal had gotten close to. He wondered what was motivating this man. He was not crazy and gave every evidence of being intelligent, though probably not well-educated. He came from a difficult family. His father was dead and his mother struggled with the three children she was left with to raise alone. Jawad was recruited for training by a person who was kind and had helped him. He provided support while filling Jawad with visions of the rewards to be gained by following the teaching of Allah. As the relationship with his recruiter grew, Jawad seemed to be sincerely dedicated to the cause and was willing to pursue the course being offered. One hitch in this scenario, that Mihal didn't like to think about, was that many of these gullible young people were proceeding with the false impression that the explosion would go outward, away from their body, and that they could survive the blast.

Mihal wondered if he would ever re-evaluate his own motives. The closest he could come to an answer was that he was doing this because he hated the arrogant Westerners, especially those in the U.S. But he was also beginning to feel the same way about many Europeans. His life would only get better when the enemy was diminished. As far as he could tell, people like Jawad acted more out of devotion to Allah and the rapturous afterlife they would be leading than hate of the enemy. *So be it*, thought Mihal. Then the uncomfortable reality set in. *Am I any different than that Kanaan fellow?*

When Mihal found Jawad, the young man said, "I have heard

something from one of the men that is disturbing. From what he said to me, I suspect he may have joined us with no intention of carrying out his promise. The man's name is Habib. I must have given him the impression that I was of a similar mind, and he told me more than he should have, at least for his own good."

Mihal heard this with some alarm. "Thank you, Jawad. This is important to know. I want you to continue observing him closely and tell me anything else you learn. Let me know if you see Habib talking like this with any of the others."

Mihal worried about how he should deal with this situation. If Jawad had, indeed, understood this man's intentions correctly, what action should Mihal take? Mihal decided to watch Habib closely for several days before acting. He would compare notes with Jawad, who would also be watching, before deciding on a course of action. A few days later, when Jawad reported nothing new or out of the ordinary in the man's behavior, Mihal decided that Jawad must have misunderstood the intent of Habib's comments. The verdict was that Habib did not appear to be any different from the others. This was a relief to Mihal, who had enough on his mind.

———————

After days that could be best described as relentless and boring, the boat arrived at Rimouski. At this tiny port in Quebec Province, it was possible to check in with Canadian Customs by phone without the need for a personal inspection. After refueling, the boat would proceed from partly salty to truly freshwater beginning in the St. Lawrence Seaway, then through Lake Ontario, the Welland Canal locks, Lake Erie, Lake Huron, and finally on to northern Lake Michigan.

Once the boat entered the St. Lawrence Seaway, Mihal thought the scenery was truly spectacular. It was late fall. The green that he was told was present in the summer was now vibrant gold and red. The leaves shone in the bright sunlight. Prosperous cities were scattered along the shoreline. Most of the homes were small, but a few were huge, like palaces. At the end of Lake Ontario, they entered another canal. This one was short, only thirty-two miles, and it had eight locks that raised the boat more than three hundred feet. This was an experience as like none he had ever known.

At the eastern end of Lake Erie, at the City of Cleveland, the boat stopped for U.S. Customs inspection. This was the first time any officials had boarded the boat. Mihal was nervous but Captain Cham was not.

———————

At Langley, Adam continued his long hours of monitoring Captain Ilyas's progress. The captain reported briefly three times a day, as did the shadow fleet that had remained in constant surveillance throughout the entire voyage. The hours of video that had been obtained were spectacularly unremarkable. Adam was eager to get a report from the Custom's officer, the first human contact with the vessel.

"Colonel Grant, this is Sam Evanson, of the U.S. Customs Service in Cleveland, Ohio."

"Good to hear from you, Agent Evanson," said Adam. "I have been looking forward to hearing your report."

"Sir, we boarded the boat without incident and carried out a superficial inspection, as you requested. The only people we saw onboard were the captain, a mate, and two crew. Their own papers and the boat's papers were in order. Their stated purpose for entering U.S. waters was to proceed to Sturgeon Bay Marine in Wisconsin for refitting of the boat, which, if I may say so, is badly needed. The demeanor of the captain indicated that he knew our appearance was a charade, but nothing was said to confirm this. He appeared to be a pretty good actor. There were several closed staterooms and other doors that we made no attempt to open. The number of microwave ovens and the extra freezer capacity suggested that the boat could manage a lot of people in minimal comfort, but we chose to ignore them. It would have been possible to hide a small army in there, and some of the things we saw suggested that they could be crammed in somewhere, but there was no reason to suspect that anyone would have taken notice of our intentional indifference."

"Thank you, Agent Evanson. We have reasons for this unusual request. They are classified now, but I suspect you were alerted to this earlier by Homeland Security."

"Yes, sir. We were informed. I expect we will read more about this in the papers."

Adam dealt with this comment with a non-committal response as he had suggested his team also do in a case like this. The truth was, when this operation played out according to plan, neither the agent nor anyone else in the country, including some of those closely involved, would know all the details or ever learn about the events from the media.

In three days, the boat would enter the Straits of Mackinac, pass under the Mackinac Bridge that linked Michigan's Lower and Upper peninsulas, and turn south through Gray's Reef passage to enter Lake Michigan. From there, giving the last buoy south of Gray's Reef passage a wide berth to the west, the boat would head due east while closely watching the depth. It would anchor in thirty feet of water off Wilderness State Park.

Tomorrow would be the final meeting of the task force. Adam could hardly wait. It had been a long month and he was ready.

Chapter 37

The boat was anchored in forty feet of water, a little deeper than predicted, one half mile off the shore of Wilderness State Park. Regardless of what these crazy people thought they would be doing, the captain's job was to deliver them safely to their destination. It was 6:00 p.m. and darkness was settling in. From the land map that Ilyas had, there appeared to be only one road coming down to the landing spot, and it was from the north, Sturgeon Bay Road. The end of the road appeared directly opposite where the boat was now anchored. With binoculars, Ilyas could see there was a sandy beach between the water's edge and tall beach grasses that hid the road where the passengers would board a bus in the morning. The park, which was said to be more than four thousand acres, looked deserted from a half mile offshore. There were no lights and no movement or signs of activity, just as it was predicted.

Mihal studied the shoreline. It appeared tranquil and unspoiled. The sights he had experienced in the last three days gave a picture of this country that belied what he had been told and were at odds with his strong feeling that he would be entering a hostile and decidedly unpleasant place. Instead what he had seen was tranquil, pleasant, and disturbingly nuanced for this man who preferred dealing in absolutes. He was mildly annoyed for liking so much of what he had experienced in the last four days. He hated the Americans who lived here, and he didn't want to like anything about them or where they lived. He was not doing well with the latter. This experience was becoming an endurance test, and he was eager to move on to the next phase.

Contemplating what lay immediately ahead, Mihal reconciled himself to the fact that his motives were in no way comparable to the people he was leading, *really boys and girls*, Mihal thought, *who would become martyrs in a few days*. He would never remotely consider doing what they were ready to do. He was dedicated to the cause, but his goal was to attain the best life for himself that he could. He was neither an idealist nor a zealot. He was a pragmatist. His feelings toward the Prophet, he had to admit, was to use his aura as a rallying cry: Allahu Akbar! The emotions stirred up by this cry in those who were susceptible turned them into no more than instruments for achieving victory over a force that was keeping down Mihal and millions like him. Mihal's actions were guided by neither love nor reverence; his allegiance was to a mostly secular and selfish cause.

Today's meeting with the captain was the last and the earliest. It was 4:00 a.m. Mihal had hardly slept, unable to turn off his churning mind. In two hours, still under the cover of darkness, they would leave the boat and head for the next stage of their mission. "Good morning, Captain. I must congratulate you on providing us a smooth voyage."

"I hope your people fulfill their ambitions, and this venture proves to be a benefit for all. It was my pleasure to be of service," responded Captain Cham. He was putting on a show, trying to sound enthusiastic, but his feelings were conflicted. Rather than a pleasure, for Ilyas Cham it was a betrayal. He was doing the right thing, but he didn't feel clean. This morning, it was even hard to get solace from the generous sum of money he would be receiving.

This interchange with the captain was awkward for Mihal. How much did the captain know? Whatever he knew, he had not interfered in any way or commented on the purpose of the trip. When this was over, he couldn't do any harm to the cause by talking; and since that might get him in serious trouble if it was determined he was an active participant, he would likely keep quiet. *I must be sure to tell Assoud what an excellent job this man did and do what I can to keep him from ending up like the Kanaan family.* "Now," said Mihal, "I have some things that must be confirmed before we go ashore. First, I must contact the people who will be meeting us on shore. We need to be certain they are there and ready to pick us up."

Captain Cham went to his safe and extracted the phone chip. He gave it to Mihal, who inserted it into a cheap throwaway phone. After dialing the number he had been given, Mihal spoke to a man who identified himself as a friend of the cause. According to plan, the man did not give his real name; instead, he provided a code name that had been devised by Fathi. This code name had also been given to Assoud and it was the only way of connecting Mihal and Assoud with the U.S.-based team. The man on the phone with Mihal was Eddie Freeman of the CIA. He was in Langley, Virginia, using a phone with an 888-national area code that would not betray his location. Eddie, who was as good with dialect as he was with electronics, told Mihal they would have ninety minutes of cover until the first light began, which would be enough time to unload the material and the people. He told Mihal to watch for a red light on the beach just before 6:00 a.m. It was the signal telling him the inflatable boats would be leaving the shore in five minutes.

Using the two inflatables, the explosives would be unloaded first, taken to shore, and placed in a van. The bomb makers would supervise the transfer of the explosives to the van, and two men would also be on hand to help with the unloading. Once this was completed, everyone on the boat, except for the captain and his crew, would be transported to land. Once onshore, all would board the bus. Left unsaid by Eddie was that instead of busing them to New York City, they would be taken to Pellston Airport where a U.S. Air Force C130 transport awaited them. Before ending the call, Eddie also gave Mihal a different phone number with the same toll-free 888 area code in case Mihal wanted to contact the team leader in New York.

Eddie immediately phoned Sahag Bagdasarian to tell him he had just spoken with the group's leader on the boat, Mihal. Sahag was the leader of the four-person FBI team that would ferry the supplies, the martyrs, and their leaders to shore. The two boats had been inflated and readied earlier. When this call was finished, Sahag alerted the Emmet County Sheriff's office, the U.S. Marshals, and the remainder of his team. He also called the Coast Guard.

Now that all the arrangements were confirmed, Mihal phoned Assoud in Peshawar with the exciting news. Things would get hectic soon, so he wanted to share this with the leader in peace and quiet. After they were on the bus, Mihal would contact New York.

Following his conversation with Mihal, Assoud dialed the number that Mihal had given him for the leader of the team in New York. Without identifying himself, Assoud offered his code and asked for the code name he expected to hear. When Assoud heard the correct response, he decided to seek further confirmation, something that had not been agreed upon ahead of time. He asked the person on the phone for the name of the man who had made these arrangements. At this point, Assoud wanted extra assurance. When Eddie heard this unexpected request, he decided it would be safe and necessary to say "Fathi Kanaan." This response satisfied Assoud, who thanked Eddie Freemen, aka the New York contact, for his efforts. Assoud was now satisfied that the first strategic phase of the project had been completed successfully. The martyrs and bomb makers were in the U.S. and the team in New York existed and was ready to deliver, just as Fathi had said. *The businessman has done as he promised,* Assoud thought, *but his fate will remain the same*.

———————

On the lowest deck, Habib, sure that he was alone and not being watched, pulled a map out of his pocket. His cousin in Dearborn had sent it to Habib when he was still in Pakistan. The map showed Wilderness State Park at the top of Michigan. This was all that the group had been told about where they would be landing. Looking at the map, Habib's best guess was that they would be landing near the middle of the park. His plan was to quietly separate himself from the crowd as soon as they were ashore. He would go into the woods to relieve himself or do whatever seemed the most natural act at the time. Once he was out of sight, he would walk south, keeping the shoreline in sight on his right. This would lead him to the end of Lakeshore Road, at the south end of the park. His cousin would be driving a silver SUV and waiting there to pick him up and drive him to Detroit. Then, it would be up to Habib to begin the task of blending in.

At CIA Headquarters, Fred Billson and a team of four were manning phones while they continued to monitor activities on the boat via the video feed. Viewing had gotten more interesting with the flurry of activity surrounding the pending departure of the bombers from the boat. Billson had heard the three phone conversations: Mihal and Eddie Freeman, Mihal and Assoud Al Walaki, and Assoud and Eddie Freeman. On a conference call, Fred Billson connected FBI Agent Ed O'Malley, who was directing the ground operations in Michigan; Marine Captain Paul George in Peshawar, who was directing activity there and in Islamabad; and Colonel Adam Grant, who was in Jeddah preparing to carry out the rescue of Ahad Kanaan. This call was vitally important because exact timing was crucial to the success of the operation. Recognizing that his role was more communication than strategy, Fred turned the call over to Adam. Each part of the operation faced a unique challenge, and success in each was vitally important.

Because there were new people on the call, Fred Billson introduced everyone. When he finished, he said, "Colonel Grant, everyone is on the line. I am turning the call over to you."

"Thank you, Fred," said Adam. "I am liaison with the CIA and also representing the Executive Branch. I have been involved in this action for nearly three months. I know you all have been briefed, so forgive me if I repeat some things you already know. I want to be sure there are no unanswered questions, no surprises, and no mess up in timing." After reviewing the details, Adam said, "Our task today is detailed and immediate. I think each of you has been briefed on your specific tasks and are ready to proceed, but before we sign off, do any of you have questions?"

"Ed O'Malley here, in Michigan. Do we Mirandize these people?"

"Definitely not," said Adam. "We will not be interrogating the transports for a while. Our goal is to detain them as quickly and quietly as possible and deal with the legal issues fairly and within the tenets of our legal system, but in due time. Despite what they planned to do, we don't want to violate any of their rights because when all of this is done, anything we do wrong today will come back to bite us after they are lawyered up."

"Paul George here, in Peshawar. Do we allow the Pakistanis we are working with to take over the supervision of the people we arrest?"

"Yes," said Adam. "This will eventually be a problem for the diplomats, but we can't worry about that now. When it comes to the capture, I am confident that the locals, with your help, can get the job done. During capture, do everything you need to, no kid gloves. These are guys who have killed before and there is no reason to believe they will hesitate to kill again. After they are in custody, it is out of our control. It will be up to the Pakistanis. How are things going with the locals, Agent O'Malley?"

On the ground in Wilderness State Park, Ed O'Malley responded, "We have had excellent cooperation from everybody. The Emmet County Sheriff, with help from the Harbor Springs Police Department, has set up a perimeter team that will cordon off the park with a buffer of several hundred yards beyond the apprehension area, and they have blocked off all access roads. This will take nearly their entire force, including the canine unit. The marine unit, maritime and not *leatherneck*, will be standing by, observing the boat while it is at anchor. The residents who have questions are being told by the Sheriff's team that Homeland Security is conducting a three-day training exercise. They will be told that no civilians will be allowed in the designated training area. There are no permanent residents in the area.

"A C130 transport plane has delivered extra FBI and U.S. Marshals. They will establish a line inside the local law enforcement's perimeter, closer to the beach. This will keep the terrorists contained in the immediate landing area. Our plan is to direct the bombers and their handlers as they get out of the inflatables to board the bus, which will be stationed and ready on the gravel road that leads to the beach. Once everybody is on the bus, eight additional FBI officers, who will be stationed out of sight in the woods, will enter the bus and maintain control of the situation. The transports will be turned over to the U.S. Marshals, who with the FBI, will deliver them to Pellston Airport. Once there, they will be placed on the C130 and flown to an undisclosed federal facility. We are all standing by, waiting for the FBI team on the beach to send the signal to the boat to begin unloading at 6:00 a.m. Eastern Standard Time UTC -5."

"Thanks Agent O'Malley. It sounds like you have everything under control. Captain George, are you set with your personnel in Peshawar and Islamabad?"

"Yes," said the captain. "We have a team of Marines and locals, numbering twenty. The compound in Peshawar will be rushed when we get the signal. The same thing will be done in Islamabad, but from everything we can determine, there is only one accomplice there. He is under observation and will be picked up, I suspect, without incident. We are also in close contact with Fathi Kanaan. Before we act, we will have him protected in a cocoon, if I may call it that."

"Thank you, Captain," said Adam. "In Jeddah, we have a ticklish situation. With the help of local Saudi police, we have surrounded the warehouse building where Ahad Kanaan is being held. For the past two weeks, we have been monitoring the comings and goings here. There is no evidence that he has been removed from the premises, and we are sure there are only three men watching him. They seem to be taking turns, but with at least two there always. We don't think they have any intention of harming him now, but they did kill his driver, so we believe they won't hesitate to kill Mr. Kanaan if it serves their ends. Our main concern is that no alerts are heard by these captors, either from the boat or from Pakistan, to freak them out. If that happens, we don't know what they will do. We will begin our operation in Jeddah a few minutes ahead of the other two spots so there is no chance these fellows will get any news that would cause them to hurt Mr. Kanaan. Keeping Ahad Kanaan from being killed is our number one active concern now."

On the boat, the deckhands assembled the group and explained they would be leaving the boat soon. According to directions given to them by Mihal, they explained that beginning at six, two boats would come out from the shore to unload the explosives. Only the bomb makers and the people running the boats would be involved in that part. When this was completed, everyone would be taken ashore in the same two inflatable boats. It would entail two trips for the welcoming party. To insure the transfer was done smoothly, they were instructed to count off in three groups of eight and one of six to make up four boat loads. Each of the passengers was to don a life vest for the short trip to shore. A folding stairway would be set up on the first deck aft for the people to use. It was important that the entire group disembark and land on the shore in the shortest possible time. The crew, they said, would remain on the boat and take it to a location that had been decided on earlier.

Now it was a matter of perfect timing and flawless execution.

Chapter 38

November 4, Friday

A brown unmarked bus departed Camp Pellston, a mid-level correctional facility in Northern Michigan, at 4:45 a.m. Twenty-five minutes later, it reached the north entrance of Wilderness State Park. The bus had two horizontal metal bars across each window. Their purpose was to prevent anyone from escaping. This feature was not something that would be noticed by the newcomers.

Once in the park, the bus rocked down the narrow gravel road and stopped at the appointed spot where the road ended in a turn-around loop. The bus carried eight FBI agents and four U.S. Marshals. The driver was an Emmet County Sheriff's deputy who was familiar with the park. The FBI agents and the marshals left the bus and deployed close by and out of sight in the woods. The driver, stayed in his seat. Following the bus was a nondescript, well-used Ford utility van with a three-ton hauling capacity that was made available by the manager of the local car dealership. The Harbor Springs Police Chief made the request, and no questions were asked. The van had only the driver, who was a member of the bomb squad from the U.S. Army. For the next few hours, Wilderness State Park and the immediate area surrounding it belonged to federal agents and personnel from local law enforcement.

Three hundred feet from where both vehicles were parked, was the beach where the inflatable boats would be launched. The stretch of sandy beach gave way to a swath of dense, waist-high, beach grass that stopped just short of the road where the bus and van waited. Several feet beyond the road was thick woods of pine, hemlock, beech, ash, birch, and heavy underbrush. This landscape had been untouched for one hundred years and was said to look as it did when the first Europeans settled there in the early seventeenth century. The first sight for today's transports, as they stepped onto American soil, would be like that seen by Jean Nicolet more than four centuries ago. Although, for today's newcomers, this bucolic scene would soon collide with the reality of the twenty-first century.

The four FBI agents, three men and a woman, who would be manning the inflatables, were selected because of their Middle-Eastern ethnicity. It was hoped their appearance would be comforting to the people they would be transporting. This team was led by Sahag Bagdasarian and included Paul Bashara, Sam Sarver, and Elaine Korman. They would be in the guise of compatriots who were sympathetic to the cause. Their task was to get everyone off the boat and onto the bus with no hint of alarm—as quickly and quietly as possible.

Everyone but the four greeters and two drivers dispersed and took their designated positions in the woods, no more than twenty feet from the road but well hidden by the trees and ground vegetation. Sahag and his team made two trips carrying twelve-foot rubber boats they had removed from the back of the van and inflated using a foot-activated pump. On the beach at the shoreline, they attached a five-horsepower Yamaha outboard to each and pushed the boats into the water. The men wore rubber boots that extended to just below their knees. The water was cold. Sahag and Paul Bashara, who had set up the red light signaling to the large boat anchored offshore, pushed off a few minutes before 6:00 a.m., started the motors, and headed to the boat. Elaine and Sam waited on shore.

While these preparations were underway, Mihal instructed everyone to leave all of their stuff on the boat except for any small personal items that could fit inside a pocket. He explained that once they were on the bus, they would be given new clothing and supplies. Mihal then monitored the removal of the explosives from the locked storage area to the main deck where the boarding ladder had been set up.

Everything was ready when the inflatables arrived. Little was said while the bomb makers helped load everything onto the smaller boats. It was understood that this material would be transferred carefully. Twenty-seven packages weighing fifteen pounds apiece were divided between the two inflatables. Each had a bomb maker aboard on its trip to shore.

Sam and Elaine greeted the returning boats, handed warm jackets to the bomb makers, and helped transfer the explosives into the van. When this task was finished, they took the bomb makers to the bus and left them under the supervision of the driver. They then returned to the shore to greet the other arrivals.

Mihal was with the first group. He seemed more agitated than the martyrs, who were docile and seemingly unfazed by their new surroundings. As each person stepped out of an inflatable boat, they were handed a warm coat, which they were grateful to receive after the cold ride on the water. This was meant as a comforting gesture; and it was later agreed that it had been a good move. Mihal directed his charges to fill the seats in the bus starting from the back. He selected a front-row seat for himself, as would a tour leader. From there he could better monitor the activity of his people.

When everyone was on the bus—except for Captain Cham and his crew—Sahag Bagdasarian, still in the guise a conspirator, welcomed them. He explained that no one would be allowed to have a phone or any weapons. Mihal assured him that nobody had a weapon of any kind and that all phones had been confiscated at the start of the journey. Of course, Mihal did not consider this decree to include himself and he did not volunteer his phone.

Being reasonably sure that at least one of the leaders would have a phone, Sahag pressed Mihal. Before he would be subjected to search, which Mihal was sure would happen, he reluctantly handed over his phone. The successful completion of this phase was immediately reported to Langley by Elaine Kerman who interpreted the high-five sign from Sahag. Fred Billson shared this news with Adam, who would soon begin carrying out phase two in Jeddah. As soon as phase two was completed, Adam would report to the team and then the third and final phase could begin in Peshawar and Islamabad.

A minute after the call was made to Fred Billson, Paul Bashara pulled Sahag aside and quietly said, "Sahag, we counted thirty-two people getting off the boat, but now I only count thirty-one—and I've counted three times."

"This could be trouble," said Sahag.

Habib Bashour walked fast along the deserted beach; cold and alone but grateful for his new coat. Although he was in a strange place and taking a big risk, he was optimistic. The directions his cousin had sent to him indicated that Lakeshore Road entered the park from the south and came to a dead end just inside the park itself and within sight of the beach. Habib was gaining confidence that the plan would continue to work out and hoped that his absence would not be noticed too soon. It had been a long journey and difficult for him to keep his true motives hidden. He was glad nothing had come from his talk with Jawad at the beginning of the trip. Habib realized afterward how stupid it had been for him to speak so candidly.

Certain that one of the terrorists was missing, Sahag walked away from the bus and made a call to the surveillance team, informing them that one person was missing. When the Emmet County Marine Patrol heard this, they immediately headed closer to shore to see if they could spot anyone walking there. "Hey, there is someone walking on the beach just north of Lakeshore Road," said Deputy Dave Pearce to his companion in the patrol boat, a twelve-foot hard-bottom inflatable, cruising just off the beach in a few feet of water.

"Yep! I see him too," said Brian Grindly, who immediately got on his hand-held and announced the sighting to the team using the frequency they were all monitoring.

Deputy Todd Mellow, who was at the south end of the park and closest to the area where the man had been spotted, headed to the entrance of Lakeshore Road off M-119, hung a right, and then headed back north. At the end of the road, he saw a silver SUV parked in a small turnaround at the end of the road with its front facing him. The deputy slowly and cautiously drove his car toward the SUV. There was no way he could keep out of sight on the otherwise deserted road. Before he reached the SUV, Deputy Mellow saw a figure trudging up from the beach and enter the vehicle. The deputy immediately called for back-up and continued toward the SUV. When the two vehicles were nearly touching, he positioned the police car so that it blocked the road. Behind him, two more police cars were coming toward him, not worried about being seen and moving as fast as the road would allow.

In the SUV, Habib's cousin muttered a profanity in Arabic and wondered how he had been talked into doing this stupid thing in the first place. For a split second, or maybe it was a tenth of a split second, he considered running. The gravel road was built on sand with no obstruction on either side. He could make a dash for it, hoping he wouldn't get stuck in the loose sand, but no, doing that would only compound his stupidity.

Having thought better of taking flight, he turned off the engine, lowered the driver's window, and told Habib to keep both of his hands clearly in sight, touching the dashboard in front of him. Not taking any chances himself, the driver put both hands on top of the steering wheel at the twelve o'clock position and waited for the officers to arrive at his car.

Deputy Mellow, seeing the shivering and disheveled passenger, took out his phone and called the number he was told to use in an emergency. It connected with FBI agent Bagdasarian. He told the agent what he had done and that it had happened without incident. He said, "This fellow doesn't speak English, but he does keep saying something that sounds like *No bomber. No bomber. Just see cousin.* The driver is not talking but his driver's license says he's from Detroit. According to the computer check on the license plate, the car is his and there is nothing out on this guy. He appears to be clean, but like I said, he isn't talking."

The deputy was told to take both men to the nearest lock-up and they would be collected in a few hours. It was clear that this was the man missing from the boat. Agent Bagdasarian told the deputy, "I don't give a damn about what he is saying. If he changed his mind, that's now his problem. We will treat him just like the others. Don't Mirandize or charge either of them yet. We have some tidying up to do here, but we should be done by noon. Just let us know where we can pick him up."

"Will do," said Officer Mellow, who then gave the FBI man the address of the lock-up in Petoskey just thirty miles south.

Habib's capture was a relief to everyone. One loose cannon could have severely tainted the entire operation. Fortunately, the people on the bus waited patiently and didn't seem alarmed by the delay. If any of the passengers knew one of theirs was missing, they did not reveal it.

During this delay, Sahag had alternated between looking purposeful and reassuring to Mihal. When his phone was alerted he stepped off the bus to take the call about the missing man. Now returning and relieved to see that everyone in the group was remaining quietly in their seats he instructed the bus driver to sound three short blasts of the horn. Within seconds, eight FBI agents wearing dark-blue windbreakers with a prominent "FBI" displayed in yellow across the back and a smaller logo in front approached the bus. Four U.S. Marshals followed close behind. Two of the FBI agents entered the bus, joining the two already on board, and stationed themselves at intervals along the narrow center aisle with Sahag and Paul. Sam, Elaine, and their driver remained with the van. The driver of the bus, who remained alert in his seat and at the ready during the entire process, was happy to see reinforcements arrive.

When Jawad realized this delay was not part of the plan and that the man he suspected as a traitor was not on the bus, he was, angry, and frightened. This unexpected turn of events felt like the bomb he had been anticipating had just detonated and he had made the ultimate sacrifice for Allah—but this was not the nirvana he had been promised.

Because Sahag knew from Mihal's mutterings that he understood and spoke at least some English, Sahag explained to Mihal that all of them were now in U.S. custody. "How many of your people speak English?" he asked.

Mihal's first thought was that he had been correct about Fathi. He was a traitor. After that split second of satisfaction at being right, his mind went numb. Then, remarkably composed, as if he had expected this, Mihal answered in excellent English, "About half."

Sahag said, "I want you to tell them the following: They are being taken into custody by the United States government on the suspicion that they are plotting a terrorist attack on our soil. They will not be harmed by us, but they will be detained in a facility while we obtain more information. You will be taken on this bus to an airport. The bus ride will be about forty-five minutes. Then you will be flown on a military plane to a secure facility where you will be kept under guard. I don't know how long you will be held or what specific actions will take place, but you should know that all of you will remain safe and will not be harmed in any way.

"There will be no more announcements after this, and nobody here will be answering any questions. When the time comes, and that will be soon, all of your questions will be answered. The fact that you have done no harm is in your favor, but you can be sure we are fully aware of your intentions. Tell everyone to remain quiet, follow directions, and comply with our requests. If they do, nothing bad will happen. Failure to cooperate will require us to do whatever is necessary to maintain order."

Mihal delivered the message in Arabic. There were a few questions, which he responded to briefly. When it seemed everyone was settled in, the bus departed for Pellston Airport. Their fates were now in the hands of the U.S. Justice Department.

Even though Habib protested his innocence, saying that he had only been onboard because he wanted to reach America and be with his relatives, he would soon join the others. His fate, too, would be decided in the federal court system. His cousin would be handed over to Federal authorities in Detroit.

———————————

Adam received word that the terrorists were in U.S. custody and the bombs were secure. It was 1:00 p.m. in Jeddah. Paul George was notified at the same time; which was 3:00 p.m. in Peshawar. Captain George's responders were separated into three groups: one was close to Fathi in Islamabad. A second was ready to pick up Mohammad, the man from Mihal's group who was left behind, also in Islamabad; and a third, larger group, was ready to grab Assoud Al Walaki and his cohorts in Peshawar. Everyone was eagerly awaiting orders telling them to act, but that would not happen until they received news that Ahad Kanaan had been freed.

It had been several hours since Mihal had spoken with Assoud. If Assoud attempted to reach Mihal, the call would not be answered because Mihal's phone had been confiscated and deactivated. Time was of the essence to prevent Assoud from growing suspicious. By Adam's calculations, it would be necessary to act in Jeddah no later than midnight and in Pakistan just a few minutes after that. It was unlikely Ahad's captors would get an emergency message off to Assoud before Adam had finished the work freeing the hostage, but there was no reason to take a chance. Adam's biggest concern now was that if Assoud learned about events in Michigan or received news from Jeddah before he was captured he would immediately lash out, and the only way he could retaliate would be to harm Ahad and Fathi. Adam resolved not to allow this to happen.

Chapter 39

When Mihal did not answer his phone, Assoud again called the number in New York. Identifying himself with only the code name, Assoud spoke. "I haven't heard from Mihal for three hours. By this time, he should be fully unloaded and have the group on its way. Can you confirm this?" He was trying to sound confident and unconcerned, but it was hard because he knew how eager Mihal would have been to deliver good news and receive the praise he wallowed in.

Eddie Freeman, continuing his role, responded to Assoud's concern. "The cell tower coverage in this rural area is spotty. It was chosen as a safe place to unload but it is known for bad cell phone reception. You must be patient. You can't expect a place to have no people and at the same time great cell phone connectivity. You will hear from him soon. And, I know the team in New York has discouraged cell phone activity by anyone on the bus to avoid any intercepts by the authorities." He ended the conversation by telling Assoud he should rest assured that everything was going according to plan.

Eddie immediately phoned Adam to let him know Assoud was getting anxious. Adam, with the Saudi team, decided they would start the rescue of Ahad around midnight; and as soon as this action started, the team in Pakistan would be given the go-ahead.

The stakeout of the building in the industrial park had been in effect for nearly a month. The Saudi Security Force, led by Captain Kamal Abad, was highly professional and extremely cooperative. Adam was impressed, greatly relieved, and happy to be able to work with them. It was a dicey thing to carry out an activity like this on foreign soil, but it was a pleasure to be working with these professionals.

From the time of Ahad's abduction, the Saudis, working closely with Adam, had monitored the activity at the building. The GPS chip continued transmitting, indicating that Ahad and his ring, or only his ring, were still there. Adam had no reason to believe the ring had been taken off or that Ahad had been removed from the building. They would soon know. Today there were two cars parked out front, indicating that all three captors were inside.

Adam and Captain Abad agreed that they would begin the rescue action at 12:30 a.m. "Which car have you selected?" asked Adam.

"The Toyota farthest from the door will be suitable. It should make a nice torch."

"Have you figured out how to get the fire going?" asked Adam.

Kamal, who had given this a great deal of thought, shared his plan. "We will place a twenty-liter plastic container of gasoline under the car's fuel tank, and connect it to a ten-foot gasoline-soaked wick. When the flame from the wick reaches the tank, it will either explode or it will simply ignite and remain a fire. In either case, the result will be the same, it will cause alarm. We expect that at least two, and maybe all three, of the men will rush out when the fire erupts. In that case, we will grab them; hopefully without any shooting, but we will be ready for that if they give us any trouble. When we see the men come out of the building, a fire brigade will arrive with bells clanging and lights flashing. The men will be too occupied to wonder how a firetruck could arrive so quickly. The firemen will be our men. In the confusion, we will swarm the men and our plan is to have them down inside of a minute. As soon as all three are accounted for, we will get Ahad Kanaan."

"That sounds like a plan," said Adam. "If it's okay with you, I'd like to be the one to get Ahad. He must be spooked after his ordeal with those goons. He knows me and will be more cooperative when he sees a familiar face."

"That could be dangerous," said Kamal.

"It's okay. Been there, done that," said Adam, who was immediately sorry, as much for the braggadocio as for the triteness of the remark.

Adam, Kamal, and five other Saudi officers stationed at a secure spot across the parking lot, watched one of their men light the fuse leading to the container positioned under the car. He hurried back to the group and, in just a few seconds, a brisk fire started under the car. In a few more seconds, the fuel tank exploded, engulfing the car in flames. Immediately, two men rushed through the door in time to see one of their cars in flame and a fire truck driving toward them in a clamor. The two men, who were looking at the flaming car in shock, were further surprised when instead of fighting the fire, the firemen had them trussed in handcuffs and forcefully dragged them away from the door of the building, all completed in just seconds.

At the instant the two men passed through the door, Adam slipped around the corner and entered a disheveled room. He knew the building was an abandoned commercial kitchen but, in its present condition, it was hard to tell. The only thing left was the faint aroma of dried fruits, nothing more. Adam thought for a split second it smelled of apricots. Then he saw a tousled man standing across from him wearing only his underwear. He was raising a large handgun. In the next fraction of a second, he would be using it against Adam. Faced with a threat that demanded reflex not thought, Adam responded in the only way he could. He aimed for the body mass between the shoulders and the waist. Adam connected with three shots to the chest. The man crumbled. Adam had no regret and this feeling was only intensified when he saw the man in the next room.

Ahad, always dapper and well-groomed, was barely recognizable. He was squatting on the floor in the far corner of the small room. When he looked up with his good eye he muttered, "Thank God."

"Let's get out of here," said Adam as he scooped up his friend. When they were outside, Adam saw that real firemen had taken over the equipment and the fire was nearly extinguished.

As Adam handed his gun to Kamal, the Saudi asked, "How many times did I shoot him, and did he deserve it?"

"The short answer is three and yes," said Adam. "Unless you wanted to converse with him in the half second you had before he shot you dead."

"In that case, Colonel Grant, I did the right thing."

"That would be an affirmative."

Before jumping into the ambulance with Ahad, Adam phoned CIA Headquarters. He immediately reached Fred Billson who said, "Adam, this is Fred. How do things stand?"

"We got Ahad." He didn't mention his injury. "One of his captors is down and two are in Saudi custody. It's time to roll with the Pakistan team."

"I'm on it, Adam. We can catch up later."

At the hospital, Ahad had a tearful reunion with Farah and their two daughters, who had returned from England to be with their mother while their father was being held captive. Lila and her two daughters remained at the house, still under the watchful eye of their CIA protectors.

From Ahad's overall physical condition, it appeared he had not suffered greatly from his ordeal, although he had lost considerable weight. The most severe damage he sustained was the injury to his left eye. It was surmised that it was caused by flying glass from the shattered window. The result was a laceration of the cornea of the left eye that was sealed by incarcerated iris tissue. According to Ahad, the eye was painful at first, but after a few days it had stopped hurting. He couldn't see anything with it though.

An ophthalmologist was called to see Ahad in the hospital. Taking him to a room with special equipment for eye examinations, Ahad was evaluated thoroughly, including an ultrasound of the injured eye. After twenty minutes, the ophthalmologist shared his diagnosis with Ahad and his family. The injury had damaged the cornea, the clear window at the front of the eye, and caused it to become cloudy. It had also torn the iris and nicked the lens, causing a cataract. That was all of the bad news. The good news was there was no evidence that the retina was damaged or detached. The corneal laceration could be repaired, the iris reposited, and the remnants of the lens, now cataractous, would be cleaned out. If possible, an intraocular lens would be inserted, now or at a later date, and the iris repaired, although it would likely remain irregular. He would be placed on oral antibiotics immediately and drops would be started later. Ahad would also receive a five-day course of steroids. If everything went as planned, Ahad's vision could be restored to near normal.

Ahad was released from the hospital emergency room to rest at home, but would have to return to the eye surgeon by 9:00 a.m. He was not to eat or drink anything. Surgery would be done in the afternoon. Still a man who was accustomed to being in charge, Ahad negotiated for a noontime arrival because he had one small task to complete in the morning.

Captain Paul George in Peshawar received the call he had been waiting for and was ready to deal with Assoud Al Walaki, but his first job was to alert the team in Islamabad. According to the plan, immediately on hearing that Ahad was safe, the team would pick up Fathi and take him to a prearranged safe house. They had been watching his home and knew the Al-Fir team, under the direction of Assoud, was also watching. Captain George had a team of four Marines ready for action. They assured him that their involvement so far had had been low key and they had not been discovered. There was no reason to hold back now, so backing up the local police, they would do whatever they had to. Within a minute of getting clearance, the local security force converged on the house to meet a relieved Fathi Kanaan. The Marines, out of uniform, were ready but remained in the background. They immediately told Fathi his father was freed and his family was safe. They elected to not mention the eye injury.

The minute Fathi was ensconced in the care of his protectors, Captain George was alerted. With a team of Pakistani Security Forces, he stormed the compound where Assoud was living. In what turned out to be an anticlimax gratefully accepted by the local forces, Assoud and three men with him surrendered meekly. They were escorted off the premises in the custody of the Pakistani Security Forces and taken to a detention center. When this was accomplished, Captain Paul George told the team watching Mohammad's house to seize him. The befuddled man was secured without incident and taken away. With this last chore completed, Captain George informed Fred Billson.

Chapter 40

_____

At 5:00 p.m. EST on November 6, thirty-five hours after the initial encounter on a deserted beach in Northern Michigan, Operation Thunderstruck was successfully completed. Thirty-nine terrorists and enablers were in custody in three countries. Only one mercenary was killed, and that happened during the rescue of Ahad Kanaan. The only serious injury to the good guys was an eye injury suffered by Ahad. All of this was accomplished with the coordinated action of nearly a hundred military and law enforcement personnel, across thousands of miles and three continents. Only those people who needed to know were aware of what had transpired and why it had been done.

The Kanaan family was safe at home, and happily reunited, except for Fathi, who was traveling from Islamabad. Adam spent the night in the same room he had used the last time he visited the Kanaans. Eager to return to Washington, Adam woke early. He had become close and considered the Kanaan family to be his friends now. They had endured a lot and were eagerly awaiting Fathi's return later in the day. Adam's job here was done, and he was ready to make amends for some things he had been neglecting in his own life.

Ahad knew that Adam planned to leave early, and there were a few things that, with the help of Farah, Ahad needed to do. When it was time for Adam to leave for the airport, Ahad said, "Adam, I don't think it is right to send you off in a cab; not after all we have been through together. If you will allow me, I would like to go with you to the airport and, after that, I will check into the hospital. Farah will meet me there. Besides, there is something I want to say. We can go in my car, if that is okay with you."

On their way to the airport, they sat in the back of a Land Rover RL4, Ahad's back-up vehicle. His usual driver was at the wheel, thankful for his time off but sorry for the man who had given his life. He was also heartened by the news that his boss had ordered a new and safer car to replace the Mercedes that had been damaged in the attack. It would have bulletproof windows.

"Adam, if you will pardon me for reading your mind, I would like to answer some questions that you might have."

"The way my mind is going, I should welcome an interpreter," joked Adam.

"Just in case I haven't made it clear, I would like to say that I take full responsibility for all the mess that happened. And, I would like to give you credit for all the good that has come out of the terrible things my family started."

"Slow down, Ahad. Don't be too hard on yourself."

Undeterred, Ahad Kanaan continued. "It started with the message I sent to the President of the United States. My intent was to get help for my son and, to a certain extent, to get me out of an ill-advised project. It sounded exciting at first—cloak and dagger—but then events got wildly out of hand. I also feel bad for what I did to Alia. I had no intention of clouding the memory of my lovely first wife, but I was desperate."

As the car approached Abdul Aziz Airport, Ahad reached into the pocket of his coat and retrieved a small, black-velvet pouch closed with a drawstring. "I gave this to Alia on our wedding day. It has been in a drawer for more than thirty years, a memory of a beautiful woman taken too soon. She had a wonderful son, who you helped save. I know Alia would want you to have this. Put it in a safe place and have a look at it later. Good-bye, Adam. And thank you." With that, Ahad gave Adam a vigorous hug.

Two hours later, settled in his seat and thinking about the equally unexciting meal choices that Saudi Air was offering, Adam remembered the velvet pouch Ahad had given him. He opened it and saw a large, unset, sparkling diamond. He was no expert in such things, but it had to be two or three carats. A crisply folded, waxed, jeweler's paper had a brief note written in a careful, feminine hand. "You told us about a wonderful woman named Erin. We thought you might have a use for this. With our love and appreciation, The Kanaan Family.

Chapter 41

November 10, Thursday

It was Adam's second day back. His meeting with the President had gone well. Although President Tripp had received regular progress reports from the CIA Director, they had none of the flavor of the firsthand account that Adam provided. Only with this account, was Phillip Tripp able to appreciate how close the country had been to a repeat of 9/11.

"Adam," the President said, "some threats can be nipped in the bud and others, for a variety of reasons, can only be stopped much closer to the point of attack. In this case, it turned out to be a combination of both. What you and the team accomplished will enable us to use our legal system in an open and transparent way to deal with the terrorists. And, the good news is they will be held responsible for a violent threat and not a heinous terrorist act.

"My concern is that the masterminds in Pakistan will get no more than a slap on the wrist; so, they may be back at their rotten stuff almost immediately. The thirty-two we got here will be dealt with in a much more satisfactory manner, and some of them may even be rehabilitated. Wouldn't that be nice?" After a pause, followed by a shake of his head, President Tripp, with a profound look of relief, finished with, "What if you hadn't been here, Adam?"

Adam appreciated hearing this from the President, but he had two other pressing matters to deal with. First was a 1:00 p.m. meeting at Langley with Robert Zinsky, the CIA Director. But more important, Erin had promised to call him later in the day.

Entering Bob Zinsky's office, Adam was surprised to see that FBI Director Phil Stark was also in the room.

"Nice to see you again, Colonel Grant," said Director Stark.

With Adam still standing, Bob Zinsky said, "Thanks for coming, Adam. Have you recovered from the recent events?"

"It depends on your definition of recovered," replied Adam. "I have a boatload of reports to finish, and I expect some folks will have questions that I won't have answers for, and then there are the trials. I look on this activity as the gift that keeps on giving."

"Please, have a seat," said the CIA Director. "Let us give you an update from the standpoint of the CIA and the FBI. Phil, why don't you tell Adam what will happen here, on U.S. soil?"

"Let me explain what is going on with the men and women who were captured in Michigan," said Director Stark. "It will be the responsibility of the federal courts to deal with them. From a legal standpoint, the terrorists were arrested in the United States after illegal entry with intent to do harm to the United States. The probable cause is the fact they had a large quantity of explosives, suicide vests, and literature describing an elaborate plot against One World Trade Center. They also carried false documents. All of these are prosecutable offenses. At their trial it is likely they will be found guilty and incarcerated, I'm

254 | Gene Helveston

not sure for how long. Since they were arrested on U.S. soil, they will be treated as any federal criminal. This is different from the enemy combatants who were arrested on foreign soil and transferred to Guantanamo Bay."

Adam replied, "That puts the matter in a clear perspective, sir, at least from the legal standpoint. Along those lines, I have a personal problem. While doing what I had to do, and acting in the only way I thought appropriate, it was necessary for me to kill one of the kidnappers. A Saudi Special Forces officer took the gun and said he'd take responsibility for the shooting. Is what I did right in the face of the law?"

The CIA director spoke. "I think this is on my plate, Adam. You were recruited by me and working on foreign soil carrying out an authorized activity. Your life was threatened by a violent person during a hostage rescue. According to CIA policy, for an action like this, you exceeded expectations by being able to apprehend two of the three men and did so without endangering the life of the hostage. In my opinion, you did what you had to do and acted entirely within the appropriate guidelines. I'm sorry but I didn't hear what you did with the gun. How you write up the report is entirely up to you."

"Thank you, sir. If it is alright with you, I will not bring that up again."

"Now, for the other reason I wanted to meet with you," said Bob Zinsky. "I am going to offer you a job, different and expanded from what you and I discussed originally. It is this: Director Stark and I want you to develop a process that will enable coordinated efforts between the organizations you employed in this recent action: the CIA, FBI, the U.S. Marshal Service, and any other agencies that you think should be included. Also in your remit would be liaison with Homeland Security, Customs and Immigration, and the Transportation Safety Administration. You have shown extraordinary skill at leadership, innovation, stamina, and dedication. There are no guidelines for how to build this kind of a service we envision, so it will be necessary for us to work with you to develop the entity we are proposing and bring it into operation. This is big, so you can take some time to think it over."

Phil Stark spoke. "Just to make sure you know that what you heard also comes from me. I am one hundred percent on board and I pledge the complete cooperation of the Bureau. We want the FBI to also be a place where you are welcome and needed. When it comes to working, you are more familiar with the CIA, but we want our agency to be a second home, if you will."

Adam looked at both men and, without any hesitation, said, "Gentlemen, I accept the offer and the challenge. I will do everything in my power to make it happen as you have outlined. I don't need time to think; I have done a lot of that over the last six months. Much has happened to me in a short time, and this has helped me come to terms with some important things in my life. You have offered me what I consider a dream job. However, I have one request. I would like to have the next eight weeks off to take care of some pressing personal matters."

A beaming Bob Zinsky stood and extended his hand to Adam. "Adam, on behalf of the President of the United States, who is totally on board and who has been working in cooperation with Phil and me, I welcome you to a new, blended family. Now, I don't want to see you until the middle of January. And if you need more time, just let me know. The job will be waiting for you."

"I second everything Bob said. The next time we meet, it will be Bob, Tom, and Adam."

"I understand," said Adam. "Thank you. I'll see you in eight weeks."

As he was driving home, his phone rang. It was Erin. She had called him a couple days ago to tell him she had an appointment to see a cardiologist about some extra heartbeats she had been experiencing. She told Adam she wasn't worried and didn't want him to worry either. She was sharing the news only because she didn't want to keep things from him. She had talked with her dad, who was a cardiologist at Jackson Memorial Hospital at the University of Florida. He had encouraged Erin to see the cardiologist in Rome and then have that doctor send a full report to him in Florida.

Despite Erin's lightness, Adam was concerned that she might be minimizing things to keep him from worrying; so later that day he did a Google search of irregular heartbeats. Two reliable sources of information caught his eye. They were postings from Mayo Clinic and Cleveland Clinic. After reading a paragraph on Mayo's website, he learned that the condition could be mild or very serious. Apart from lowering caffeine and reducing stress to eliminate the abnormal heartbeats, nothing else he read was reassuring. To him it seemed like everything was binary. You could live or not. It was bad, or it wasn't. The treatment was invasive or it was simple and required nothing more than a lifestyle change and medication. Adam turned off the computer trying to decide whether he should be relieved or if he should be more concerned than when he started his quest for more knowledge.

Before Adam could do much more than chase this information around in his head, trying to make sense of it, Erin was calling again.

"Adam, I will be coming home for more tests. Dad insisted. I couldn't talk him out of it. I feel great, and I don't want you to worry. I love you, Adam."

Adam responded, "I love you too, Erin. Where and when are you flying in? I'll meet you there."

"I will be in D.C. in three days," said Erin.

"Okay. I'll be there," said Adam. As he said good-bye, he knew he had to find a jeweler, pronto.

Chapter 42

November 13, Sunday

Adam was standing in the foyer of The Admirals Club at Washington Dulles Airport. He had stationed himself strategically just inside the entrance doors, where he would be the first to see anyone enter the facility. Behind him, the arrivals board indicated that American Airlines Flight 3277 from Rome landed ten minutes ago. This sprawling airport, that he was sure had been designed by a committee that didn't agree on much, was not a place that could be navigated quickly or easily, but this should be enough time for Erin to be at this fairly central point.

He was right. A few seconds later, the large glass door separating the concourse from the Club's foyer slid open automatically. For a split second, it framed Erin and his heart raced. She saw him immediately and covered the few steps between them like a sprinter coming out of the blocks. They embraced, and both spoke the endearing words of two people who were ecstatic to be in each other's arms.

After half a minute, Adam could wait no longer. Straightening his arms to move Erin back so he could see all of her, he said, "You look great—but how do you feel? I have been worried sick."

"Adam, of all the things I think I know about you, it's that you are not a worrywart. I feel good and am embarrassed to be the cause of the fuss. My dad didn't even wait for the report from the doctor in Rome. He demanded I come home immediately—so here I am."

"What did you hear from the specialist in Rome?"

Erin gathered her thoughts for a second. She wanted to be honest, but even more, she wanted to be reassuring because she could see that Adam was anxious. "The doctor in Rome was very nice. He did several routine tests, mostly centered on the electrocardiogram findings, because he wanted to get an idea about how the internal signaling system in my heart was working. The problem is that everything was normal. As he was explaining it to me, all I could think of was a poem, or maybe it's a nursery rhyme, that seemed to say exactly what the doctor was telling me about my heart: *There was a little girl, who had a little curl, right in the middle of her forehead. When she was good, she was very good indeed. But when she was bad, she was horrid.* I guess my heart is that little girl. During the testing, it was behaving."

"From what I read online, what you are telling me may explain why you felt crummy before and feel fine now—it's just that *something* wasn't right when all of this was going on. At least it doesn't sound like you have any of the serious underlying causes for this kind of behavior, and that means you may be helped by medical treatment, even short-term, or maybe just changing a few things in your life, but definitely not anything that would involve something that was serious." Adam didn't want to use the "S" word—surgery.

"Now who's the doctor, Adam? What you just said is what my dad told me on the phone before I left Rome."

"Let's get on the plane and just enjoy being together in Miami," said Adam.

"Let's."

Just outside Baggage Claim at Miami Dade County Airport, Adam spied two people who he thought had to be Erin's parents. He was right. The woman was short and strikingly attractive. The man was tall and distinguished-looking, with thinning hair that looked like it had been redder and fuller in his youth. He looked like someone who didn't have any difficulty being in charge. Erin had a combination of the best DNA that each of her parents, an Irishman and a woman whose mother was Korean, had to offer.

During the joyful family reunion, Adam hung back appropriately and watched as the emotions of all three tumbled out unchecked. During this brief interlude, he realized that for the first time since he had seen Erin across the great seal in the lobby of the CIA Headquarters, he was just *looking* at this extraordinary woman. After that first meeting, all their time together had involved intense personal interaction. Some were moments of pure pleasure and others sheer terror, but all were charged with energy. As he looked at Erin, Adam knew she was the person he wanted to spend the rest of his life with. For him, she was perfect in every way. He found both her mind and entire being enthralling. As far as Adam was concerned, she was a person who simply couldn't be improved.

The reverie ended when he heard Erin say, "Mom and Dad, this is Colonel Adam Grant, who I have told you so much about."

Adam immediately offered his hand and addressed them formally. "A pleasure to meet you, Doctor O'Leary and Doctor O'Leary."

"Enough of the 'doctor,'" said Erin's mother. "It's Marian and Brian."

"And Adam," said the Colonel.

Adam and Erin were in the back of the Volvo XC70 wagon. Adam was behind Marian, who had her seat forward. There wasn't much legroom in the backseat of this model. It was extremely practical when it came to cargo space; just not legroom in the back. But that was okay because ninety-five percent of the time it served no more than two passengers. And being next to Erin was all the comfort Adam needed.

They traveled down 112 to Interstate 195 and exited right after passing over the bay heading for the Bal Harbor Condominiums. Arriving at their destination, Adam saw a beautiful high-rise facing the ocean. Erin had pointed out an article that featured the building in the in-flight magazine. It said that this building was on the site of the former Bal Harbor Club, a landmark of the first iteration of Miami Beach.

After parking in their designated underground space, the four proceeded to the elevator that took them to a personal elevator lobby that served their apartment on the 15th floor. The apartment was elegant. Worthy of a spread in *Town and Country*. Marian took them both on a quick tour, more for orientation than bragging. This was Erin's first visit to her parents' new home. The couple had moved in just six months ago and Erin had been looking forward to seeing the place she had heard so much about.

It didn't disappoint. Her mother explained it had been described to them by the Realtor as a flow-through plan; the price notwithstanding, they fell in love with it and made the decision to buy it on the spot. To the east was the Atlantic Ocean and beaches, and to the west was Biscayne Bay and the City of Miami. Between these two views, the condominium was just about anything a person would desire when it came to luxury living. Adam did some quick mental arithmetic and concluded that even with the income of two doctors, and no other obvious significant indebtedness evidenced by them driving a reasonably priced three-year-old car, these digs would take a big chunk of their take-home pay.

After the tour, Adam was shown to his room. My room not

our room, thought Adam. He was just old-fashioned enough to think the arrangement was fine, for now.

Marian said, "I'll bet you're both famished and could use some dinner. It will be ready in thirty minutes."

Being a resourceful homemaker, as well as a successful career woman, Marian had turkey lasagna in the oven that she had prepared ahead of time. She and Erin put together a fresh Italian-themed salad. A French baguette and a California red wine completed the dinner, which was enjoyed by all.

Finally, with coffee being served, it was no longer possible to put off the medical talk. Brian started. "Erin, you look great, and I am sure you feel fine now, but I have scheduled an appointment for you with Dr. Kirk Peal. He is a specialist in electrophysiology. This means he deals with everything about the electrical workings of the heart." Her dad paused. Almost apologetically he continued, "In the simplest terms, the heart is like a toaster. It needs electrical stimulation to work and has internal regulators that deal with making the toast light or dark or somewhere in between, and it even has settings to deal with bagels. It responds differently and appropriately depending on how you set it to regulate the electrical flow." Seeing everybody listening and not put off by this simple explanation, he continued "Like a perfectly good toaster disappoints if you don't set it right, a perfectly good heart, in the physical sense, doesn't work properly either if it doesn't receive the appropriate electrical signal. The difference is that the decision about the proper electrical signal is made automatically by the heart itself. Last week, your electrical signaling process was misbehaving, and that's why you are here. Since then, your heart has automatically and on its own reverted to sending a normal signal, and is now working perfectly. We should be doing everything in our power to keep things that way. My guess is that after your appointment tomorrow you will be given a low dose of a specific medication for the short-term, and then you will be checked on a regular basis. Your appointment with Dr. Peal is at 10:00 a.m. tomorrow. I am sure you will like him. He is both smart and a very nice guy. Now, if you allow me, I am just going to be your dad. Dr. Peal will know what to do next."

With dinner and the postprandial medical talk over at eight thirty, Adam and Erin decided to take a walk on the beach. They were alone and had already discussed each other's work on the plane. With their shoes left on the steps that led down to the beach, they kicked sand with their toes as they walked. Erin started. "Adam, I have made a decision."

She seemed to be awaiting a response. Adam complied. "And that would be …?"

"I am going to ask for a transfer back to Langley. I enjoyed my time in Rome and, if I do say so, I am doing a decent job, but, Adam, it's not just me. I …"

Before she could say any more, Adam spoke. "Erin, please stop and let me say something."

"Okay." The response from Erin was soft.

"Erin, I have been waiting to tell you something, but I wanted to do it when it wouldn't affect any decisions you might make about work." Then, doing his best to say as much as possible in the fewest words, Adam explained to Erin the opportunity that had been offered to him. "It is finally a real job," he said, "not just another short-term assignment that has a good chance of getting me killed. It will be a real position, permanent and important, and I won't be tied to a desk." He knew Erin would agree that a purely desk job for him would be out of the question, he would go bananas. "This job is like what we did in North Korea, and what I did in the Middle East, but I won't be relegated to the trenches, I'd be there just some of the time, and that would be my call." Adam was so excited to finally tell someone about his job offer that he could hardly contain himself, but he wanted to be honest with Erin. He would not promise something that he couldn't deliver. Somewhere in their relationship was the unstated but unwavering promise to be honest.

When she heard his news, Erin was happy and relieved. "Adam, that sounds wonderful! You deserve it. We can talk about the fieldwork later, but I support you one hundred percent."

As Erin looked at this man who meant so much to her, Adam reached into his shirt pocket and retrieved the black-velvet pouch that he had gotten back from the jeweler only the afternoon before. The stone was now in a platinum setting in a ring size that was his best guess. Without any planned behavior, he found himself sinking to one knee and saying, "Erin, will you marry me?"

Erin's smile and tears of joy provided the only answer he needed.

About the Author

Eugene M. Helveston, MD, is emeritus professor of ophthalmology; founder of the section of Pediatric Ophthalmology; and former Chairman of the Department of Ophthalmology at Indiana University School of Medicine, where he provided patient care and teaching, and carried out clinical research.

After authoring hundreds of professional papers, three medical textbooks, and a nonfiction book in 2016 titled *The Second Decade: Raising Kids to be Happy, Self-Sufficient Adults through WORK,* he turned his attention to writing fiction. *The Golden Pelican* was published in 2017.

A native of Detroit, Michigan, Gene currently resides in Indianapolis with his wife, Barbara. You may contact him at ehelveston@msn.com.